Bonds from Addiction

By Daniel Arthur Johnston

ISBN 979-8-9922737-0-0

Self-Published by Daniel Arthur Johnston

Printed in U.S.A. by IngramSpark

If you're struggling, seek help.

If you're lonely, seek family.

You're loved.

~ Prologue ~

I write to relate. With so many questions of who I am and who I want to be swirling around my head, sometimes I just want a shortcut to the answers. The scenario could be that of a hard-working family man offering the world to his young. It could be about embracing fame and using it for a greater or evil power. Or what if I was leading a group of misfortunate students who were angry at the world? Could I change them? Would I succeed or fall into the villainous roles that have played out so many times in the past?

The truth is: I'm all of them. I intellectualize. I want to challenge all the truths and lies that surround me. Although it's impossible to enter the thought processes of others, I can start with that individual process I want to invade and build a character around it. In my stories, my dreams, my fantasies, or even my nightmares, I will be those characters and see what triggered me to be who I am.

Growing up in the eighties—the last decade without public internet—was a great time for imagination. There wasn't a game console in every household trying to direct your thoughts or strip your attention away from the great outdoors. Where there was a tree, there was a spaceship. In the forest, we'd conquer the enemies of our fortresses with weapons made of sticks and pinecones. If our fort fell, we rebuilt it better and stronger. We'd augment the shit out of it to the point where the ratio of wall thickness to open space was so small you felt like a beaver.

History class taught us about various eras and how people fought and dressed. I couldn't remember names or actual events, though. So, it was up to us to recreate this history to the best of our knowledge. I'd recruit knights from around the neighborhood. No healers or magicians. Just knights. If you could swing a branch, you were in.

The only thing that would interfere with our kingdom was that wicked whistle, a battle horn if you will, that would alert us that our playtime was over and we needed to retreat back to our homes.

Every childhood should be like mine. No one should enter the big hectic city life until they're at least working age. Youths are sucked in, neglected, and rarely reminisced. I could be biased, though.

After all, I'm a knight.

CHAPTER 1

~ Roll For It ~

Another night at my local spot. It's been my go-to place since college, although I don't remember many of those nights. As an engineer who likes to dabble with writing, I find frequenting these establishments on a regular basis helps fuel my imagination, much like Hemingway. Truth be told, I have more dreams while I am awake than when I'm asleep.

I prefer this bar to others for many reasons. One reason is the hilarity of this useless skylight that rarely performs any function. During the day, the moving clouds periodically reveal a massive beam of sunlight through the window. As everything in the bar quickly brightens, my vision turns white, and I feel as though I am fainting.

After the immediate head rush, I glance around to see if any angels are descending from the heavens. Like in the movies, I expect all deaths to trigger this effect. I mean, somebody has to come down to retrieve those poor souls. In reality, though, all I see with the additional light is filth collecting in the corners and fingerprints smeared across the glass surfaces. Clearly, the popularity here isn't correlated with its cleanliness.

My friend and roommate, formally known as Sir Francis or 'Cis,' joins me moments after my arrival. He's escaped his dungeon once again. At least, that's what I call the kitchen he works in. In relation to my work-from-home cushion-soft desk job, everything probably feels a bit more restrictive. The restaurant has quite amazing food that leaves their kitchen. They can't seem to function, though, without working each employee down to the bone. I work a portion of the hours that he works. He makes a portion of the money I make. I go home for the holidays and he forgets they exist.

At the end of the day, though, neither of us lives luxuriously. He doesn't have much surplus cash beyond monthly costs. I have some, but I tend to fill my idle time with activities like work and drinking cheap beer at a dive bar. We live on different sides of the spectrum: white-collar versus blue-collar. In this bar, though, there's no spectrum. You're either here, or you're not.

"Good evenin', Brey!" the sarcastically-excited Cis calls out.

"Another day in paradise?" I respond with a half-sympathetic, half-tired grin.

"Another day in labor. Another dish to serve. Another dish to clean." He pauses as he stares blankly at the floor next to me as though he forgot his next recited line. With a quick inhale, he lifts his head and continues, "I need a drink!" Cis turns his head and quickly makes contact with our friendly bartender, Angie.

Angie is in a similar place as Cis. The owner of this place is about as distant as an AA member. Angie occasionally does have some barback help, but is typically working solo regardless of how busy it is. What makes her our favorite bartender, though, is her nerd history. Bartenders can have many labels and reputations, but a former D&D Priestess is not one of them. Based on some of her stories, she's a killer dungeon master, too. Beyond this side of her, I can't say I know too much about her or her past.

The thing I like most about D&D is how a room lights up when there's an abundance of creativity. It's a sensitive energy, though, as it only takes one person to bring the whole thing down. It's like when you're at the bar with the locals, and all of a sudden, the 'cool kids' walk in.

"What will it be tonight?" Angie asks us among a sea of waiting patrons.

"I'm feeling fancy tonight," Cis jokingly replies.

"PBR?"

"Bud Light."

"Make it two!" I shout over the small crowd.

Angie looks me up and down and laughs while saying, "I should have known." Perhaps we are what we drink. I stopped by the gym before coming here, so she's commenting on my shiny blue and gray gym clothes. They do look similar to a familiar aluminum bottle.

A pet peeve I have about the bar is when groups leave single-seat gaps. There were a few wasted seats tonight, so we migrated to the server station. It doesn't seem like it'll get much action tonight. This at least gives us a place to stand and chat while still being able to share some words with Angie in between her hustles.

Naturally, though, we don't sit idle for long. Some asshole ordered a drink, then went and sat down in the back. Angie asks if one of us will deliver his drinks. I accept that role, though, as Cis already spent his day making food for probably the same ingrates.

There are days that Cis takes his opportunities to shine, though. He typically plays the role of barback, which means he does most of the thankless jobs. He's able to show off his mad slicing skills to everyone as he tears up lemons and limes. Sometimes, we even jump on the dishwasher to help there. These jobs are much more entertaining when they're optional.

There are two reasons we thrive at doing this during our visits. One is Angie. We love her company, and we hope assisting her makes her love ours. Second, since we both live together, we need to justify leaving our apartment. I would typically prefer to just stay home and maybe game a bit while drinking beers and watching something in the background. In our groove, the three of us make a pretty fierce team and are a force to be reckoned with.

Cis appears extra worn out this evening. Thoughts seem to fill his head, and the world appears to be resting heavily on his shoulders.

"What's up, man? Things alright?" I try to keep him in a positive mood as his emotions play a big part in my life. Not only is he my roommate, but he's like my right side. If it drags, I drag.

"I've just been thinking that maybe there's something we're missing out on. I was listening to Bill today," who is the owner of the restaurant he works at, "and I couldn't figure out what made him successful. He isn't bright. He isn't a hard worker. He isn't charismatic."

I cut Cis off and say, "He's courageous and lucky." He looked up at me with a glance like I was out of my mind. I explain, "He took a risk of opening a place up. He lucked out by hiring someone like you. Even though it's not your sole responsibility, you wouldn't let the place fail."

"There's got to be more than that."

"That's it, man. He's lucky. Look at all of his employees, including yourself. You practically live there. You are responsible for that restaurant's success."

"Maybe," he hesitates as he hangs his head and rapidly taps the bottle he holds with both hands, "Let's do something. Something *big*."

"How big?"

A big grin stretches across his face as he pulls a twelve-sided die out of his pocket. Similar to rolling dice in D&D to see how successful you are at performing an action, we like to roll a die once in a while to see if we *should* do something. Depending on the size and risk involved, we lay out a number for ourselves along with a well-defined legend. If we hit that number, we follow through without ever looking back.

Cis shakes the die around in his hand as thoughts swish around his head. As he continues shaking his closed fist up and down, he glances up toward the ceiling and then back down at me again.

"Lucky seven says we go cross country." God only knows what this journey would entail, but that's only a one-in-twelve-shot chance of needing to know. I nodded with a smile and took a swig from my beer.

He launches the die into the air. It was a bit higher than usual. Perhaps it gave him more time to change the rules or the numbers. The die bounces onto the bar and then over onto the floor by Angie's feet.

Angie bends down to get a good look at the die as it rolls under the ice chest behind the bar. She knows better than to just grab it without seeing the proper number first. She's not new to this.

"Seven," she says with a half-grin, "Fucking seven." She nods her head slowly and gives me a quick wink.

Almost in unison, Cis and I slam our beers down onto the bar, raise our clenched fists into the air, and cheer loudly. There was almost a ninety-two percent chance our night was going to be the same as any other. But here we are, ready for the extraordinary! We also didn't care to get confirmation of what Angie saw. Maybe it was a seven. Maybe she felt like we needed to get out.

*

Without hesitation or question, we both make it through the front door of our apartment and head straight to our bedrooms. It's agreed that we'd have the night to pack anything we could fit into a single duffle bag. Beyond that rule, Cis and I each have to secretly write down a few places we want to see on our trip. In the morning, we'd plan our routes accordingly.

Being a freelance software developer and writer, I have the freedom and work to complete at will while traveling. I just finished a contract, so this is happening at a perfect time. Cis has the burden of informing his boss that he will not be returning to work. While his expenses are a mystery, my decent savings should keep us moving.

Angie asks to meet for brunch in the morning so she can say her goodbyes. While we'll miss her frequent company, I suspect it'll only be a matter of weeks before we're back to our normal routines.

I hear the growing voice of Cis in the other room.

"No! I will not be in today, tomorrow, or any day after! That's what quitting *means*!" Like many times before, I assume his boss is taking his resignation and turning it into a request for more shifts. He's a bit of a bully. And bullies—young or old—don't seem to understand when enough is enough. They'll tear you down until you are broken and then take you down a few more steps. When you're finally done, they just go off and find another soul to torment. Fuckers.

I hear from the other room, "Okay, fine. Put me down for whatever fucking shifts you want. Except for Friday morning, set that aside for you to go fuck yourself!"

SLAM!

Most people don't know the feeling of slamming down a phone anymore. After one of our alcohol-fueled tangents one night last year, we decided to always have a house phone that we could slam. It is perfect for moments like this.

"He took it quite well," Cis yells to me as I could hear his packing continue. It sounds a bit like a child throwing a tantrum.

I laugh to myself as I take a final inventory of my duffle bag. There are some jeans, cargo shorts, a bathing suit, one hoodie sweatshirt, t-shirts, undergarments, and one semi-formal attire. Any situation we may run into should be covered!

I pause for a moment as my eyes run across the old family photograph I keep framed on my dresser. For me, it was a much simpler time back then. Maybe not the clothes, though. They were hideous. I went to school, played with the kids in the neighborhood, spent time with family then slept. All along as my days cycled, so many things were happening around me. I'm not sure if keeping secrets from a child is right or wrong, but it would have been nice to know that the life I knew would quickly spiral out of control.

WHAM!

Startled, I snap out of my thoughts and look over at the door. There stands a drunk Cis holding the top of the door frame, swaying his body back and forth. The frame creaks on every swing, buckling from the weight of his body.

"This is no time for deep thoughts," he says, "Clear heads. Clear roads. That's all we need!" With the flash of a grin, he swiftly makes it back to his room.

"You've got this," I say to myself as I lift myself off the corner of my bed. I bounce a few times on my toes to trigger a little extra blood flow in my body.

Now standing in the bathroom, I stare at a plastic bag sitting by the sink. I start gathering the obvious bathroom supplies that I'll need. My one sure way of remembering everything during a trip is to pack the night before. As I go through my morning routine the next morning, I can figure out what I forgot to put in my bag. I always tend to forget my toothbrush as it's the only thing with a permanent fixture that it calls home. My muscle memory is programmed to put it back into that same holder no matter what state my brain is in.

It's far easier to pack when you know what's on the itinerary. Going on a planned weekend trip to visit family has no mysteries. And there are certainties like knowing if electric outlets will be available. The same applies for things like toilet paper. My paranoia starts to take control of my decisions. I pack my electric shaver as well as my shaving cream, razor, and back-up blades.

Then the thoughts go wildly off track on what could occur on the trip. I pack up the big jugs of shampoo and conditioner. The band-aids stare me down. I start daydreaming of illnesses we could come down with. I pack meds, nasal sprays, antacids, a twelve-pack of soap, dental floss, flashlights, batteries, candles for when the batteries are dead, matches for the candles…the bag wasn't going to cut it.

"Cis! We have a situation!" I yell out.

"Use this," Cis says as he appears around the corner with an old hockey bag of his. I suspect my thrashing around was already screaming for help. "Maybe just leave a small corner in that bag for my stuff?"

He smiles and disappears into the shadows of the hallway.

*

We pack for another solid hour before reconvening in the kitchen with our gatherings. A large pile of clothes builds up in the middle of the kitchen. These all require a run through the washer and dryer before the night is up.

Cis pulls out his D12 again.

"One through six, you're on laundry duty," he says as he rolls the die across the table. It bounces around a few times, clicking and clacking on the wooden tabletop. It makes its final landing on the now infamous seven.

"Shit," Cis mumbles under his breath as he stands up from the table. He stops in his tracks. He spins around and says, "One through six, you're folding." He rolls an eight. "Son of a bitch."

Cis reaches his hands down, palms up, and table flips an imaginary table. We're firm believers that good sportsmanship is about as alive as chivalry. It's okay to be miserable about losing. No one likes it.

He reaches down again and bear-hugs the pile of clothes. With a drooping head and an emphasized sigh, Cis turns away to do his duties.

"You dropped some socks," I say.

"Get fucked."

I stand up and make my way back to my room. As I pass Cis's bedroom, I get a nasty whiff of stale beer. Five or six empty beer bottles hang out on his dresser, a couple on their sides. Based on my limited memory, I think it's fairly safe to assume those were consumed in the short time since we've returned from the bar. I give him about thirty more minutes of drinking before he either crashes or begins to slur his words. I gather the bottles and bring them to the kitchen. After a quick rinse, I toss them into our growing collection of returnables.

We grew up in the same place doing the same things, but his drinking escalated far beyond mine when he got sucked into his career path. It was a 'chicken or the egg' situation. I couldn't tell for sure if cooking was really his passion or if he just felt like he belonged there due to his lifestyle of drinking heavily. In most kitchens, his problem probably goes unnoticed.

Another quirk that Cis has is he's very selective about who he wants to take orders from, especially in a kitchen. He is quick to determine if someone warrants respect based on a few traits. One is consistency in their attitude. If they act bipolar, he's gone. He wants to be loved or hated, not both. Especially not on the same day.

The other trait he looks at is the basis of their decisions. If they seem logical, whether correct or not, he can manage his expectations. When ego rules, he bails. He's very good at his job but needs that room to fly. If he gets that, his loyalty can't be beat.

Cis could be put in charge of running his own kitchen if he just smiled and nodded a bit more to the owners. He's known to regularly sacrifice any brownie points he has to keep the owners in check. His concern has always been around keeping his team happy. From my understanding, most of his arguments with those 'superiors' end when they just play the rank card. Keep at them, Cis.

A couple loud thumps come from the laundry room. I assume it's from the washing machine's doors, but anything is possible in our household. I watch the door patiently to make sure Cis comes back unscathed.

A loud beer burp echoes from around the corner as Cis turns the corner.

"Goodnight, man." Cis gives a quick dismissal wave. I turn in for the night.

CHAPTER 2
~ The Plan ~

RRRRINGGGGG.

Before the first ring finishes, I swat my side table, attempting to silence my phone. I make just enough contact to instead knock the phone on the floor.

RRRRINGGGGG.

A grunt quietly leaves my mouth as I roll over on my stomach to give myself better reach. After a couple attempts, I managed to pull the phone close enough to grasp. The first thing I notice is that it's not my alarm going off—it's Angie. And it's six in the morning. Who calls someone at six in the morning? I think it may be illegal in some countries.

"Hello?" I say into the phone, "Everything okay?" As it is rolling out of my mouth, I start to think that maybe something is wrong.

"GOOD MORNING!" Angie says in her outdoor voice, followed by an excited giggle, "What time are you two leaving?"

"Leaving?" I ask slowly as I try to remember myself.

"You and Cis are still going on that trip, right?"

"Oh shit. Yeah."

"Well, let's grab breakfast first! Call me when you're up and ready."

"Sounds good," I say with a little more energy. We share byes and hang up.

"CIS! Wake up!" I scream, but I hear no response or movement in the other room.

I fight for the energy to sit up in bed to avoid falling asleep again. My head shakes back and forth like a rattle. As I strain to stabilize, I hear the growling of a bear. It's followed by the squeaking of Cis's bed, then some dragging footsteps. I drop my legs off the side of the bed and finally sit up.

"I know I had a few too many last night, but did we really plan to wake up this early?" Cis says as he wipes the sleep from his eyes.

"No. You can blame Angie. She wants to meet us for breakfast before we leave."

"I'll be ready in twenty," Cis says with a nod as he turns and heads to the bathroom.

I glance at the packed bag and box sitting innocently on my floor. I glance at the creature in the mirror.

Here we go.

*

We say our goodbyes to the house as I lock the door. With the enormous hockey bag and work backpack encumbering me, I waddle to the car. I hope this isn't the beginning of a complete disaster.

"You ready for this?" I ask Cis, who is off in his own world.

"I'm still trying to figure out what's going on," he says.

"Well I hope you figure that out soon as I'm following you, my fearless friend and leader." We smirk at each other as we toss our stuff into the trunk of my car. A bit of my concerns for this trip are muted by the presence of a reliable friend and a reliable car.

As we briskly gather into the front seat and close the doors, I lean into the steering wheel and glance at Cis as I turn the key. He sarcastically taps the dashboard with both hands. "It's not too late," I say to Cis as I place my hand on the e-brake lever. "I can pull it and stop everything."

"Then all of that packing would be wasted time." Cis's eyes shift over to me. "We can't have that."

Then something shifts in his hangover, and he's filled with a small burst of energy. Cis rolls down the window, reaches out with both hands, and starts slapping the roof.

"WOOO!" Cis screams out the window. I'm fairly certain he just realized he didn't have to return to his personal hell again. It's arguable what's more exhilarating: leaving behind a shitty job or leaving behind heaps of technical debt. Both can be breathtaking.

"We need to figure out our itinerary at breakfast," I say.

"Agreed. I suppose I should have planned a bit more before the dice roll."

"Well, you'll have another shot at it."

"That I will."

As the first note plays on the radio, Cis reaches over and turns the volume up loud. After a few seconds, he leans in and starts singing, "Loving you...isn't the right thing to do..."

I back out of the driveway and start moving forward in our adventure. As the lyrics play, I wonder what the song is really about. It sounds like the guy loves some girl who only wants to have benefits—nothing more. If it's about something so depressing, why is it such an inspirational song? While listening to it, I feel like I could put on one of those flying squirrel suits and glide happily through the clouds.

"You can go your own way," Cis continues his audition and queues me up.

"GO YOUR OWN WAY!" we belt out together.

I'm starting to question my decisions a bit less now. This is the right thing to do.

*

We pull into the local diner, and I'm immediately taken aback by the rare sight in front of me. For the first time in the last one hundred years, the diner was getting a renovation. Perhaps it was only some fresh paint, but that counts. That definitely counts. Maybe in another hundred years, they'll do something about the broken tiles littered through the place.

Turning around the corner to find parking, I see Angie sitting on the back of her refurbished muscle car, playing around with her phone. I pull the beast into the spot next to her.

"Gotta love these parking spots," I mutter as I carefully open my age-worn door to avoid hitting Angie's shiny black car.

"Good morning, boys!" Angie hops off the back of her car with her arms wide open.

"Aw shit. Angie has been liberated!" Cis announces as he excitedly goes in for the first hug.

"You look so much different in the light!" I say as I go in for my hug.

"I feel different too!" Angie spins her keys around her finger a few times before catching them in her hand.

"Thanks for coming for our send off!" I tell her as I gesture towards the door.

"You guys don't even know," she says as she puts the key into her trunk. As her trunk pops open, there's a moment of confusion and anticipation. Sure enough, there's a large duffle bag full of something.

"If that's a dead body, I'm out," Cis says as he slowly takes a step back.

"YOLO," I reach in and grab the bag, "is this a going away present?"

"If you consider me as a going away present...I was sort of hoping you'd have an extra seat in the car? Sorry if my optimism last night steered me wrong!"

I look at Cis, and he's already looking at me trying to read my feelings on it. Without much hesitation, we both look back at Angie and exclaim, "Hells yeah! You're in!"

"Are you sure you don't need to roll on it?" Angie says out the side of her mouth with a slight grin. I grab her bag out of her trunk, and as I turn back toward my car, I catch Cis in my peripherals.

"Perfect twelve," he says as he breaks into his happy dance.

Angie pulls Cis and me in and lays her arms across our shoulders as we make our way to the restaurant's entryway. She releases us as we approach the silver entryway. The pause in her step and her playful nod to the door is quite clear, although Angie must not have seen the death certificate. We use chivalry's last dying breath to entertain her anyway and open the doors for her.

"Good morning, welcome to Abel's Diner! Booth or bar?" the very alert host says with a genuine smile. His voice sounds clear over the oldies blasting on the radio and the bustling staff slinging dishes to tables.

"Booth!" we all answer. It's too early, and we're too hungover to hear that other word again. She gathers three menus and brings us over to a well-lit laminate booth. It has the traditional red, white and black color themes.

Tossing the menus down, the host says, "Faith will be your waitress today. She'll be with you in a moment!" It is clearly another hint from above that we're doing the right thing.

"So what's the plan?" Angie asks before even looking at the menu.

"We didn't quite get that far!" I say as her eyebrows furrow in response. "I'm thinking we each write down a few places we'd be interested in seeing. Then we can build out an itinerary?" Cis and Angie nod as they turn their focus on the menus in front of them.

"Good morning! I'm Faith, and I will be taking care of you today. Can I start you off with something to drink?"

"Coffee with cream. And water. Lots of water." I say.

"I'll have the same," Cis says with some hesitation as he glances down at the off-white mug in front of him. He probably really wants a drink to kill his hangover.

"I'll have a coffee and…who's driving?" Angie asks.

"I can," I say.

"I'll do a bloody mary as well," Angie breaks the ice.

"Okay, give me a bloody mary too, please." Cis looks a bit relieved knowing booze was coming too. I don't think bloody marys are necessarily his drink of choice, but they're socially acceptable at breakfast.

"Should we make it a hat trick?" Faith looks at me as she bites her lower lip in anticipation. Her hand softly taps a pen across her order pad.

"Nah. I'm apparently the DD for our trip."

Faith's face perks up, "A trip? Where you all headed?"

I laugh as I tell her, "We actually don't know yet. Will let you know by dessert!"

Faith smiles as she turns away.

I stop her. "Actually!" Faith pauses in her steps. "Sorry, but could we borrow three pens, please?" I smile at her with my fingers visibly crossed as she turns slowly around.

"Of course, junior," she says softly as she walks behind the bar. She ducks out of sight and rises a moment later with pens in her hand. Faith scoots over to our table and drops them in my hand, "Drinks will be up shortly!"

"Thanks! You're a real charmer!" I say with a nod and hand pens to Angie and Cis.

"Okay!" I slap both hands down on the table. "Use these pens to write down your three favorite places to visit on the back of your napkin, then turn your napkin over! No discussion until we're all finished."

"Yes, captain!" Cis says. He chuckles, then quickly gasps for air as if he's seen a ghost. His face goes blank for a brief moment, followed by a forced grin. Cis ducks down to start his list with one arm curled around the napkin to hide it from us.

Angie and I make eye contact. She appears a bit uncomfortable with what she just saw. I asked him about it a while back. He says he gets these jolts of anxiety, much like a zap of electricity. It's short but strong. It feels like the walls of his throat are being inflated. I'm guessing the endorphins of laughter are the trigger. I pass it off as being normal to Angie.

As I look down at my napkin, my brain goes blank as I try to think where I'd like to see on this trip. I guess it depends if I'm looking to dork out or impress these two with my selections. There are so many options to choose from.

I spent a lot of time playing in nature growing up, so perhaps I should hit one of those colossal national parks. I mentally map out the ones I can think of: Yellowstone, Yosemite, Zion, and Grand Canyon. If I write down the Grand Canyon, I wonder if they'll give me Las Vegas as a bonus since it's close. Or perhaps I put Las Vegas, so it's guaranteed. Then maybe I can weasel in the Grand Canyon as a bonus stop. I'm quite the gambling type, but to risk gambling with gambling? Not happening. Also, truth be told, I'm not a fan of being stuck in a car. I choose Yosemite and Las Vegas as my first two locations.

As a software engineer from the East Coast, I only hear rumors of the human mill called Silicon Valley. The home of people manually automating manual work. I hope the insanity isn't just a communicable sickness. I'd hate to get hardwired with entitlement and depression the moment we enter. I don't really have justification to prioritize anything else, so this becomes my third location. I look back up at Yosemite and decide the short distance feels like a cop-out. As I scribble it out, the napkin starts to give away. I choose Yellowstone in its place.

I lift my head up to see Angie gazing out the window with the pen to her lips. Her eyes are still, but she's clearly calculating something based on her focus. Those same green eyes brighten up as she lifts one finger up in front of her face. Without pause, she dives back down to her napkin to scribble down her findings.

Cis appears a bit more unraveled than Angie. Based on his slumped shoulders and defeated look on his face, you'd think he is designing a heist with no prior knowledge.

"You doing alright?" I ask him.

"I'll be better once Mary shows up," he says as he picks up his pen again. His hands tremble down to the napkin as he scribbles a couple words. I try to avoid looking, but my eyes shoot straight down and see New Orleans and Chicago. They're not places I would have thought to pick, but interesting choices.

"Hallelujah!" Cis rejoices as Faith makes her way back to the table with our drinks. He watches intently as his drink is placed in front of him. It's clear he wants nothing more than that alcohol flowing through his bloodstream.

"Have you decided on breakfast?" Faith asks.

"I'm not going to lie. I completely forgot to look," Angie says.

"Could we please have three more minutes? I def—" I cut myself off. Before I can finish, Faith smiles, nods, and disappears from our table. Before she even gets to the kitchen, Cis downs half his drink. He lets out a sigh of relief then turns his attention to the menu.

"There it is," Cis says as he points down at his menu. "The one dish that really defines the love and care a kitchen provides: Eggs Benedict."

As we make eye contact, he continues with his lesson, "Hollandaise is easy enough to make fluffy and delicious. It's also easy to give up after the sauce breaks once or twice. Then poaching an egg? The concept is easy. It's not difficult to poach an egg. It is also easy to give up on a nice poached egg, though, after the egg splatters into the water and looks like a circling Milky Way. And getting an egg that's not undercooked and has a runny yolk? That takes a bit of finesse." I don't really have a response, so I just slowly nod and smile.

"I guess I'll have that too. I'd hate to leave this place without knowing how much they love me," I say.

Soon after, Faith comes back to the table and we place our orders. She disappears back into the air like a happy banshee.

A moment later, Angie oddly folds up her napkin as if she's making origami. She lifts her hand to reveal her first, "New Orleans, baby! Home of Mardi Gras, beignets, and cajun food."

"Opa!" Cis pulls his hand down to show he also had New Orleans as his top pick. With a pen woven in his fingers, he reaches across the table and high-fives Angie.

"I guess we'll have to stop for some beads and Tums," I suggest. "My first pick has a bit of a different vibe. Yellowstone Park." The two nod approvingly. "While I'm excited to see the geysers, I'm also excited to send this bison back to his natural habitat," I say as I glance over at Cis.

"Show me the way to the fermented fruit!" he responds. Cis makes eye contact with Angie and asks, "What's your number two?"

"You may see a bit of a theme here. Las Vegas!"

"Ha! I guess we're not too original in this group." I reveal Las Vegas also as my number two.

"Well, now. I guess we're in good company. Why Vegas for you?" Angie gives me an inquisitive look.

"Gambling, for sure. Are there other reasons?" I give a similar look back.

Cis jumps into the conversation, "Shows, buffets, hookers…shall I go on?"

Angie sits up straight and lays her hands flat on the table. As she starts to softly tap her fingers, she innocently tells us, "My parents met in Vegas many years back."

"You're from Vegas!?" Cis asks in an excited shock.

"No, no. Neither are my parents. My father was a pilot that was stationed there for a bit." She grins softly as she continues, "My mom was just visiting the city with some friends from school. Coincidentally, they were staying at the same hotel, the Mystic Facade, one night, and my mom got locked out of her room. My dad was on his way out when he saw her nervously sitting in the hallway waiting for security to come."

I make brief eye contact with Cis. After years of knowing her, this is definitely the most personal story we've really heard from her.

"There were some rowdy people at the hotel that night. My dad sat opposite her in the hallway and let her know he'd keep her company."

"Sounds like a one-night stand turned into parenthood!"

She cuts Cis off, "Actually, no. They exchanged addresses and numbers and became long-distance friends. They didn't see each other again until two years later after my mom graduated. My dad happened to be in town that week and came by her graduation. Then somewhere after that, it became parenthood and marriage."

"They sound like a majestic couple," I say. "So you want to find that hotel?"

"Yes, but that's not all."

"Carry on," I say with a smile as I sit back in my seat.

"My mom got sick when I was six and passed." As the words left her mouth, it was as though a deafening breeze came across the table. It's never the turn you expect to hear in stories.

"After she passed, she was cremated. In lieu of a traditional funeral, my dad and her relatives each got a necklace that had a vial of her ashes hanging like a pendant. They all promised to each other to bring her back to visit the locations of all of their favorite memories with her. So…" she pauses briefly, "my dad brought us here."

With our undivided attention, she continues, "We went to the hotel and sat in the same spots they sat in. This is where I learned about the story for the first time. Then, I remember sitting on his shoulders as we walked down Fremont St. Beyond how magical Las Vegas felt, it was how my dad was on that day. While he appeared deep in his emotions, he also seemed burden-free after finally fulfilling that promise," Angie looks down at the table as a small tear collects in the corner of her eye.

I pause for a moment to see if she's going to continue. "It sounds like he knew exactly how to celebrate her life," I say to fill the void.

"Absolutely," she responds with a nod.

With a furrowed brow, Cis asks, "So, how did this become number two on your list? It sounds far more important than New Orleans!"

Angie gives out a soft chuckle.

"It's my dad's fault really. He always told me to be the star of my own dream before being a supporting actress in someone else's." Angie pauses, looking lost in a thought as she stares through the salt shaker. "He always dreamed about bringing us all back to Vegas. Money never came easy to him, though. Unfortunately, the money only came with my mother's passing."

"I like that," I say and quickly rebuttal, "The part about starring in the dream…not the timing of the money."

Cis jumps in, "So where's your dad now?" He looks her sincerely in the eyes.

Angie looks up, directing her attention at him. "He lives here in town."

"Oh?" Cis looks impressed with the answer.

"Yeah, he's partially retired. He works as a handyman in exchange for room, board, and a little stipend." Angie shrugs and looks casually out the window.

"That sounds a lot like not retired," I say as I pray quietly in my head that my retirement looks more like cocktails on the beach.

Angie gives out a light chuckle. "He does like keeping busy."

"To each their own!" Cis says.

"Yes, to each their own!" Faith pops back in with each of our dishes lined up on her left arm. Her body is clearly weighed down on the one side, but she gracefully keeps the plates perfectly balanced.

"Eggs benedict for you and you," Faith says as she serves the plates from her arm to the table, as if she was throwing a disc. As the plate lands in front of me, the smells of the buttery hollandaise and greasy hash browns fill my nostrils. This will do!

"And an omelet for the lady." She places the last plate down in front of Angie as she says, "Anything else I can get you at the moment?"

I look toward the wall side of the table and see a selection of ketchup, hot sauces, jelly, and butter. I look back and say, "I'm good!" The other two nod in agreement. Faith gives a quick grin with a hurried nod, then heads away from the table. As she accelerates, her dirty blonde hair bobs up and down, strongly accenting the bounciness in her step.

Next to me, Cis is examining the restaurant's efforts. He dabs his fork into the hollandaise and puts the tip of his fork into his mouth.

"Hmm," he simply says. Cis nudges the side of the egg. It rolls like a stone and settles back into its original location. With a vertical dab of his knife, the yolk slowly bleeds out of the egg. He puckers his lips and pulls in his fingers for a chef's kiss. His hands slow down, his lips lose their pucker, and he lifts one finger.

"Should I be impressed or annoyed with this?" a wide-eyed Angie questions.

"The latter. And so will he when his food is lukewarm by the time he actually eats it," I say.

"You can't rush excellence; it needs to flow naturally," Cis says as he stabs his fork through the whole benedict. He smiles as his knife glides through the firm egg and crusty English muffin. It crunches as he lathers on some extra sauce.

"The finest of mother sauces," he says as he fills his mouth. His eyes stay on his plate as he chomps down on his food like a hungry Neanderthal. He tilts his head side to side as his eyes shift upward above Angie's head.

In a far less theatrical fashion, I begin eating my eggs benedict. The hollandaise is certainly fluffy with a hint of lemon. It's quite good, actually. It's everything I pictured from Cis's description and more.

"How have I never been here before?" Cis continues, "This is quite amazing." I nod in strong agreement.

"How's your omelet?" I ask Angie, who's been quietly eating across the table.

"The omelet is great, but it needs something."

"I've got what you need," Faith says as she passes by our table. She dashes behind the counter and over to the pass. Her back blocks our view. However, I see her grab two ramekins and then fill them. Faith turns around and heads directly to our table.

"Salsa and sour cream," she says as she places them in front of Angie, "Give that a try, and let me know if it helps."

Angie smiles and blotches a bite of omelet with a dab of each.

"It's perfect. Thank you so much!" Angie says.

"Anything for you, love," Faith says in a flirtatious yet playful manner. She gives a quick wink and bounces off.

We probably look like ostriches with our heads in the ground with how hyper-focused we are on our food.

"Brey, what's your last place?" Cis asks as he looks up from his plate.

"We're both two down. You catch up first," I say back to him.

"Yeah, let's hear it!" Angie adds on.

Cis rubs his hands together and then holds them outward as if he has a well-prepared speech.

"Next up is the windy city itself, Chicago. Home of the bean, some great dining, and '95 Bulls!" It turns out it wasn't much of a speech at all. At least he had a bit of enthusiasm in his voice. It's hard to talk bad about those ninety-five Bulls, so I refrain from making any comment.

"Any specific restaurants you're eyeing?" Angie asks.

"There are a few places I've heard a lot about. Some of our line cooks have bounced around the country, and they hardly shut up about it." Cis's voice trails off a little as he finishes the sentence. It appears it took about twelve hours for him to realize he just quit his job and those line cooks are no longer *his* line cooks.

Before he gets too lost in his thoughts, I speak up, "My last one is the *great* Silicon Valley. While I'm thankful to not live in that world of competitive burn-out, I would like to take a walk and be surrounded by company logos I only see on my phone."

"While we're in California, my last one was Napa Valley," Cis says with a smile.

"I missed out on this opportunity," Angie says, "my last one is the home of the Gateway Arch and the Cardinals. Baseball, not football."

"St. Louis," I say.

"St. Louis," she repeats. "There's also someone I want to see there."

"Who's that?" Cis asks.

"A cousin. There was a period of time when we did a lot of family things together, went to concerts and such. Then she moved, and that period became sealed in time. We didn't really communicate much after that. It'd be nice to catch up," Angie claims.

As I smile at her, I tell her, "You clearly put a lot more heart and consideration into your choices than I did."

"Or me," Cis says.

"It's been a while since I've got out. Gotta make the most of it!" she says.

I look around the table and notice our plates are mostly clear. I draw up a quick sketch of the US and map out our potential route.

"I think this route will work: Chicago, Yellowstone, Napa Valley, Silicon Valley, Las Vegas, New Orleans, St. Louis, then back home. That sound good?" I suggest, "It'll give us a bit of a counter-clockwise trip around the states."

They agree. After settling our check, we head out to drop off Angie's car at her place. I can't say I'm excited for the much longer second leg of the trip, but I'm looking forward to spending time with Cis and learning a thing or two about Angie, our mysterious bartender.

CHAPTER 3

~ The Windy Road ~

Ksssst!

Cis cracks open another can in the backseat. The car begins to smell like a can redemption station.

Glug glug glug.

Cis empties another beer into his mug. He stashes the incriminating evidence inside the trunk by way of the folding seat next to him. Extra care is used when putting the seat back vertically again to avoid it accidentally latching. After succeeding with the task, he leans back, lowers the brim of his hat, and takes a long swig from the mug.

"Drink anymore, and you just might forget the trip!" Angie says from the passenger seat.

"Don't worry, I'll probably remember some good stuff," he says without lifting his brim, "Also, I could use a pit stop soon!"

"Roll for it," I yell back to him and look for his response in the rearview mirror.

Cis grunts as he pulls the D12 from his pocket. He tosses it on the seat next to him. Angie looks back and watches it settle in the crevice where most lost change ends up.

"Ugh, twelve!" she says with a bit of disappointment in her voice.

"Okay, since I can't make your bladder magically drain, I'll find the next place," I say, "Rules are rules."

Cis's thumb rises into view in the rearview mirror.

"What do you think a 'one' would have meant?" I glance over at Angie.

"The door he's leaning on would have popped open on him. He'd fall out of the car, taking 3d6 damage, but in the process, he would piss himself. So if he survives the fall, he'll be relieved."

CLICK!

I look back and see that the door next to Cis is now locked. He must find humor in his actions as a slight grin quickly appears on his face. It's quickly covered by the mug as he takes another drink from it.

"Rest area in one mile," Angie says. I can see Cis shift in the backseat, preparing for launch.

I slow down as I veer into the ramp for the rest area. Cis's legs start to bounce.

"You look like you're about to piss yourself," I say as I purposely decelerate. A grunt echoes from the back. As the car comes to a halt, Cis swings open his door and jumps out in a hurry.

"You're mean," Angie says. I look over at her, and her green eyes glow in the light. They always turn heads at the bar, but it's different now. The sincerity of her father's story showed a new, vulnerable side of her we've definitely never seen before. The only ones looking vulnerable in a dive bar are the ones half in the bag. It's in moments like this, she feels less like a non-player character and more of a member of our party. I do start to question who's the protagonist here.

Angie's door opens more gracefully. Our paths meet at the front of the car, where we stretch a moment. It's a beautiful sunny day, probably in the low seventies. A gentle, cool breeze carries Angie's delicate aroma. I smell hints of roses and peaches. A pause comes with the breeze, and I'm left with the emanating smell of burning oil from the hot car engine.

I jog slightly ahead to grab the door for Angie. Like water behind a dam, as soon as the gate is open, a swarm of people starts flowing out. It feels like a well-prepared trap every time I find myself holding the door for extended periods of time.

The men's bathroom is fancier than most. Cis is at the first urinal, one hand orchestrating his efforts and one stabilizing him firmly on the wall. I get into position at the next urinal and quietly carry on my business. There's a mixed smell of the urinal cakes and stale beer. In my peripheral view, I see Cis's head bob up and down.

"Dude, did you just nod off at a urinal?" I laugh as I glance briefly over at him.

"Uh…no." He joins in on the laugh as he zips up. As he walks away, he mutters, "I totally did." He takes the die out of his pocket and rolls it across the sink counter. He nods, then washes his hands. I'm afraid to ask Cis, but I'm pretty sure he just rolled on whether he should wash his hands or not. There's no room for a catastrophic failure on that roll.

As I approach the sink, I'm reminded of the worst use of any invention ever: motion sensors for turning on and off sinks. I wave my hands around like a lunatic—flinging soap all over the bathroom—just to get a tablespoon of tap water. It feels like an insult upon injury that the water pressure is actually quite nice in those little spurts of water I get.

Leaving the bathroom, I see Angie standing by the vending machine. She's pulling her hair back into a ponytail. In the dark bar, it looks espresso colored, but it's a bit of a dark blend in the light. Her bent arms expose her athletic physique. I go to the gym just enough to know how much dedication it takes to sustain a healthy lifestyle. Like all things in life, there's always room for improvement.

"Anything good?" I ask as I walk up beside her.

"Yeah, but I can't decide," she responds as she shifts her lips back and forth.

"Stand by!" I say as I do a quick jog out to the car. I return with the disassembled ashtray full of loose change. I tell her, "I've been saving this for my kid's future college fund, but I think they'll understand that this was slightly more important."

I pump a small handful of nickels into the machine. This is the only time I find value in them. Nobody wants to spend the time counting them out at a counter. We collect our fallen loot and walk toward the car. Cis is sitting comfortably on a picnic table like a dog in the sun. He sees our arrival and joins us.

"Want me to take us to lunch?" Angie asks as we get close to the car.

"I would love that," I say. I unlock my door and then toss her my keys. I fall into the car, and the overwhelming smell of beer once again fills my nostrils. Angie and I concurrently roll our windows down half-way.

Ksssst!

Cis holds the can low and out of sight as he refills his mug.

"Give me a sec!" he says as he grabs a crinkled paper bag from the floor of the car. He fills it with the stash of cans from the trunk. Cis starts to look around like he's doing a drug trade.

"Wait a second," Angie says with her hand raised. "Okay, go." She clenches her fist like she's communicating silently to her squad, and Cis hurries to the trash outside and unloads the evidence.

"Teamwork," I chant as Cis playfully shoves the bag into the trash.

Angie asks me, "So what did you bring for tunes?"

"Anything our phones can play—I have an adapter." I hold up the end of the cord to show her.

"Okay. What do you have on your phone?" Angie asks as she glances down at my phone in the center console.

I pick up my phone and navigate to my playlists. I clear my throat as I recite, "Allow me to present my list. First up is 'Hit the Snooze.'"

"Sounds exhilarating. Anything on there that wouldn't put me to sleep?"

"It has hits from musicians like Jim Croce, Green River Ordinance, Train, Kelly Clarkson, Gordon Lightfoot, and many, many more." I look over at her initial reaction and can only assume acceptance based on her slow nod with her lower lip puffed out.

I continue down my list and say, "Next is 'Grungin' Rock.' It's pretty much how it sounds. Alice in Chains, Linkin Park, Chris Cornell, Pearl Jam, Sublime, etc."

"I like the lineup so far. Go on," she says. Her voice sounds a bit more optimistic.

"'Rap it up,' which is actually just Eminem and a couple dozen non-Eminem songs. And that brings us to the last properly populated list. 'Boot Stompin' Fun' is my collection of country music. It's quite limited to the time period where I was really into it."

"Give me a shuffle on the first one. We can change lists on each passing of the keys," Angie says.

"You got it." I smile as I turn the playlist on shuffle.

As the strumming of 'Hey Girl' by O.A.R. begins, she excitedly says, "Ooo, I love this song!"

We crank up the volume and sing along like some carpool karaoke. Cis tries to cover his face and get some sleep in the back. His bouncing leg must mean he's digging the song. I'm not sure why we listened to the hit-or-miss radio for so long. Here we are, though, not looking back. It feels like my soul just opened up a little bit. The road trip has officially kicked off.

*

Cis startles awake and pulls himself up quickly. I look back and see him struggling a bit as he takes another swig of his beer. It's likely related to those shocks of anxiety. He says when it happens, it makes his throat feel like a one-way path moving up. That's for both air and stomach contents. Drinking anything helps open up the road to be two-way. It controls it, but these incidents seem to be more frequent as his drinking has accelerated.

Angie and I share a concerned look. It's clear there's an issue, but not sure it's something either of us can control.

I try to change the subject to my recent recurring kick.

"Have you listened to Savatage before?" I ask.

"I don't believe so," Angie says slowly as she stares blankly ahead.

I change the music to Savatage's Handful of Rain album. I skip ahead to my personal favorite song of theirs, "Alone You Breathe." It's also the song that introduced me to both the band and the album.

As the piano intro ends and the guitar kicks in, Angie asks, "Who is this again? The sound is so familiar!"

"It's Savatage. I'd categorize them as theatrical metal. The lead singer and guitarist are two of the founding members that were brought in to create the Trans-Siberian Orchestra."

"Yes!" she exclaims as she slaps the steering wheel. "I totally hear it!"

"I'll play the song 'Chance' next. It's like a metal version of Bohemian Rhapsody—in the sense that there are very isolated sections of the song."

"Nice!" Angie smiles and taps her thumbs on the steering wheel along to the melody.

I turn backward to see how Cis is doing. He is starting to nod off again from a seated position. As he startles himself awake, he looks up and realizes I'm watching him.

"Whoa," he says loudly over the music, "creepin' much?"

"Just close your eyes. I like to watch you sleep." I wink and turn back around. It sounds like Cis had something else to say, but the music just drowns out his voice.

I watch the cars outside my window as we gradually move past them. Most faces I see are in their resting positions. A couple faces are singing softly to themselves. It's not a very vibrant crowd today. It's wrong for me to judge, though. I tend to do my best thinking when I'm just staring at the road.

Angie reaches forward and turns down the music. "Do you have a dream?"

"I have a lot of dreams. I'm usually being chased, though, so they might be classified as nightmares."

Angie rolls her eyes as she taps her fingers on the e-brake lever. "Career-wise, I mean. I know you've talked about writing code, writing a book, but wondering what your end-game looks like."

My goals have always felt pretty short term, so the question catches me a bit off guard. "Honestly?"

Angie's eyes jump between me and the road. "You can lie, but I'd prefer the truth."

"I don't really know. I'd love to have something published. I'd love to run my own start-up." I pause as I try to get a better sense of what it is that I actually want.

"Okay, so nothing big?" she says and smiles.

"The hardest part is finding something I'm super interested in. I've written a lot of throw-away projects in hopes it'd create a spark. I've even had three or four LLCs with the full intention of doing something with them. I ran out of steam before I got anything close to production," I say as I think about my past projects.

Like they say: If you want to go fast, go alone. If you want to go far, go with others. I've been preparing for that breakthrough idea. My focus hasn't really been becoming the best at a single thing, but rather being comfortable enough at every part that I can demonstrate my ideas. Each layer may not be perfect, but it's good enough.

"And for the text?"

"Pretty much the same. Finding a subject to write hundreds of pages about is difficult. I'm a slow reader and an even slower writer. It doesn't take much for me to hang up my hat and move on to something else." I say as I glance over to Angie. "And honestly, I tend to use it as a way to alleviate stress. I suppose it's a positive sign that I don't write too often."

"That's fair," she says.

I shift my weight to turn towards Angie a bit. "What about you? Where do you see yourself when you hit cap level?"

"I'm a glutton for punishment and service. I would like to run my own quaint little cafe. Maybe a rotating menu that has healthy spins on traditionally unhealthy food and drinks," she says as her eyes occasionally turn to look at me. "I may not lean too healthy, but definitely not a bar and definitely not pub food!"

"I heard Cis may be looking for a new job when the trip is over," I say loudly for Cis to hear, but his deep breathing hints that he's probably asleep.

"As for the dream," I say, "I think you should do it."

She smiles as her eyes squint a little. She looks at me and says, "I think you should too."

"To our dreams!" I grab my hours-old coffee and tap it against Angie's water.

*

Concluding our many-hour trip consisting of rest areas, food breaks, and driver swapping, I pull the car up to the hotel's entryway. Cis is groggy but awake in the backseat. I give Angie's arm a gentle shake as she just dozed off in the last thirty minutes of the trip.

"I'll be right back. Going to check in," I say softly, then head inside. As I approach the entrance, the doors slide open. I'm blinded by fluorescent lights and a polished white floor. A desk sits off to the right that has ugly wood paneling. It reminds me of the Griswold Station Wagon from National Lampoon's Vacation. Two individuals chat behind the desk. Their conversation ends as they look toward me with genuine smiles on their faces.

"Welcome!" they say in unison. The young man continues alone, "Are you here to check in?"

"I am. I booked one of the suites. Brey Anders," I say to him as he starts punching things into his computer. Tacky gold vases stand behind the desk as decorations. They're in dire need of some patch work and a fresh coat of paint.

"Ah, yes. Three guests. One night." I advert my judging eyes to catch his eye contact as he looks up from the humming monitor.

"Yes, and I wanted to ask. Do you have a cot that can be rolled in?" I inquire with my fingers crossed visibly above the counter. The suite we got comes with a king size bed in the loft and then a pull-out couch.

"We do. I can get one sent over immediately," he says. He continues to punch things into the computer, collects my card for incidents, and then gestures toward the elevator with my room key. I thank them and head back to the car.

"All set. Just gotta park," I say.

As we walk in, I tell them, "I grabbed a suite for us. Angie, you can take the bed upstairs in the loft. Cis, you take the pull-out couch, and I'll grab the cot that they're bringing over."

"That's not necessary. One of you can grab the bed, and I can take the cot," Angie offers.

"My die says, 'no,'" Cis responds.

"Bullshit. You didn't even roll it," she calls him out.

"I saw it," I say, "I guess that's final then." I flash a smug smile as we load onto the elevator.

"Toss our stuff in the room and get a nightcap?" I ask Angie as we make our way back to the lobby.

"Of course!" Angie's eyes widen, her shoulders rise, and she nods slowly at me like the answer should have been obvious..

"I'm in, too!" Cis says as he trails behind us. Honestly, I was expecting him to be the first to crash tonight. He must be twelve-plus beers deep already, just from the car ride here. I suppose he did take several naps between them, so maybe he's starting off a lot fresher than Angie and myself.

We make our way down the hallway toward our room. As I swing our door open, I get that initial "hotel smell." It's not a bad smell per se. It's just the dull fragrance of the staff's cleaning supplies. The amenities seem sufficient. It has a small kitchenette with a bar and seating for two. There's a bathroom to my right and then stairs that disappear into the darkness toward the loft. An ancient couch sits in front of the TV. It's enough for us.

I hear a squeaking sound coming from down the hall. After we put our stuff down, I peek down the hall. It's the hotel staff member pushing a cot toward us.

"Excellent timing," I smile to the woman pushing the cot, "I can take it from here. I appreciate it." I take the cot and push it inside the living room area behind the couch. The springs look old—rusty, even—but it should hold my weight for the night.

"I can totally take that," Angie says again with a bit of guilt in her voice. Cis turns and holds a finger up as if to shush her.

"That's nonsense. Brey clearly deserves that!" Cis says. He turns away and drops his stuff next to the couch. He looks back at me and says, "I'm a good roomie. I'll sleep where I was assigned and not fight you for that old bag o' springs." I shake my head as I unlatch the top of the bed, and it shrieks loudly as its sides fall down.

"Bed is made. Let's go!" I say. I'm sure I'll need a few hard drinks to make this cot feel like a proper bed.

Angie comes down the stairs after dropping off her bag. We head to the conveniently placed bar next door. It's a dive bar with a couple dozen patrons and about the same count of neon signs. The standing room is ample for the current headcount. There are two bartenders gradually moving around. The male bartender is a bit of a hipster. He looks like he just got off stage from a showing of S.E. Hinton's *Outsiders*. He very much has the vibe of Sodapop. The female bartender matches his love for denim with overalls over a white top. They don't seem to communicate among themselves much, but they have a strong chemistry as they weave back and forth behind the bar.

Cis is naturally the first one to belly up to the bar.

"Good evening, what can I get for ya?" the male bartender asks Cis.

Cis points to a board for specials and asks us, "Shot and beer?"

We agree, as it'll get us closer to bed faster.

"Three specials, please—Jose and Blue Moon," Cis orders for us.

"Absolutely. Want to start a tab or clear out?" the bartender asks him. Cis slides over his card to start a tab. I can already tell this nightcap is going to be a long night. The bartender puts a salt shaker and some lime slices in front of us. He swings by the register and then returns soon after with our shots.

"On your marks," Cis says as he passes around the salt shaker and distributes the lime. I lick my hand and sprinkle some salt on it. Tequila is a perfect example of how funny the concept of hard alcohol can be. It obviously tastes fucking awful if there's an assumed three-step process to take a one-ounce shot. Some say that more expensive alcohol tastes better, goes down smoother, yadda yadda. It seems you only pay top dollar to reduce the gag effect. I'd rather get the shot over with and get back to something that has a favorable flavor.

"Ugh, I can't believe I've spent so many years serving this shit to people," Angie says through a cringed look. She quickly chases it and puts her shot glass on the bar.

"Ping pong!" Cis says he notices a table in the back. He looks back to me and asks, "Wanna play?"

"Sure! Sign us up!" I said happily. I've always been a fan of the game.

Cis disappears over to the table to inquire. After a bit of discussion with the current players, he comes back and tells me it's just a couple pissing around with no score and no timetable. He seems a bit agitated, but I agree with Cis. If you have no etiquette, you're probably a piece of shit. Patience isn't a virtue. It's a waste of time. I shrug and turn back to Angie as Cis deserts us again.

"Just for the record, this,"—I wave my arm across our view—"is what I picture for your dream."

"If this is ever my dream, please just put me out of my misery," she says.

Watching the patrons of the bar, I'm guessing they're all regulars. They sit mostly spread out but share some small talk as they pass each other. It feels like a place where lonely people come to forget about their days. The only folks that don't match this are the ones loitering around the ping-pong table. Cis stands closely beside the table and converses with them between plays.

"So, what drinks will your quaint little place be serving?" I ask Angie. I realize our previous talk about dreams ended well before it was exhausted.

"Healthy mocktails, for sure. Freshly squeezed juices. House-infused seltzers. Marinated or pickled fruits that work as both garnish and flavoring. I've played around with it at home. We don't have a juicer or vacuum sealer at the bar, so I haven't tried recreating anything there."

"Vacuum sealer?" I asked.

"Yeah, you can use it on things like cucumbers. You fill a bowl with a pickling liquid and cucumber slices. Through the vacuum process, the air and water get displaced from the cucumbers, and the liquid gets sucked into those areas. It's a fun technique!"

I can vividly picture her doing this at the small restaurant and looking fulfilled with her work. It's a beautiful sight. I snap out of my thoughts as I see Cis walking backward toward us. The boyfriend from the ping pong table is pushing him in our direction. I can only imagine what happened to escalate it to this point.

"Okay. That's enough," Cis says with his hands up. A moment later, he repeats, "Okay. That's enough. I mean it." The boyfriend seems unconvinced by Cis's words and continues to push him.

Cis plants his feet on the floor behind him. He pulls his arms in and places them on the guy's chest. Then Cis shoves him forcefully backward. He stumbles back five or six feet and then falls backward onto the ground.

"I said 'enough,' asshole," Cis says, and he turns around and sees us.

"What the fuck?" I say to him, unknowing of the situation. "Why don't you sit down and chill?" I pull a stool out for him.

"Fuck that," Cis says as he pushes the stool away from him. He high-tails it out the front.

"What the fuck is that guy's problem?" the boyfriend says as he stands up and wipes the collected dust off his pants.

"If I had to guess, you," Angie says dismissively. The guy scoffs and returns to the section of the bar where people seem to like him. She looks at me and asks, "Should we go check on him?"

"Nah," I say, "it'll probably just fire him up more. It's best to let that tequila shot wear off a bit. Then there should be room to reason with him." I take a deep breath and try to exhale any remnants of stress that are building up. I like Cis a lot. He's a brother to me. Things just tend to escalate a lot quicker with him when he's been boozing it up all day. I suspect he's not allowed in the bar anymore, but at least everyone got to walk away freely.

"So if I open up this new quaint little place, will you write the first review for it?" Angie asks. She tilts her head slightly to the right as she looks at me to accept.

I recite in a critic's voice, "This quaint little place is doing seriously big things! Its menu of fresh mocktails and organic farm-to-table food is spot-on delicious and satisfies any type of craving, any time of the day. And if you need an extra pick-me-up, just sit at the counter and have a conversation with the dreammaker herself, Angie. Ten out of ten. I eat here every meal." Angie just smiles widely and leans in for a hug.

"Thank you," she whispers. My head gets immediately wrapped back around that scent of roses and peaches.

"Wow, my first hug!" I exclaim. "Just wait for the final draft—it'll really make you blush!"

Angie pulls away smiling and asks, "Shall we go find our friend?"

I nod, and we start toward the door. As we get close to exiting this run-down place, Angie turns around, clearly looking for someone.

"Hey, hipster!" she yells across the bar. The regulars at the tables begin to look at each other, trying to determine who she was yelling at. She points to an old guy sitting at the table closest to the ping pong table and yells, "Could you tap that guy for me?" She then points to the guy who is still playing peewee-level ping pong at the table.

"Hey you, the girl wants you!" he yells at him with his worn raspy voice. As the ping pong guy turns to look at Angie, she extends her arms sharply to the guy. Her middle fingers shoot up as her eyes get happily wide.

"Have a shitty night, fuck face!" she yells at him. Angie drops her arms, turns toward me, and starts giggling. She puts her hand on my upper back and guides me out the door. What a hero!

We make our way back to our hotel room where we find Cis crashed out on the couch.

"Found him," I say to Angie. We give each other a look of relief, knowing that this night could've ended a lot worse. Now we can settle down to sleep this night away.

CHAPTER 4

~ First Destination ~

Most of the time, it's not the worst thing to move around in your sleep. It is when you're a light sleeper and sleeping on a cot that sounds like a barking seal whenever you shift or breathe too deep. I could have probably slept another three hours, but my tolerance for the noise has depleted. With one more extremely loud metallic screech, I flip my legs over the side of the bed and sit up.

"Quiet down there!" Angie yells kiddingly from the loft.

"Yes, ma'am," I say as I struggle to stand. My legs are a little numb, a little sore. I hear a small shuffle sound from the couch. I turn to see Cis sit up. He looks at me, moans softly to himself, then falls back over.

"What's on the list for today? I'm hungry!" the voice from above echoes through the room.

"I need a beer," Cis continues to moan from the couch.

"I think your liver needs a break," I say.

"I agree with Brey," Angie says as her feet thump down the stairs, "Dibs!" she says as she jumps into the bathroom and closes the door quickly behind her.

"Ah fuck," Cis says as he rolls back over. I laugh as I grab my hotel key and bee-line it for the lobby bathroom. If you can't have two bathrooms, you need to have a strategy for moments like this. Always know where the next closest bathroom is, be it the hotel lobby or a nearby gas station. It's almost as important as knowing where the emergency room is.

This hotel is past its glory days. The smells of chlorine and mold plague the halls. Hurray for indoor pools. Even the walls of the rooms are a smoker's white—something that should've been painted over when cigarettes became banned inside hotels. For the size of the room, though, the prices are inexpensive, and it still attracts assholes like myself.

I walk into the bathroom and get hit with another wave of nastiness. Somebody's colon has exploded from clearly too much spinach and turnips. I pull my shirt over my nose and do everything in my power to finish fast and get back to the room.

Cis lifts his head over the back of the couch as he hears me open the door. After realizing it was me and not Angie, he grunts and lies back down. The shower turns on and I can see the last of his patience disperse into the stale hotel air.

"Okay. Okay. I get it." Like a zombie, Cis migrates out of the hotel room.

"Bring an air freshener!" I quickly yell over the banging of the closing door.

Just like that, silence. I sit on the edge of the couch as I let the outside voices creep into my head. Was this trip a mistake? Did I just remove that one responsibility from Cis's life that kept his alcoholism at bay? I really hope not. This already feels like a trip that's going to change the course of our lives. I just hope it's credited with something positive.

"Everything okay?" Angie asks from the doorway of the bathroom. Either she takes a really fast shower, or I just completely zoned out for a bit.

"Yeah, I hope so." I didn't have to explain my thoughts any further. Angie collected her things from the bathroom and walked over to me. She rests her hand lightly on my shoulder.

"My dad always told me: I can keep juggling as long as I'm willing and able, but in the end, things will land where they need to be," Angie says. She pulls her hand from my shoulder, gives a sharp nod, and then carries her things back up to the loft.

As the group reconvenes, I scoot my bag and cot into the corner. The place looks a bit more like a hotel room again and not an overcrowded shelter. I'd typically press on Cis to do the same, but I'm no longer convinced he'll be in the condition to set it back up when we get back.

"Okay, who's rolling for breakfast?" Angie says as her eyes dart back and forth between Cis and myself. Cis digs deep into his pocket and pulls out his lucky D12. He rattles the die in his cupped hands, pulls them close to his face, and blows on them.

"Twelve—we can find a nice brunch place," he says after a deep breath.

"Six—franchise pancakes," I add in.

"One—hotel lobby's rubbery bagels and unrefrigerated yogurt," Angie says as she raises her crossed fingers.

"Are the crossed fingers in favor of or against the one?" I ask.

"Definitely against. I'm also not sure there are four numbers between the hotel's continental breakfast and a franchise pancake, though. I'm really hoping for a ten or higher," she says.

Cis rolls the die, and it lands on a four.

"Fuck…" we say in unison.

After a bit of brainstorming, it was decided to treat it mathematically for all fairness. We hit one four out of a possible twelve, which means we're looking at a place with a rating of one and a half stars out of five.

*

It turns out it's brilliantly difficult to find a one-and-a-half-star rating in a location like this. We scrolled through the first two hundred restaurants and didn't even reach the realm of three stars. The only sort features we could figure out through the website put priority on good places. It's fair. It makes sense they don't want to be responsible for patrons eating unrefrigerated yogurt, but let us live a little!

Fate isn't always kind. Today, we trade down our dice roll in hopes that karma will give us a boost for dinner. I find myself in the hotel lobby, picking through the assortment of low-budget carbs and sugar. As promised, the bagels are rubbery. The yogurt, however, resides in a small refrigerator. And the coffee is hot. Regardless of these saves, it still feels like a 'one.'

"Eat up, friends," Angie says to us, "We've got a giant bean to go check out."

I lift my bagel up as a toast and then chomp my teeth into it. It takes a bit of tugging to rip this gluttonous tire apart. I could liken its consistency to a mix of beef jerky and a hacky sack. I only hope the deliciousness of the cream cheese outweighs the pain of my sore jaw muscles.

"I'm not even sure this is capable of soaking up my excess stomach acid," Cis says as he bends his bagel in half. He releases the bent side of it and it flings back almost into its original shape.

"Try the stale muffins. That'll help," I say as I toss him a muffin. As the muffin coasts in his direction, he puts up his hand to block its flight path. Crumbs scatter on impact.

"Should've added more butter," Cis says as he looks down at the busted-up muffin lying next to his plate. He shakes his head and backs away from the counter.

"Shall we eat on the way?" I ask.

"Right after you clean up after yourself," Angie says, pointing at me and then the scattered muffin. I try responding, but she quickly shushes me. She points again to the crumbs. I grab a nearby trash can and swipe the crumbs and remaining muffin into it.

As Cis hits the bright sun rays on this beautiful day, he shrieks a bit. He looks back at me with his shriveled blue eyes as though he is seeking asylum inside the hotel. The glare off his dirty blond dome looks like he had his tips iced. I gesture for him to carry on toward the car.

Meanwhile, it is apparent who slept on the bed last night. Angie walks energetically—not weighed down by anything. The moderate waviness of her hair looks curly when pulled back in a ponytail. The contrast is stark with Cis, who is trudging along like a troll through a swamp. I can't blame him, though. I imagine it's hard to truly love life when living with a constant hangover.

The drive over to the land of the bean is quiet. The radio is playing, and soft voices sing along. The area is quite nice. It's like a chunk of the city was taken over by nature lovers. We park down the road from the bean and make our way to it.

It's bigger than I imagined. Based on the mass of people surrounding the metallic-looking bean, pictures feel pretty cliche, also a bit touristy. You have about three hundred and fifty distorted people in each shot. But yeah, not every day you can take a picture where people vary in size and shape. They range from the Slender Man to Violet Beauregarde—post-blueberry transformation.

"Can you take our picture?" Angie asks a woman next to us. After she hands off the camera, she guides us closer to the bean. Her arms extend and lay upon our shoulders as she pulls us both in a little. Through her wide smile, she whispers, "Smile, ya fuckers." As quickly as I can smile, SNAP!

"Here you go," she says as she hands back Angie's phone, "Let me know if you'd like another." I hover over Angie's shoulder as she opens up the picture.

"You got the fucker to smile!" I exclaim to Angie as I give her a pat on the shoulder. "The best I get is a grimace. Huge accomplishment!"

"That's because you're not funny. And your timing sucks," he says, grinning.

"At least you crack yourself up," I say as I direct my attention back to this ungodly-sized bean. It's more impressive the higher you look—once the fingerprints seize.

"I wonder if my dad knows about this," Angie says, "He'd get a kick out of it. He'd also feel bad for the people that have to wash it every day because people can't keep their hands to themselves."

"Like this asshole?" I point over to Cis as he's slowly mesmerized by the reflection as he puts down one finger at a time on the bean.

"Think he's seen a mirror before?" Angie responds.

"Probably not. I bet it'll blow his fucking mind."

"Yeah, yeah, I hear ya," Cis says without diverting his attention from the bean, "Wait until the guys hear about this."

"To make sure we're on the same page here," I say slowly, "You know this isn't a metallic rock that fell from the sky. Right?"

"The pyramids didn't fall from the sky either," Angie says. She winks and smiles at Cis.

"Yeah, dick," Cis says sternly as he makes eye contact with me.

She got me there. I smile and think about what kind of process it would be to make something so curvy and shiny. My brain hurts trying to picture it, as I've never fabricated anything of this size. And metal just feels so permanent.

"I'm gonna find a bathroom," Cis says as he points to some buildings to the west. "Then would you two care to walk over by the water?"

"Sure, we can start walking down that way and wait for you once we hit water," Angie suggests, and I agree.

As Cis scurries toward the street, Angie and I take a final look at the massive bean in front of us. I snap a quick photo, and we start heading toward the street.

"Did you have to go?" Angie asks.

"Nah, I should be good for a while."

We arrive at the street and head east on it. I expect to see Lake Michigan. However, I'm quickly disappointed by the view—cars, roads, and a bridge. The sky opens up, though, so I'm hoping there's a chance we are headed in the right direction.

"I hope Cis has a working compass," I mutter as I consider his path probably won't be as straight as ours.

"We all have cell phones," she says back.

"True."

I glance over my shoulder and see a remarkable view of the city. As I spin my head forward again, I quickly catch Angie side-eyeing me. She gives a smile as she looks up to the sky.

If you remove the traffic from the walk, it's actually quite tranquil. Down the road, we come up to the Great Lake and it's definitely sizable. I can't say I've ever seen a yacht club on a lake before. We're in a whole new territory of greatness, I guess.

"Hangry Stork—quite the boat name," Angie says, "Give me your best guess on who owns that."

"Who owns it?"

"Yeah."

"Hmm…let's see." I think about it for a few moments. "I'm picturing the boat is like a hospital delivery floor, short on food. Everyone is clearly hangry. Babies sound like endless sirens. I think it's owned by the head nurse."

"How much would they sell it all to you for?"

"They really just want some time out, so they're willing to go cheap. Maybe a gift certificate to Chilis?" We share a brief laugh. Then I point to another boat, "Bitter Blue—same question."

Angie smiles as her eyes lock on a tall, bearded man jamming out at the stern of the boat. "You mean the one with the guy playing the harmonica?"

"Ah, yep!" I smile at the idea that he must be living his best life.

"First off, they must've bought it with that name as he's clearly loving life."

"I mean, it's their boat. They could just rename it," I say.

Angie looks disappointed as she scoffs at me. "You never rename a boat."

"Why not?" The curiosity in my voice causes it to jump up an octave.

"It's bad luck! It's like rolling with disadvantage for the rest of your life!"

I laugh and nod. That would be quite unfortunate.

"As for these people, I bet they set the bar for everyone in the community. Pursuit of happiness? They fucking wrote the book."

"Price?"

"Their lives aren't for sale. They'll laugh you off the docks. That's not a simple luxury for them—that's their way of bonding with life. When they walk on shore, they call it sea legs. But it's actually Mother Earth rocking them back and forth, ensuring them they'll be back out on the boat before long."

"Damn...that's deep," I say as I watch the guy wail some bluesy tunes on the harmonica. No doubt, he found his place in this world.

"Okay, back to—" Angie starts to say when she's cut off.

"Dang! That guy's good!" Cis says as he comes storming down the road. He has a large coffee cup in one hand, a paper bag in the other. His mood has certainly lightened up quite a bit.

"Didn't bring me one?" I ask as I point to the coffee cup.

"I thought it'd be too early for you," he says as he opens his bag and I see some bombers in there.

"It's not even lunchtime yet," I say, slightly frustrated. My internal fingers are crossed, hoping his drinking doesn't put a damper on the day.

"Well, the hangover wasn't going to cure itself. Let's walk!" he exclaims and walks ahead of us down the path.

I sigh quietly and shrug in Angie's direction. She mirrors my motions, and then we begin following after him.

His steps are a bit jubilant now, but no doubt they'll become sloppy with time. If I could wish one thing for anyone in the world, it'd be for Cis to reach this level of contentment without the alcohol. I can understand why it's labeled a disease, but I think that also gives too much justification to people who don't try to fight it. It doesn't have to be terminal.

Cis moves to the side of the path and puts down his bag and coffee cup. He pops off his coffee cup lid and quickly refills it with one of the bombers from the bag. His eyes dart around to make sure no one spots his shenanigans.

Not much is being spoken as we walk further down the path. Everyone is a bit distracted by their own thoughts or vices. At least thirty minutes and a few thousand steps must've passed as we come up on a small park.

"Pardon me. I must relieve myself," Cis says as he veers off the path. His seal broke a couple beers ago.

"Shall we head back and find some food?" I ask Angie, who is distracted by the vast size of the lake.

"Yeah, sounds good," she says without losing eye contact with the water.

"Something up? You seem deep in your thoughts," I say.

"We should do something." Angie turns sharply towards me.

"Oh? What's that?"

She continues with her steady eye contact. "About him. We should at least talk to him. Is this normal?"

"I honestly don't know. He was at work a lot of the time, so when I saw him drink, I thought he was just relaxing after a long shift," I say.

"I definitely think we should say something, together," she quietly says, "but let's wait until we're at another location. I'd hate to ruin the home of the '95 Bulls for him." She nods over at the side of the path as Cis joins us again.

"Feeling better?" I ask Cis.

"Always when I see your face," he says as he pretends to pinch my cheeks from a distance.

"It's time for some food. You got a place lined up for us?" Angie asks Cis.

Cis nods with a sly grin and gestures for us to follow him.

*

As we entered the restaurant, I couldn't help but think that we were walking into a speakeasy. From the street, the windows are tinted dark. The hallway to the restaurant is shared with a laundromat and a locksmith. It kind of reminds me of being in Tokyo train stations as a tourist. We're trained to expect less in those venues, but sometimes, the greatest gems really are in what I perceive to be the rough.

The mood changes as we approach the entryway. As we walk within several feet of the door, the host swings the door open, wearing a suit and a large smile. Inside the restaurant, the layout is bright and very modern looking. It's a small location—it may hold only about thirty patrons.

"Welcome!" the host says as he works his way around us from the door.

"Hello," we all exclaim at slightly different times.

"I've got a reservation. It's under 'Cis' for three," Cis says as he edges his way to the stand.

"Of course! Follow me!"

The host walks very formally, almost like he's ice skating. It quickly becomes apparent that it's part of the culture here as all of the staff seems to be gliding across the floor. There are large, colorful paintings of abstract art placed by the tables. If Picasso were a graffiti artist, this is the art he would've created. The contrast between the staff and the decor is remarkable. I can only compare it to ballerinas dancing in full leotards at a nightclub, bumping some heavy bass.

"This place is fucking amazing," I whisper to Cis, "Good taste!"

"Uhh…yeah," Angie says as she looks around wide-eyed, "I really don't know how to act in a place like this."

Cis smiles proudly. I don't think he gets too many wins, so to share a piece of his passion with us? That's a huge win for him, and us. I want to just focus on the experience, but my case of curiosity is severe. How much does a place like this cost?

I lean into Cis and whisper, "Did you happen to check the prices before?"

"This one's on me," he whispers back. "Just enjoy the show."

The host glides into a spin as we arrive at our table. His left hand captures a chair that he pulls out as his right open hand presents the chair to Angie.

"Dang, AI got really good," Angie says as she shares a smile with the host and takes her seat. She bounces a couple of times in the chair as the waiter scoots her chair in. Cis and I plop down in our chairs.

"Is this your first time visiting us?" the host asks as he slides into where a fourth chair would've been.

"What gave it away?" I rhetorically ask. The host casts an authentic smile at me. His hypothetical glass is certainly overflowing with happiness. It's nice to see people who truly enjoy where they are in life and don't need to bluff their way through with arrogance.

"Sparkling or still this afternoon?"

"Any preference, Angie?" Cis looks over at her.

"I'm fine with either," she responds.

"Okay, still water sounds great. Could we get some lemon slices on the side?" Cis inquires.

"Of course," the host glides his way back to the server station.

"Do you think Faith bounces too much to work in a place like this?" Angie asks. Cis and I laugh and nod in approval.

"I could see this atmosphere working, though, with bouncy people as well," I say.

Cis quickly follows with, "They may need to install some suspension on the trays, though. Otherwise, those plates would be a mess!"

As I study the menu, I have to revisit my phone a lot to look up some of these terms. It feels like I'm doing research for another thirty-page paper. I'd also label this type of restaurant as more of a dinner place, and I am quite surprised they even open for lunch. It just seems like too much effort, given the time of day.

Another gentleman shows up at the table with water.

"Welcome! I'm Josh, and I'll be your server for this experience," he says as he starts pouring water into our glasses. "If you haven't seen our cocktail menu yet, our mixologist comes up with some of the most amazing things you'll ever taste! Also, if you decide you'd like to start on the food menu, we also make suggestions for both alcoholic and non-alcoholic drinks that pair perfectly with each dish." He pauses a moment as our eyes pass over to the food menu. "And one last thing before I open the floor. This is the part in the speech where most servers would give you the daily specials, but since our menu is updated every other week, we treat all menu items as specials."

"I'm sorry, did you say every other week?" a wide-eyed Cis asks the waiter.

"Yes, sir. And believe it or not, sometimes it's every week. We believe in slow movement and aim to get eighty percent of our produce and meats from local farms and vendors within a hundred miles of here. That leaves us to the mercy of the harvest gods and the sorrow of the local butchers."

"I'm wildly impressed!" Angie exclaims.

"She speaks for all of us," I say.

"Do you have a tasting menu for lunch?" Cis asks.

"Not a tasting menu per se, but we do have a sampler meal, which includes two appetizers, two entrees and two desserts. Of course they're small portions of the regular-size menu items, but I assure you that it won't leave you hungry!"

"Is this heaven? Am I dead?" Angie asks as she looks at each of us.

*

Lunch will go down as absolutely mind-blowing, and it's a restaurant that I'll forever remember. The drinks really are incredible, and they trigger Angie into some brainstorming. Each of us has a sampler meal with all unique options. I can honestly say that all six appetizers, six entrees, and six desserts are unbelievable. Mixed into that, the laughs are plentiful too.

We leave the restaurant and just start walking in a completely random direction.

"What else is on the agenda, Cis?" I ask Cis, who's trailing a little behind.

"Oh! I got something!" he says as he looks up from his phone. "Follow me." He walks past Angie and I. I look at Angie, and she seems content with whatever is next.

After walking briskly for several blocks, we come upon a place that has a pirate theme to it. The sign is rough wood, stained quite dark, and has an actual ax sticking out of it. Cis turns toward the door. He reaches out and pulls back on the door, but his hand misses the vertical door handle, and he stumbles back a few feet.

"Are you sure you want to be throwing an ax?" I ask him.

"If it wasn't a drunken sport, they wouldn't have a bar inside," he says over his shoulder. He steps forward and promptly opens the door.

"Fair," I said as I gestured for Angie to go in first. I follow behind her.

The sign is not misleading at all. Indoors, it's very dark except for the light silver fences set up around each station. Large busted-up boards with spray-painted targets sit on the back of each bay. Some heavy classic rock rings over the speakers, but not too loud.

Cis walks up to the sign-in host, who happens to double as the bartender. The bar looks like it's salvaged from previous owners. Planks replace the normal bar tops. Some old beer barrels replace the base of the stools. What was once likely the server's area is transformed into the sign-in location.

The host is dressed to look tough, but her smile dissipates any intimidation. Besides, if she was plopped into any other setting, I would've taken her for a biker instead. Her genuine smile makes me question if this area of Chicago is all happy or if we're just getting lucky.

"Welcome in! Looking for a bay for three?" she says as she looks over our shoulder to double-check her count.

"Yes, ma'am," Cis responds.

"Great! Have you thrown axes before?"

"Yes," Angie says from behind. Cis and I both turn to face her. She looks caught off guard and explains, "I used to help chop wood in my earlier years." It was far less engrossing than our vivid imaginations set up for us.

"Sounds like you're a few steps ahead of these two then," the host says with a wink to Angie. "I can get you set up on bay four over by the window. I'll give you a run down in a moment, but if you have any questions after, my pirate name is Stash. Just give me a yell. For now, though, let's go over weaponry. As you can see on this wall behind us, we have a full assortment of your typical sharp objects like axes, knives, and throwing stars. We work with a local blacksmith artist who also creates these other pieces for us."

The host walks over to the shelf behind her. She lifts up a metallic object that's shaped like a broken bottle.

"That must be for the ranged DPS in a bar fight?" Angie asks, which causes Stash to light up.

"Exactly!"

Stash continues onto the next object that looks like a wooden stake and says, "And this is for when you're in a bar of vampires!" Down the line, we saw several other spiked objects, including a club and coffee mug. There was even a laptop with three razor-sharp edges.

"This is for those tough days at work where you just want to yeet it against the wall," Stash says as she pretends to fling it across the room.

"That's perfect for this one," Angie says as she points to me.

Cis pulls out the twelve-sided die from his pocket. He holds it up to Stash and says, "So we carry around this die here. We roll it occasionally and base our following moves on the result of the roll."

"Like LARP?" Stash asks.

"Exactly!" Cis responds. He continues, "If we each roll the die, could you give us a weapon of your choice? A twelve would be the one you'd expect to score the highest, and a one would be a real dud of a weapon."

"Absolutely! Let it roll!" Stash says excitedly as she rubs her hands together.

"Okay." Cis looks around as he warms up the die in his right hand, "Let's roll for initiative."

He plops the die down on the counter. It bounces awkwardly as it hits divots in the wood.

"A nine," he says as his die comes to a stop, "I'm feeling pretty good about that one."

"Okay, give it here," Angie steps up to the counter. She gives the die a bit of a backspin in the air, and it lands on a five. Angie shrugs and hands me the die.

I blow a burst of warm air on the die, shake it, and toss it across the counter. It lands, unfortunately, on two, so I'll be waiting for the last item.

"Okay, here's how it'll play out. You're going to roll three times. Each roll will represent a weapon, and we'll go in the order of you, you, and you. No repeats in weapons," Stash says as she points to Cis, Angie then me. She picks up the die from the counter and inspects it. After feeling confident that it's not weighted, she hands it to Cis.

"Let's fucking go!" Cis says as he tosses the die high in the air. The die rotates rapidly in the air and lands smack on a divot. It shoots the die over the counter, just like with Angie at the bar. Cis leans over the counter to take a look.

"Ten, let's go," Cis smiles as he pulls himself back from the bar. Stash hums as she turns toward the back wall. Her focus is clearly on the knives and axes as they seem the most weighted toward success. She pulls down a blade that looks like a Celtic cross with a hilt. The edges of the cross are sharpened, and it looks quite deadly.

"I think I'll go with this for you. The weighting on it isn't perfect, but as you can see, the area that has to hit the target is quite forgiving." Stash hands the ax to Cis and then picks up the die from the ground and hands it to Angie.

She swiftly rolls the die, and it lands on a five. Her shoulders sag with the news.

"Ooo, now things will get interesting. Tell me," Stash looks at Angie, "Are you a flower girl?"

"Ha. I assume you're not talking about the young girls in a wedding. And I enjoy some fresh flowers from time to time," Angie says as she nods to Stash.

Stash opens a drawer and pulls out what looks like a metallic mace in the shape of a rose. The pedals are of various heights and look incredibly sharp.

"This one is one of my favorites," Stash says as she holds it up for Angie to see, "The weighting on it is nearly perfect. However, it's not forgiving. The mace has to hit like this, or it doesn't stick," Stash explains as she holds it horizontally in the air.

"Okay," I say, "the suspense is quite possibly killing me."

Stash giggles as she hands me the die.

"Here goes everything." I hold the die between my middle finger and thumb and flick the die wildly into the air. I take a step back as it hits the ground approximately where I was previously standing. I see a twenty as it's first hitting the ground. I can only imagine how cool that weapon would be. It bounces a few more times and then settles.

Everyone goes silent. Even the music is just a silent vibration in my chest. I open my mouth to say something, but only air passes out. My head begins to droop and shake involuntarily left and right.

Breaking through the silence is a loud, roaring laugh from Cis.

"A one," Cis says through his laughter, "a fucking one!"

Stash slowly grinds her teeth in pretend dismay, but the look is quickly replaced by a large smile and even larger eyes.

"I know exactly what you're getting!" she hustles back to a drawer in the back. She turns toward us with something behind her back. "Now," she says, "I understand we just met, and I haven't built up any goodwill yet. Please don't hate me."

She reveals my weapon from behind her back. It's a fucking metallic rock shaped slightly like a unicorn head. Cis and Angie both burst out laughing.

"I'm supposed to stick the wall with that dinky-ass horn?"

"Unless you're strong enough to split the wood with the dull end." Stash's words only make Cis and Angie laugh harder. The fucking thing is the size of a baseball, and the odds of hitting the wall with the horn is probably one in one hundred. I smile at the irony of it, but this is going to suck.

"Okay," I say in defeat. "Bay four. I'm going to need a beer for this. Could I get whatever IPA you recommend?"

"Ah yes," Cis breaks away from laughing, "We'll take a pitcher, please. I guess the least I can do is pay for it."

We settle up with Stash and set our weapons and beers down on the counter by our bay.

"This rose screams, 'barbaric with good intentions,'" Angie says as she admires her rose.

Stash comes by after we've put our things down and offers some direction. All of her demonstrations she performs with a normal ax, which doesn't give me much confidence in my fucking rock. She does show the distance, swing, and timing for the rose mace, so at least I'm the only one with some room for shitty excuses.

My turn has come. I approach the line that she recommends throwing from. Given the weight and size of the rock, I turn sideways and look over my left shoulder like a baseball pitcher. I extend my arm back and launch the rock at the back wall.

THUMP!

The rock bounces off at the same velocity as it hit. It spins violently and then pierces the floor in front of me. I just stare at it through an angry squint.

I hate rocks.

CHAPTER 5

~ The Night Has Come ~

After throwing that rock for a couple hours, we determine it's time to leave. The air feels great outside, and the sun is now blocked by the towering buildings around us. We begin our journey toward our next landmark before actually knowing where that is.

"Shall we get a snack somewhere?" I ask Cis, who looks a bit like a disheveled child coming down from a sugar buzz. He's completely worn out but still too hyped up to settle down.

"Yes! I'm down for anything!" Angie says.

"Let's…" Cis starts to speak, then softly gasps. He clears his throat and starts over. "Let's go to the Hancock place."

"Oh my God—yes! I've actually heard about the bar that overlooks the world," Angie says. I'm not a fan of heights, but I also don't want to limit this trip to frivolous things like that. In support of them, I do a quick search on my phone for directions.

"Well, that's convenient. We're actually halfway there already. It's about fifteen minutes away," I say.

The walk makes it quite clear that the alcohol is starting to take over control of Cis. He stumbles a bit but at least stays vertical and stable enough not to alert anyone other than Angie and myself. It's a quiet walk—just what we need, I feel.

We approach the tower and travel up the elevator to their sky-high restaurant. They're just opening for their dinner service, and Angie convinces the host to give us a corner seat. Cis and Angie take the seats next to the windows and gawk at the views. Excitement rings as they point out things they recognize to each other.

I, on the other hand, have my seat about six feet from the far corner of the table. I'm so far back that staff and other guests have to walk between me and the table to get by. This is one of those places I'd have no problem experiencing through pictures. My heart beats loudly, but I try not to let the anxiety win the battle.

"Dude, you gotta see this." Cis waves for me to come closer but doesn't actually turn his body or head from the view.

"I'm good," I say as I pull my legs back to let another patron pass by.

"No, seriously! You have to check this out!" his voice gets louder, stirring up the light crowd of senior citizens and business suits.

"No, really, I'm good," I reply.

"Good evening," the waitress pops in behind me, "is this your first time dining with us?"

"Yes, but we're just here for some apps and drinks," Cis says as he brings his focus back inside.

"I can help with the apps, but I was advised not to serve you any drinks," the waitress said in an apologetic voice.

"What? Are you fucking serious?! Who told you that?" Cis's face starts to turn tense and red. "I hope it wasn't fucking you," he says as he points the finger at me.

"It was my manager," she quickly said. It was me, actually. I know we're already in the intoxication stage. I didn't know we were in the red zone.

I imagine the shots near the end of the ax-throwing place probably kicked in on the walkover.

"Then bring that buffoon over, I have some words for him," Cis says sternly to her.

"I actually think it's best that you leave," the waitress responded. She didn't seem like the type of person to tolerate such behavior. Good for her.

"You know what," Cis stands up sharply, tipping his seat back, "fuck this place. Fuck all of you!" As he starts to walk away from the table, he trips slightly over his chair. He catches himself and then storms to the elevator. I quietly thanked and apologized to the waitress. I give her a tip for the headache and follow after him.

Angie is used to being around drunks of all types. I'm impressed by her patience as she tries to be supportive of Cis without being an enabler or a parent to him. She strikes a wonderful balance, which is, of course, why everyone loves her.

As we get to the elevator, Cis pulls the die out of his pocket.

"Anything lower than a nine, and I'm going to take a shit on the floor," Cis says as he tosses the die in the air. I reach out and snag the die out of the air.

"No. No one is taking a shit," I put the die in my pocket as I herd Cis into the elevator. I keep my arms extended to avoid any runaway scenarios. Once I hear the door close behind us, I lower my guard and turn to see Angie by the elevator buttons. Her face remains patient, but her eyes show a growing concern for our friend. Like a werewolf, he transforms in the night. When he awakens in the morning, the path of destruction left behind is but a faint memory to him. To the rest of us, it's another bloody battle in a never-ending war.

"Well, that place is fucked. Where to?" Cis asks.

"My feet could use some downtime. I vote we hit up the hotel for an hour or two," I say.

I physically felt fine. I didn't actually want to go to the hotel. However, it did feel absolutely necessary in order to maintain some level of mental health for Angie and myself. Alcoholics and day drinking never end on a positive note.

"Okay. I'd like to grab some beer on the way back," Cis requests.

"Let's just go back for now. I don't need long and we can come back out after."

Cis agrees to my recommendation, and we stroll back to the hotel.

Angie is clearly trying to remain quiet but gives me a satisfied nod. While I'm a bit desensitized to Cis's drinking, this trip is definitely shining a new light on it. It's normal for those who drink to have a beverage after a long night of work. Unfortunately, for alcoholics, "one is too many, and a thousand is never enough."

And for Cis, every night is a long night.

*

I sit on my cot with my laptop, warming up my legs. Work can be a real blessing when you want things to pause for a moment around you. I hear a slight snore coming from the couch and see Cis's hand dangling over the top of it. It's probably safe to say that he's out for the night. I sit and watch his hand twitch and picture him reaching out of a grave like a zombie. Perhaps a phoenix would be a more appealing visualization for what I hope is in store for Cis.

"June twenty-fifth," Angie says as she comes down the stairs holding her laptop.

"That's the day after tomorrow?" I turn to ask her. I frequently lose track of the date.

"Yes."

"Is there importance to this day?"

"Not yet," she says as she sits down next to me.

"I suppose a new tradition is starting?" I ask her, thinking she came up with something fun to do in Chicago.

"Not for us. For Cis," she says. She turns her laptop to show it to me. It's a rehabilitation center based out of Jacksonville, Florida. "I may or may not have given them a call and they have room for Cis."

"Oh…perhaps we should run it by him?" I ask. I'm curious how he'd take it.

"Here's the thing. Even if he agrees to this, it's sixteen hours away. That's a lifetime for him to come up with excuses not to do it. I think we should start driving first thing in the morning and tell him we're headed to New Orleans."

"Okay, wouldn't he notice the street signs?"

"Probably not. We'll get him on the eat, drink, sleep routine like on the trip here. If and when he realizes it, we'll pull over and have the talk."

"So what's the twenty-fifth if this is happening tomorrow?" I ask.

"His sobriety date. Potentially. Also, halfway to Christmas."

I pause for a moment as I stare through her laptop screen. I pull the die from my pocket.

"No," Angie says as she covers my hand with hers, "this is something we need to do. Cis needs a pivotal moment in his life, and he needs it right now. And while I'd love to go party it up in New Orleans for real, I think we both know how that would go."

- 68 -

"You're right," I reply as I put the die back in my pocket. My hands begin to tremble slightly as a tear forms in the corner of my eye.

"Let's do this," I say as I close my laptop.

Angie rubs my back with one hand. She stands up with a loud creek from the cot. We both give a soft chuckle as she migrates back upstairs to the loft.

"Get some sleep—long day tomorrow!" she yells down over her heavy footsteps.

CHAPTER 6
~ Road to Revival ~

I awaken to the sound of someone stirring around in the bathroom. My eyes slowly focus on the clock in the kitchenette area of the room. It's five in the morning. It's not strange to require bathroom breaks this early, but then the shower turns on. I glance over to the couch and can see the arm of the zombie. It must be Angie in there.

After drifting off for what feels like a second, I awaken fully to the bathroom door opening. Angie comes out with a cloud of steam and a towel around her head. She appears fully ready to take on the day. We make eye contact and she gives a tired grin. As she approaches the cot, she squats down to get close to me.

With one hand on the cot for balance, she whispers, "I think we should start the journey south so we can hopefully get there before needing another hotel."

"Yeah. Makes sense," I groggily say as I sit up in bed. I get a whiff of her hair as she stands up and it's the classic Angie smell, only it's further enhanced by the wet hair.

"You smell good," I say as I rub my eyes.

Angie shifts her head back to look at me. "Oh good," she says with a soft laugh as she heads up the stairs.

"Yo, Cis! Wake up!" I say loudly. I hear a grunt from the couch. Cis sits up with squinty eyes and messy hair. He patiently looks towards the faded digits on the microwave, probably waiting for his eyes to focus.

"It's only five!? Why are you waking me up, you monster!" Cis drops back into the couch cushions.

"We're getting an early start for New Orleans. Angie would like to reach there tonight, and it's a long ass drive." I pause for a second to hear his reaction, which never comes. "I can wake you again once I'm done with the bathroom," I say as I stand up.

"The hell you will." Cis hastily rises from his comfort zone and moves into the bathroom. I guess he didn't want to visit the lobby again. He pops his head out for the moment and asks, "Isn't there supposed to be a few places between here and there?"

"Plans have changed. We're going to zig instead of zag." I say as my hands demonstrate the change of path.

As Cis uses the bathroom, I pull together my clothes for the day and make sure everything else is packed. I sneak down to the lobby for a quick bathroom break and the much-needed coffee bar.

The hotel starts serving coffee for free rather early. I imagine it's to keep the overnight staff awake and relatively alert. I put together three coffees: two regular and mine is half regular, half decaf. I like the gradual change of energy. The same applies to alcohol. I'd prefer to drink an excessive amount of low-percentage beer before I'd enjoy getting sloppy with hard liquor. It avoids scenarios where jitteriness and anxiety take over.

I struggle to open the hotel door while holding the three cups. With a few kicks to the bottom of the door, I gain the attention of Cis, who comes to the rescue.

"Delivery!" I say as he takes two of the cups from me.

"Angie! There's a coffee down here for ya!" Cis yells up the stairs. Angie looks over the edge of the loft and catches my attention. She fingers for me to come up.

"I can bring it up," I say as I close the door and grab her cup back from Cis. As I come up the stairs, it's dark except for the light illuminating off of her laptop screen. She waves for me to come closer while also holding up a finger to ask for my silence.

The glowing mess of the laptop turns into a legible website. It appears to be from the rehab clinic. She points to a section that shows the supported health insurance.

Cis and I both signed up for insurance through the government. With his chef work and my freelance work, insurance is a perk not many have the privilege of getting. While anything from the government isn't perfect, it may just pay off. I point to the screen and give a thumbs-up to Angie. She's been in contact with the clinic, so I imagine she's making sure he doesn't have to declare bankruptcy in order to have a chance at sobriety.

"Enjoy! Gonna take a shower and should be good to go in a bit," I casually say as I bounce down the stairs. I don't want to look suspicious to Cis, so I avoid eye contact. I grab my clothes from the cot and head into the bathroom.

As the door closes, I feel relieved of the pressure. I'm really bad at hiding things. I honestly see no reason to lie because it's such an exhausting task to keep up with. Angie is right, though. It's a long drive, and who knows what will happen if he knows the truth. For today, I'll just be a loyal follower and see where she takes us.

After a quick shower and shave, I turn off the water and hear talking outside the door. I get dressed and open the door. Angie and Cis are in the living room chatting about New Orleans. It's mostly the regular mentions of beignets at Cafe Dumonde and the French Quarters. I drift back into my thoughts once they start talking about the value of beads during Mardi Gras.

I look into my own eyes in the mirror. I really hope this person I see is someone who can pull off what feels like a heist. It's an attempt to strip Cis of this nasty disease. We may not be vaccines, antibiotics, or even superheroes, but I think there's hope to rid him of it. Fuck alcoholism.

"Okay, just about ready," I say as I work my way into the living room and toss my dirty clothes in my bag. I scan around the room and point out that Cis's phone charger is still in the wall. He packs it up and finalizes stage one of leaving the hotel.

"I can grab the keys and check out," Angie offers. I hand my key to her.

"I checked out on the app, so you only need to toss them in the drop box," I say. She raises her arm in acknowledgment and heads out the door.

"Are you all sure we don't want to make a couple of stops on the way? I mean…New Orleans is across the country!" Cis exclaims. I'm sure if the stakes were lower, we'd have a few destinations and sleepovers between here and there. That's not the case, though.

"We'll be good. We'll rotate drivers and stop for food along the way," I explain as I turn my attention back to my bag. I pretend to rummage around in it a bit so he won't be able to figure out from my eyes that there are some hidden agendas.

"Can we start with one of those food stops?" he responds.

"Absolutely. I'd kill for something to go with this coffee." I pick up my bag and walk past him toward the door. I push the door open for Cis and continue down the hallway.

"I'll be right behind you," Cis says as the door shuts. Seconds later, I hear the crisp sound of a beer cracking open. I guess he wasn't going to wait to kill the hangover. I'm also caught off guard, as I have no idea where that beer came from. Out of curiosity, I slow my pace down. Less than a minute later, I heard a loud burp and another "ksssst" sound. My man was holding out on us. Good for him.

I meet Angie, who's out by the car now, and we sit, checking our phones while we await for Cis to arrive. The brisk breeze washes away my tiredness, much like a cold shower. It brings a level of clarity to the morning. I can only compare this feeling to when you sit alone at the bow of a moving motorboat. The wind is deafening, as though it's protecting your thoughts from any outside opinion. As you skid across the water, you might as well be on top of the world. You're untouchable.

Cis finally arrives. He's chewing gum, which he rarely does. I know the reason, and I'm sure Angie does now, too, considering he reeks far more of beer than what any mint could output.

"Ready for a square ass?" I ask him.

"You know it!" he says.

We fill into the car like sleep-walking synchronized swimmers. The doors slam in unison, and we're locked in for the road trip. Goodbye, Chicago. You were fun, for the most part.

*

I drive for the first few hours with no music or talk. Cis is surprisingly awake still, but the beer is slowly becoming the victor in the battle against the coffee. Occasionally, his head starts to drop, and then he awakens quickly. He gives a cough followed by some intense swallowing. I don't know how much rehabilitation can fix it, but I hope we find out.

Angie was alert for the first hour but decided to get some shut-eye as we'll be swapping the driving responsibilities throughout the day. She has a rolled-up sweatshirt as a pillow against the door of the car. Her body leans into it, much like a mermaid pose. The waves will definitely be crashing later today. I'm afraid the skies feel a bit ominous at the moment.

I like playing a game where I go ridiculously deep into my thoughts. I argue with myself about various scenarios until I'm completely annoyed. Then, I put my "trust in fate" by turning on the radio and letting the lyrics guide my direction. As I turn it on, it's easy to identify the song "O-o-h Child." As they sing, "we'll put it together and get it undone," I realize there's no turning back now. I look in the rearview mirror and see Cis asleep. "Things are gonna get easier," bud.

"Trust in fate" has been a motto of mine for many years. Perhaps I'll dive deep into that at some point, but for now, my focus is on the single point of failure in the backseat. In the spectrum of how things are going, I'm faring well.

Cis and I go way back. He was my first friendship that didn't end when the school year did. Whether he liked it or not, that responsibility remained his for many, many years. Next year will mark a quarter of a century.

Our interests over the years varied a bit, but it didn't stop us from continuously crossing paths like a thin, tight braid of hair. We had our first drinks together back when we were fifteen. Those frequented our crossing paths as much as anything else had. Our lives were so close at times that you would assume we were in parallel universes based on how different things turned out for each of us. "Nature versus nurture" with another questionable feat.

We've had our fights over the years. It was never anything physical, just me getting mad at Cis for acting like a selfish prick. And vice versa from time to time. Those fights dissipated long before we moved in together. And with his work hours, we have a lot of time to ourselves. When he is home, I'm usually working on code or writing in the privacy of my room.

I have to figure out when I'm going to grab another coding contract. They offered to extend it indefinitely, but I chose to take a break to work on my novel. I feel like I'm living in my own novel now. It's a novel of uncertainty, mysterious loveable figures, and I fucking hope a happy ending. I really do.

*

Just outside of Indianapolis, we find a diner off the highway. Angie looks a bit refreshed after splashing water on her face in the bathroom. Cis's face is glazed over. I'm sure I'm somewhere between the two of them.

The waitress has come and gone with our order. I think we're all a bit sick of eating out. It's easy to romanticize a life where you never have to cook, but the excessive use of butter and salt is typically not part of that dream. Would it be so bad to have delicious food that isn't trying to kill me?

Talking about killing, Cis's Bloody Mary shows up with our coffee and juices. The biggest jokes are all of the obstacles that he'll need to dodge in order to get to the booze. I'm surprised he doesn't instruct them to hold the garnishes and spiced tomato juice.

"I should be good to drive until Nashville. Shall we plan to stop for lunch then?" Angie asks.

"That should work. It'll probably be around three-thirty by then. I suppose a late lunch, so we can follow it with a late dinner," I say.

"When is playtime?" Cis asks as he sips on his drink.

"It's now. Look under that enormous green stalk," I point out as he maneuvers around a long piece of celery.

"Angie, how do you feel about cheeseburgers as garnishes for Bloody Marys?" Cis asks.

"I suppose if I wanted someone dead, that's a non-suspicious way to complete the task." Angie pauses for a moment. "If it were up to me, alcohol would be eliminated from breakfast altogether."

Cis jokingly gasps loudly.

"I'm glad it's not up to you," he says.

"Honestly, it's really just a marketing choice by large booze makers. It's a free pass to let you drink beyond your limit the day before because POOF! Next morning, we'll fix your shit with more shit! Then you have some people who can carry on with their days. Others, though, propel into a nasty pattern of day drinking that leads to people wanting to shit in restaurants," she says with a grin.

"Doesn't your business thrive from boozers?" he asks.

"I take no pleasure in it. And it's not my business. It's like a bear trap that I got snagged in years ago."

"Are we the teeth of the trap?" I ask.

"More like the scars that will remain when I finally free myself," she says.

Cis and I both laugh as we look at each other. Simultaneously, we ask each other, "We're scars!?"

"Not like the scar from a tragic accident," she pulls her shirt aside and shows a scar by her collarbone. She points to it and says, "This was from my first time falling into a bowl. Hurt like hell, but it reminds me of those simpler days. It was an early step into my skating phase."

"Then I hope we're an early step into something you'll happily remember," I say.

"Me too," she says with a smile. "Me too."

Angie's cell phone rings. She hurriedly heads outside to answer the call. We can't hear her conversation, but her body language says something isn't going well.

"Think that prick finally realized she's not working?" Cis asked, referring to the owner of her bar.

"Probably something like that." I begin to mindlessly fidget with a straw wrapper that was on the table. My hands like to keep busy when my thoughts are all over the place.

A thousand scenarios flow through my head. Maybe it's her dad, and something bad happened. Is this as far as she goes with us? Or maybe the clinic filled up, and we actually have to go to New Orleans now.

"Going to hit the bathroom," I say as I scoot out of the booth. I approach the entrance where the bathrooms are and wait for Angie to finish up her call. I'm not in Cis's line of sight, so hopefully, he doesn't catch on.

Angie comes through the door and catches eye contact with me. After a long sigh followed by a hearty chuckle, she quietly catches me up on everything that's transpired since morning.

We briefly visit the bathrooms and then return to the table, where Cis is working on what appears to be a mimosa.

"Everything alright?" Cis asks Angie.

"Yeah, just something—" Angie starts to speak as the food arrives. Saved by the bell! She quickly turns her attention to the server and helps direct the plates to the right person. It's no Chicago food, but it'll get us to Tennessee.

As the servers clear the area, silence comes across the table. We probably look like we haven't eaten in days with how badly we're devouring our food. To be honest, though, there's really no reason to savor it. Restaurants put salt and pepper on tables because of cooks like this. If bland was the target, then they nailed their bullseyes.

The food was eaten, cleared, and paid for so quickly that Cis is still finishing his second mimosa. The biggest downfall to traveling with drinkers is how often they need to take breaks. I'll try to save up some patience though by sleeping through as much as I can. It really does feel like a marathon ahead of us.

Cis realizes we're waiting on him, so he chugs the last bit of his drink and steps away from the table.

Angie waits for Cis to leave our view. She turns back and gently asks, "Are you sure you're ready for this?" Her eyes hold a lot of sympathy. I'm sure she's ready to support me however I respond.

"Probably not, but I also can't imagine a better time," I say nervously.

"It's fair to have nerves. It's day zero. The anticipation before the jump is always the scariest part," she says, "I think we'll be a good team through this."

I smile at Angie. It's easier to hang onto my dwindling faith when she is around. If she thinks there's a reason to believe, nothing can get in our way. I raise my hand for a high-five, and she meets me halfway.

We rise from the table and reconnect with Cis by the door.

"There's a convenience store across the street, Cis," Angie says to him as we exit the restaurant.

"Don't need to tell me twice," he says as he redirects his trajectory.

"We'll pick ya up," I say as I continue to the car with Angie. I hand Angie the keys and then get into the passenger side.

"I don't want him to have buyer's remorse," she says as she sits down and puts the key into the ignition.

"Buyer's remorse? He won't regret buying alcohol," I say out of the side of my mouth as I get settled in my seat.

"I don't mean for this purchase. He doesn't realize this could potentially be his last day of drinking. I don't want him to feel like it was wasted," she says while looking at me. She turns back to the wheel and says, "Let's just hope he buys into the plan."

"Yeah, I agree." It's one thing to ask someone to postpone an activity. It's another thing to ask them to never do it again. "I hope we're more convincing than the disease."

We pull the car across the road into the parking lot of the convenience store. Cis comes out with a double-cupped coffee and a brown paper bag under his arm. The smile on his face is like a kid who just got asked to a dance by their longtime crush.

Cis enters the car, separates the extra cup from his coffee then hands the coffee forward.

"I didn't want to be too obvious. Not sure about the laws around here," he says, "Also figured the caffeine may come in handy for you."

"Thanks," Angie says, "I'm glad to be part of the cover-up. I'm sure someone will drink it before too long!"

"As will I!" he proudly exclaims from the back.

*

Cis is sound asleep in the backseat as we finally hit our destination in Jacksonville. Angie and I each have a bit of energy left in our tanks, thanks to the on-and-off naps we've each had. We have a cooler full of half-melted ice, liquor, juice, and beer. Angie had me pick it up in Nashville, claiming it'd be too late to get anything once we got to New Orleans.

The trip was timed well, as we coincidentally passed all border crossing signs while Cis was sleeping—at least all of the ones that would've suggested our true destination. Due to the confidentiality surrounding the day, I'm mostly in the dark, too, since we couldn't get into any details. I imagine the truth will all start to unravel soon.

Angie rolls onto a side street and kills the engine.

"Ready?" she turns to me and asks. I nod with a bit of uncertainty as I turn to look in the back seat.

"Yo, Cis! Time to get up!" I bellow into the backseat. He slowly opens his eyes, but his body remains still.

"We in New Orleans?" he asks. He looks out the window, but this dark side street is anything, but identifying. Our current view is just of single story homes with cost-efficient vehicles parked up and down the street.

"Not exactly," I say. He sits up and looks around. We're just out of sight from the clinic, so he's not tipped off.

"Where are we?" he asks as he rubs the sleep out of his eyes.

"One sec," Angie says as she exits the car. She opens the backdoor and Cis pulls over his pile of stuff as she takes its place.

"Brey and I think you're an amazing friend, wonderful chef, and just an all-around great guy," Angie starts saying. Cis's eyes grow wide.

"Is this a threesome or an intervention?" Cis asks. I laugh as Angie stays focused.

"It's the latter. We've watched you transform into someone else during this trip and it's not the same person we came on this trip with," she continues as Cis's face turns tense, "We would love it if you would check into rehab."

Cis sits up and starts breathing a bit quicker. "What the fuck?! Was this the whole reason I was invited on this trip?"

"Not at all," I say. I didn't think now was a good time to remind him it was his idea.

"Do you know how far a rehab place would set me back? I don't even have a fucking job! No job. No insurance," he says. He starts stuffing his loose items into his bag.

"Angie made some calls. The clinic can help you get insured," I say to him, "and if there are additional costs, we already agreed to cover them." I pull up the headrest of my seat as it feels ridiculous talking around it.

"So it's all decided?! You ditch me in some shitty corner of America and continue on without me?" He pulls his lumped up belongings onto his lap. If flight is his intention, it doesn't seem too far out.

"Not exactly," Angie says.

"No. That's EXACTLY what this is!" His voice fills with irritation.

I hold out my palm to stop him. "We're going with you."

"Why would you come with me?" Confusion overtakes his irritation.

"No matter how enraged your barbaric ass is, you still need your bard and cleric for this adventure," I say, "And believe it or not, we need you."

"Yes. We love you, and we need this to happen and we need it to be successful. This isn't the end of our journey. It's simply a side quest," Angie says.

"What about your jobs?" he asks in a more serious tone.

"Medical leave for mine. Brey is already on break," Angie tells him. "And what's more inspiring for a book than a trip to rehab?"

I laugh. I know about as much of the insides of a rehab clinic as I do my body. There's some therapy, probably some horses, and maybe healthy food to revitalize our livers and brains. Perhaps I can change my novel to a bunch of scouts singing kumbaya in front of a well-lit campfire.

"Listen—I understand I've been an ass at times," Cis says calmly, "but you two really don't have to do this." He pauses for several seconds and then says, "I'm willing to go."

"Hooah!" I shout out. I shake my car seat out of excitement.

"Opah!" Angie shouts as she squeezes his shoulder.

"One last thing to do then," I say to Cis. Then I turn and smile at Angie.

"Hopefully, get out of this car? My ass hurts," Cis says as he squirms around a bit.

"Even better. We've got a story to sell. Never trust a skinny chef, right?" I smile as I jump out of the car and go back to the trunk area. Angie climbs into the front again as I pop the release for the backseat to flop down.

"What's behind door number one!?" I hear Angie excitedly ask Cis.

I jump back into the front seat for the big reveal. With my legs crossed, I sit backwards with my back to the dashboard. Cis pulls down the seat and sees a styrofoam cooler. It stands a bit too tall, but he's able to slide the top off and slosh around in the icy waters. His face lights up as he pulls out a handful of nips.

"I need a better view of this," he pulls on the fragile cooler to slide it into view. The styrofoam chips off like it always does. With a little more care, he's able to jimmy it halfway into the backseat.

"Is this Christmas?" he asks with a delightful look on his face.

"Nah, it's just the Christmas party," I say, "Now stop being greedy and pass some shit out!"

"Okay, okay! For the bard of the group, here's your own copy of *Tequila Mockingbird,*" he says as he tosses me a nip of tequila.

"You went bard before the cleric? Bold move," Angie tells Cis as she waggles a finger in his direction.

"I needed time to come up with a new pun," he says, then pauses as he stares at the available booze in front of him.

"I got one," I say excitedly, "how about some vodka for the saucy cook?" Cis holds his thumb out sideways then points downward in a disapproving gesture.

"I expect more from the Bard, but I don't have all night," he says as he cracks it open and downs the shot.

"Okay. I got it," Cis clears his throat in preparation, "Let the fun begin!" Cis tosses Angie a gin. "Take two, but don't call me in the morning. Alcohol you!"

"Okay, okay. Lime not good at puns, but you'd really Schweppe me off my feet if you have some tonic to go with it," Angie recites. Cis and I applaud the efforts as he scurries in the back to find her sly demands. As Cis rummages for the tonic, he comes across some beer first. He hands me one and slides another between his legs for temporary storage.

"Quick question," Cis says, "if we all get shitty, how do we get to the club of quitters?"

"We walk," Angie says with a quick smile, "we're only two blocks away from it!"

"Didn't realize I was drinking with a couple of geniuses," Cis says as he cracks open his beer. He puts the can up to his mouth and just leans back.

"How about that tonic while you're still somewhat functioning?" Angie asks with a playful, disappointed look on her face.

"Oh shit," he says as he quickly puts the beer back down. "I totally forgot what I was doing."

"No kidding," I say as I raise my beer in a toast, "To Cis: the guy I'll never forget. From the guy, he's already forgotten."

Cis locates the tonic and hands it to Angie. She has the gin already locked and loaded in the cup. Just as quickly as the tonic touches the gin, the whole drink is gone.

"Whoa!" I nod multiple times to Angie as I'm inspired by her dedication to getting drunk. "Someone is on a mission."

"Give me that bottle of Pinot, please," she requests. Cis hands her the bottle and the corkscrew. Like a true ace, she pops the cork out and then proceeds to chug probably a glass or so worth of wine straight from the source. Cis and I watch in awe as we wonder how far she'll go. With a loud belch, she lowers the bottle and passes it to me.

"Okay, grab me one of those Bud Lights," I say, "This is a combination that only few know. You chug a little red wine, then follow with Bud Light."

"You chase your wine?" Cis asks me with an awkward look on his face.

"It's more like a diluter. Similar to juice with hard liquor," I say, "When you drink the light beer right after, the red wine doesn't get taken over by the beer. It instead expands into this mixed drink that fills every corner of your mouth. It's a blessed feeling. And, of course, it fucks ya up sideways."

As Cis is handing a beer forward, Angie snags the beer and the wine out of my hands. Without any hesitation, she puts the bottle to her lips and tilts her head back. After four or five seconds, she lowers her head, swaps out the wine for the beer then fills her mouth with it. Angie gently swishes the beer as she stares downward, contemplating what she got herself into.

With her cheeks still full of beer, she gives an approving nod to me and then swallows. She hands me the beer and wine slowly. No words escape her open mouth, but the intent is there.

"Speechless?" I ask her.

"Uh-huh," she says, "That's actually pretty good. It removes any burn of alcohol, so the bottle probably goes down like sangria."

"Okay, I have to try now," Cis says as he reaches for it. I give the wine and beer a quick chug, then pass it off to him. He proceeds to go back and forth a few times between bottle and can.

"Does it get your approval?" I ask him.

"Yes, and I'm glad we're all going to rehab after this. This'll fuck ya up before the cock goes a doodle!"

We drink through another bottle of wine, six or seven nips, and finish the twelve-pack of beer. The only remains are puddles in the bushes from where we relieved ourselves. This session requires treatment like a delicate acid trip: only positive talk.

"Well," I say, "fuck. It'd be much cooler if we were just going to bed."

"They don't have beds?" Cis says with a slight slur.

"Of course they have beds," Angie confirms, "I didn't actually ask though. Fuck. I hope they have beds."

I collect our trash and any remnants of alcoholic products and discard them quietly in a trash bin down the street. My car will hopefully be safe here for however long we're in for.

"Are you all ready for a new life?" I ask them as we collect our belongings from the trunk.

"I'll miss this," Cis says as he looks back and forth between Angie and me.

"It's only the alcohol going away," Angie says. She pats him gently on the back and gives a quick shoulder rub. "We got this," she says, then turns to Cis. "You got this."

CHAPTER 7

~ The Gateway ~

With the sun preparing for another rise, we drag ourselves to the well-lit entrance ahead of us. The building isn't branded by any means, but probably for privacy purposes. As we get closer to the door, a placard reads "Pond Point" to the left of the door. Two security guards, probably twins, make their way to the entryway. They're identically tall and wide—I imagine they could become a wrestling tag team if the security work doesn't pan out for them.

"May I help you?" one of the brothers asks.

"I sure hope so," Angie says, "We're a little later than expected, but alas, we're expected. Angie, Brey, and Cis." She points to each of us as she says our names.

"Yeah, you're definitely late," the other brother says.

"Did the security academy teach you to be so observant?" Cis asks through his tired eyes.

"Don't mind him. It's been a long night," I say as I hold back my laughter.

The security twins wave for the nurses behind the receptionist's desk to come forward. A blonde middle-aged woman and a black man, who looks far more fit than the security team, arrive at the door.

"Welcome to Pond Point!" the woman says with a large smile on her face, "I'm Shelly, and this is Daymond." She points to the black man, who smiles graciously with a gentle bow of the head.

"And this is Jamal and Micah. They're part of the team that keeps us all safe," Daymond says as he holds a hand out to the security twins. They both give restrained nods.

"Let's have you all take a seat up here at the desk, and we'll get you checked in," Shelly says as we follow behind her.

"We'll take those," Jamal and Micah say as they reach out for our bags.

"You better not steal any of my panties," Cis says as he squints his eyes and hands over his bag to Jamal.

"You can have some of mine if they do," Angie says as she hands her bag to Micah. Micah reaches out and takes my bag as well.

"Light packer," Micah says as he hauls off with my packed hockey bag.

Jamal and Micah walk behind the counter and start opening the bags, still in our view. They step away from the bags and let Shelly and Daymond conduct the searches.

"We only allow clothes and medication to enter the facility. It's on record that medication isn't a concern for any of you. Anything suspicious, like alcohol or drugs, gets destroyed. And anything beyond that will be locked away with your luggage until the end of your stay," Shelly explains to us.

"What is this?" Daymond pulls a small red circular pill from my bag.

"It looks like an old Tylenol that's seen better days," I tell him.

"I don't know, it looks suspicious," he says as he holds it up with his long delicate-looking fingers for the twins and Shelly to see.

"Yes. It looks suspiciously like Tylenol," I repeat. "I also have no sentimental attachment to that Tylenol, which probably expired four years ago. Just toss it." They continue to look at it in hopes of identifying it. This is going to be a long morning.

"He's probably right. Just toss it," Shelly finally says to them as the twins remain huddled over it.

"Anything else I should know about in your baggage? Anything sharp?" Daymond asks me.

"Just my wit." I wink to him.

"I'd happily lock that away," Jamal says while clearly suppressing his urge to smile at himself.

"Okay," Shelly says, "we have a couple forms for you all to sign, and then we'll show you to your beds. As you can imagine, people are sleeping, so please be quiet as you make your way in."

We all nod in response.

"For HIPAA privacy reasons, we're going to separate you all now and go through the rest of the intake process individually. You will see each other again in the morning or possibly in the afternoon, given the time."

Angie walks off with Shelly, while Cis gets pulled aside from another individual who we hadn't met yet. I get the pleasure of Daymond it seems.

"Again, welcome to Pond Point," Daymond says, "Your time here is completely voluntary, and as such, you have the right to take or refuse any medicines or medical treatments offered."

I nod and start to wonder what treatments he's referring to. I hope it's not shock therapy—it'd probably drive me to drink.

"Let's start with a quick picture so we can identify you throughout the day," he says as he points at a webcam on top of his monitor screen. It's too late for smiles, so I just look up at it. He fidgets around with the mouse and keyboard a bit. With one final hard click, I can hear a printer warming up under the counter. Daymond slides his chair back a little and watches it.

"Okay, we require patients to keep these badges around their necks and visible at all times. It's used for identification during head counts and medication time. It's also used by security to make sure only the appropriate people are within these walls," Daymond says as he pulls out a printed sticker with my name and photo on it. He slowly pulls away the sticker and adheres it to a badge with a Pond Point-branded lanyard to it, then slides it across the desk to me.

"For tonight and tomorrow night at the least, you'll be in one of our monitored rooms with one roommate."

"Monitored?" I ask as I look around to see the glow of screens coming from behind the desk.

"Yes, there are cameras. Our medical staff keeps an eye on new patients. Seizures can happen when withdrawing from alcohol. Our trained staff will come in if they have any suspicions, but otherwise, they won't enter your room," Daymond explains.

"What happens after tomorrow night?" I really don't want my stay to be televised.

"You'll move to a non-monitored room but still with a roommate. And because you're coming in for alcohol, we will prescribe you a benzodiazepine to avoid the risk of seizures as your body works through the withdrawal," he says as he shuffles through a couple of the papers in front of him.

"I'm good. I don't want the medicine," I say clearly.

"It's strongly recommended for alcoholics coming in."

I look at Daymond and he's staring at me like a teacher stares at a student when they're not following every order. "I'm good. I don't want the medicine," I repeat in a more stern voice.

"We need to avoid seizures among our new patients," he starts to explain.

"You just told me I had the right to refuse medicines. So, I refuse." I hold my eye contact to let him know I'm serious.

"I understand what you're saying. I just don't think you've fully considered—" Daymond says as I cut him off.

"Where's Shelly?! Clearly, your policies are broke, or you are hard of hearing. I'm NOT TAKING YOUR MEDICINE!" Who is this guy? He's turned me into an enraged and drunken Cis. For fuck's sake.

"Okay, okay. No need to yell," Daymond says as Micah moves in a little closer to me.

"There was a reason to yell. You couldn't hear me," I said.

"Okay. I'm going to need you to sign these forms that let us bill your insurance for your care here," he says as he tries to keep calm. He slides over the papers with a pen. In my peripheral vision, I see Micah move in a little closer again. Perhaps he thinks I'm going to stab this guy. It certainly wouldn't affect his dull senses.

"Is my care going to improve, or is this already your best foot forward?"

"Please, just sign the forms so we can get you into your room," he says.

As I sign the forms, I hear Angie laughing in the other room with Shelly. She apparently got the winner here. The person who was with Cis walks around the corner and sits down at a desk. It appears Cis, the troubled one, made it first across the finish line to bed. Or he got kicked out already. Either way, what a guy.

"Thanks," Daymond says as I finish the forms. "It looks like you had most of the expected toiletries, so they've been assembled in this bathroom bag here. We added some shampoo, conditioner, and a bar of soap." He slides a small black bag across the desk to me.

Typically, I would look in the bag to verify the list, as I already don't trust him. I'm too damn tired for that, though. I nod as I pull the bag closer to me.

"And we put all of your clothes in the dresser of the room you'll be staying in. Feel free to grab what you need from there for the night. If you'll come with me, I'll show you your room and bathroom," he says as he stands up and comes around the desk to me.

I follow Daymond down the fluorescent-lit hallway that strongly resembles a hospital with a touch of added hospitality. His long black braids sway back and forth as he hurries down to my room. He stops at a door then gestures for me to be quiet. Slowly, the door opens. The light reveals two full-size beds on the right wall, evenly spread out across the room. On the left, each bed has a small dresser across from it. Somebody sleeps quietly in the near bed.

Daymond closes the door quietly, and I follow him to the bathroom. It's remarkably similar to a dormitory bathroom at the college I attended. The smell has a strong resemblance, except it lacks that additional stench of stale beer.

"You can get ready for bed and make your way there. Since it's nearly morning, we'll let you just sleep until you're good. Then, just come up to the front desk. Someone can catch you up on the schedules there. Again, welcome to Pond Point," Daymond says with far less excitement than Shelly had. I think I annoyed him over the medicine. To be fair, though, he fucking annoyed me first.

*

My body slowly awakens. It feels like I slept on a soft, puffy cloud far from civilization. After dealing with the cot at the last hotel, I'm sure a bed of nails would've felt peaceful. It's nice being at a real hotel. I roll over and open my eyes. To my dismay, my focus and memory snap back to reality. I'm not in a hotel. I'm in rehab.

I hear faint chatter down the hall from probably a dozen voices. None of it is familiar, but I do wonder how Cis and Angie are doing. I remember there are cameras that are watching me, so I lay very still to avoid attention.

I decide I've delayed long enough, and I kick into a higher gear. I grab a change of clothes, my toiletry bag and head back down the hall towards the bathroom.

"Wait up," I hear from a recognizable voice as footsteps approach from behind. I turn around to see Cis. His hair is messy and his eyes look like they were recently sealed shut.

"Oh hey! How was your first night?" I ask him. His eyes shift around to activities happening down the hall.

"The bed was better than that couch for sure," he says. I nod intensely.

"Seen Angie yet?" I ask Cis.

He looks back at me. "Not yet. I just woke up."

"How was your guy last night who checked you in?" The medication conversation still annoys me long after it should have ended.

"Pretty incompetent. I may have dozed off once or twice as he read the forms one word at a time. Sounds like he's never done intakes before. Strangely enough, most people show up on their own and not in little parties," Cis says with a grin on his face. I shrug and nod to Cis. I suppose I can cut them some slack.

"Where's your stuff? Not showering?" I ask Cis as I realize he's not carrying anything.

"Nah, not now. Going to get some coffee first and relax a little," Cis says.

"Nice—save me a cup." I hold up my bundle of clothes. "I'll be headed that way as soon as I'm done."

We break apart, and I do my typical morning routine. I brush my teeth, shave, pee, then take a shower—almost always in that order. As I finish up my three-minute shower, the door swings open hard to the bathroom.

"Yo! This place fucking sucks! We need to find a new rehab!" Cis yells to me.

"Whoa! What happened?" I yell back.

"There's no fucking coffee! Just decaf from six to ten in the morning!" Cis continues to speak quite loudly.

"Seriously?" I ask, but try to avoid escalating further. "I'll be out in a moment and will walk down."

Realizing this may be the best part of the day, I let the hot water drizzle on my head a little longer. The plumbing here could use a urologist, but at least the water is hot. As fast as those words travel through my head, the water starts to fluctuate between ice cold and blazing hot. I turn off the water. I chalk it up as a test by the administrators. They're probably trying to see how close to the edge I am.

I get dressed, then drop off my dirty clothes, towel, and toiletry bag back at my room. My nerves start to build up a little as I look around the bare room. The sheets have been removed from my roommate's bed, which means he's either graduated from the monitoring rooms or he died—hopefully the former.

As I start coming down the hall, I can hear Cis clearly over the other voices.

"Why is there no regular coffee!?" he asks.

"It's a drug. We don't want to encourage people to just trade addictions," some unfamiliar voice says.

"What about the decaf?" he says. I can tell by his voice that he's quite irritated.

"That too can interact with people's medications."

"But not between hours of six and ten in the morning? Do you have an interaction easement with the coffee during that time?" he asks.

"Listen, you're just intellectualizing. It's a normal defensive mechanism," she responds.

"Well, if someone INTELLECTUALIZED when they came up with these horrendously stupid rules, we wouldn't be having THIS conversation," Cis loudly says. "And what about that generic Kool-Aid that's being spun around like a slushie all day long? That doesn't interact with drugs? For Christ's sake, you're giving people diabetes with that shit! At least coffee has antioxidants!" he says in his final appeal.

"You're intellectualizing," she says.

Cis angrily shakes his head, then turns around and walks away. He visibly exhales as he appears to be recollecting himself. The woman who was speaking with him sees me and turns my way. As she spins to face me, her curly black hair bounces across her back like rocks skipping across water.

"Good afternoon," she exclaims, "Have you been by the front desk for the schedules yet?"

"I haven't," I say, "I was looking for some coffee."

"We only have decaf coffee available to patients from six to ten in the morning," she says.

"Yeah, I'm sure you have dumber policies here than that, but it does set the bar pretty low. Also, who are you?"

"I'm Janette—the coordinator here," she says and is saying a bit more, but I stopped listening. If she can't offer me coffee, she's useless to me. As she continues to produce noise, I turn away and head to the front desk.

I approach the front desk, where a nurse sits. She has short, dark brown hair and wears a headband like Rambo. Her name tag reads "Raye." I start to open my mouth when Cis appears out of nowhere.

"Raye, as in a ray of fucking sunshine?" he asks the woman who looks like she belongs in a militia.

"Hilarious. Fuck around and find out what happens here," she says. I want to laugh, but her face looks like a no-laugh zone.

"Is this the right place for schedules?" I ask her to change the subject.

"Yeah, I'm here for the same thing," Cis says.

"As am I," Angie says as she also appears out of nowhere. She puts a hand on each of our backs.

"No touching other patients," Raye tells Angie.

"Oh, right," Angie says as the forced guilt causes her lower lip to cower from her top lip. She pulls her arms close to her sides.

"Hold out your badges," Raye says as she looks over the desk for them. We hold out our badges, and I can't help but look at Angie and Cis's photos. Cis has a hilarious fake smile and squinty eyes, much like a kindergarten school photo. Angie looks naturally happy and beautiful as always in hers. It looks more like a well-prepared senior photo.

"Did you brush your hair before that shot?" I ask Angie as I glance down at her badge.

"Well, of course, I have to wear this thing around," she says. I point at Cis's badge and let out a forced laugh.

"Did they use your passport photo for yours?" Cis asks me. I have no response, as it absolutely appears like that. Forced pictures are the worst, and even more so when the photographer is a useless jerkoff.

"Here are each of your schedules. Most events are larger group activities. However, the items with the thick border are smaller group activities. These include therapy sessions, and you'll see your assigned therapist in parentheses under the title," Raye explains as she points out the box on Angie's printout.

"Francis squared," Cis says. He points down to "Frank," written under his. My therapist is Carol, and Angie's is Alan. Hard to judge a book by its cover, even harder to judge a person by their name.

"Lunch will be served momentarily, so feel free to make your way over there. Your first group reflection session will be at two," she stands up and holds out her hand, pointing to the cafeteria. Not the warmest lady, but I can't imagine we'll see too many of those.

Cis pulls us aside before we enter the cafeteria.

"Okay, new game," he says as he pulls out his die from his pocket.

"Wait a second! I thought I—" I say and am quickly cut off.

"You did. I saw them toss it in your bag for lock up," Cis says with an evil grin on his face, "I might've rolled successfully for sleight of hand. It's mine once again!" He lets out an evil laugh.

"So…" Angie looks down at the die then back up to us, "what are we rolling for?"

"Our reactions to lunch," he says.

Angie and I give out an "ahh" in unison. It's a fun idea. Anything to bring some happiness into this place.

"Twelve means it's the best meal you've ever had. One is the worst. This starts when you first see the food and ends after you leave the cafeteria," Cis explains to us.

"Roll for initiative!" I whisper to avoid the staff overhearing.

"Give me that," Angie says. She takes the die from Cis and shakes it in her cupped hands. She fully extends her bottom hand to create as much of a flat surface as she can. She lifts her hand briefly and we all see a lowly two.

I grab the die from her and repeat the process. A six! So far, we're not looking like a grateful group.

Cis takes the die from me and rolls it for himself. He pulls his hand back and shows an eleven. I laugh out loud as Cis quickly stuffs the die back deep into his pocket.

"Let's see what we've got!" Cis says as he leads our party into the cafeteria.

As we enter the cafeteria, there's a one-man serving line on the left. A small placard at the beginning of the line holds a piece of paper with today's menu.

"Just what I NEEDED! Oh God, a cheeseburger! Please tell me it's American cheese on it!" Cis says excitedly to the lone worker behind the line. The worker unenthusiastically nods.

"Is that even cheese? Gag," Angie says with a disgusted look on her face, "Could I get a side of latex with that?"

"It's a cheeseburger," I say in a monotone voice, "They're made with cheese and a burger, usually found between the top and bottom of a bun."

"I mean, just look at that masterpiece!" Cis says as he points at the hotel pan full of about thirty shingled burger patties. He tells the server, "I would love one of those juicy, flavorful patties of heaven!"

The server pulls the top shingle off to reveal that the overlapped parts of the patties are completely raw. Clearly, some idiot thought they should cook the burgers like that.

Cis gulps then stays with his demeanor, "Fantastic! Black and blue is my favorite!"

"You all have mad cow disease if you think I'm touching that raw garbage," Angie said. I'm fairly certain she isn't acting anymore. If she is, this could be an Oscar moment.

"It's partially cooked but mostly raw. It's a burger," I say indifferently.

Angie laughs and points at the squash next to it, "Is that shingled squash raw too? I'm not a chef, but I'm pretty sure 'shingled' is not a cooking technique."

The cook just looks down at the food, seemingly a bit embarrassed. Considering there's no kitchen in this facility, he must have driven it in. Which means it's raw food or no food.

"Oh no, that's salamander-kissed delicata squash, so fresh and delicious that it doesn't even require salt or pepper. You can see the chef here finely chopped each piece a slightly different width to give the illusion that it was on purpose. Amazing," Cis continues. He's clearly crawling in his skin.

He leans over to us and whispers, "What sort of gateway to hell did you bring me to?"

I whisper back, "Just walk through it. The food will cook quickly on the other side."

"Where's Shelly?" Angie asks, "There's no way she'd allow something like this to happen."

The server pulls the burger hotel pan out of the serving line and returns it to the hot box behind him. He pulls up the corner of Saran Wrap on the remaining hotel pans and uses a spatula to pop up the top patties. After a little detective work, the server yanks one of the pans out and puts it into the open space on the line. Then like a true amateur, he starts messing around with the hotbox temperature. I assume he wants to turn it into a portable oven. He advises it'll be a few minutes.

Cis notices this and says, "It's like the Ritz Carlton in here. The burgers are perfectly steamed to order. If it's gray, it's okay!"

Some sessions must have just ended as people start multiplying in the cafeteria.

"Oh hey! We have new friends," a woman says as she appears with a small group of others. She introduces herself as Sarah and the others as James, Rico, Steve, and Amy. I'm fairly certain I'll forget their names within the next minute or so, but I'll try to hang onto it.

"Nice to meet you. I'm Angie. These are my friends Brey and Cis. We just got in early this morning." She covers the side of her mouth and whispers, "Is the food always awful?"

"The bacon is edible," Steve says.

"Yeah, sometimes the eggs aren't completely dry," Rico says.

"The food is pretty bad all of the time," James says, "but the fellow patients are pretty wonderful. So we stick around the place for each other."

It's unfortunate there aren't Yelp reviews for institutions like this. It's a true test of Cis's will. If he can survive on low-grade raw processed meat, anything on the outside will be fine dining on a beach.

"What brings y'all in here?" Amy asks with a drawl. She has a bit of the southern belle thing going.

"I came for the food," I say.

"Alcohol. All three of us," Angie says.

"Drink of choice?" Steve asks.

"Mainly beer and shots—some wine on occasion," Angie replies, "And yes, I'm speaking for all three of us as I was actually their bartender." She winks at us.

"How about yours?" I ask Steve.

"Favorite drink? Oh, no. Alcohol wasn't for me. I'm a pillhead. Opioids," he says.

"Bourbon was mine," Amy says with a sly grin on her face, "Nobody questions a respectable drink like that."

"Nobody?" Rico says with a chuckle. Rico appears to be the eldest in the group, probably has a decade or so on me.

"Well," Amy pauses to correct herself, "Nobody did 'fore that officer."

"Ah, court-ordered to be here?" Cis asks.

"Nah, my lawyer recommended coming here and delaying my hearing. He thinks if I'm a good girl here and fix my shit, they'll be nicer to me out there."

"And you're going to do exactly what they recommended," Sarah says as she waggles a finger in Amy's direction. Sarah comes off as a go-getter, perhaps a little bossy in her everyday life. She has shorter auburn hair, slim build, an energized smile, and must be here for Valium or some form of downer.

"Your drug of choice?" Steve asks. He clearly knows but is prompting her to give us a full inventory.

"By choice, cocaine. By fate, anything that got me high. I prefer uppers to downers, though," Sarah explains.

"Food is ready," the server announces. There's a mixture of cheers and grunts.

"I'd like a cooked burger and the sides," I return to my monotone voice and place my order with the server.

"Oh, man! Great choice, my friend!" Cis exclaims. He pats me hard on the back. Our new friends chuckle as they know he's being sarcastic. The server scrapes together the food on a plate and hands it to me. It's really hard to picture how this food is passable by any health inspector. Thanks HIPAA.

The burger looks like it was boiled for thirty seconds. A good bun is nicely toasted to give it a little crisp. That isn't the case here, though. The bag of buns was clearly tossed into a microwave for a minute until it hit peak moistness. And the smell, my goodness, it's like I walked around with the bun in a soaking wet shoe all day.

"Surprise me," Angie says to the server, "There's no way I'm custom ordering my food poisoning today." She turns to me and asks, "Do you know if there are lawyers here? I need to write out my will before I sit down."

Janette comes around the corner after hearing about the server's misfortunes. She goes behind the counter and speaks with him quietly.

"The food being served is safe to eat. Please proceed like normal," Janette says and walks away.

"I'm sure Janette is certified ServSafe with a boatload of experience in this field," Cis convincingly tells the line, "Let's just all take it easy and eat some of these delicious servings. Then we can all meet at the bar after for shots of apple cider vinegar!"

Joining the two of them here sounded like a great opportunity. With no food or coffee, though, it's going to wear me down fast. We've barely been awake an hour, and I already feel a bit trapped. I suppose I'll just stay focused on the endgame.

We sit down together with our new friends. Through the small talk, I notice Cis isn't really eating, and his energy level has dropped.

"Excuse me for a moment," he says as he stands up and walks to the bathroom. Angie and I share a concerned look but pass it off as just a bathroom break.

"So, Brey and Angie, where you all from?" James asks us.

"The suburbs of Boston—born and raised. I had a couple escape plans that temporarily worked, but my dad is back there. So, it was never long before I went home for extended stays. Then, on one visit, I got put in charge of a bar, and then time slipped away," Angie said with a soft smile.

"I hear ya. It becomes your community: friends, family, lovers, and haters. And some liquid gold to blend it all together," the quiet Rico speaks up.

"Alcohol too?" I ask him.

He nods and says, "And whatever prescription drugs showed up to the bar that night."

James stays quiet as he eats his food. He shakes his legs rapidly, but no one else seems put off by it. I just accept the tremors as a natural occurrence and take a bite of the pig food in front of me.

After several bites and some small talk across the table, I notice that Cis never rejoined us at the table. I excuse myself and walk over to the bathroom I saw him head to. The place is empty, stalls and all.

I stop by the front desk and ask if they've seen him. I assumed if he took off, they might say something along those lines. If he did leave, he snuck out well, as they didn't even see him walk by. I patrol the halls and even check his room, but no sign of him.

When I return to the table alone, Angie has a concerned look on her face.

"Did you find him?" she asked nervously.

"I didn't. I have no idea where he could be," I say.

"He could be out on the patio by the pond. That's where the smokers gather before sessions, after sessions, and pretty much whenever they're awake," James says to me as he points around the corner.

As I walk out the door to the patio, I see Cis sitting alone on top of a picnic table. His feet are rapidly tapping, and he has a pack of cigarettes in his hands. I walk up to the table and sit on it next to him.

"I thought I had it, but I don't," Cis says to me in a shaky voice.

"Have what?" I ask. It's clear the idea of sobriety is catching up to him, but I want him to guide this conversation. Honestly, I have no idea what to say.

"The strength to overcome this shit. I probably would feel fine outside of here, but this place is suffocating," he says, "I don't want to go back to smoking, but I need something. I feel like I'm in a tower defense game, and it's just wave after wave of anxiety." He rotates his arm in front of him to emphasize the repetitiveness of it all.

"Do you want to talk to the doctor here?" Anyone else would definitely be more equipped to properly handle this. Knowing Cis's ability to run, I don't want to say the wrong thing at this point of the journey.

"Fuck that. They'll turn me into a zombie."

"That's fair. Then give me that so I can pack that shit. This can be tomorrow's problem to fix," I say as I grab the pack of cigarettes from him. I pack them against my right wrist.

I open up the pack and give him a cigarette then take one. Jamal comes from around the building.

"Hey! No sharing things in here. Give him back the pack." he says to me. His voice is serious, but body language suggests he's just doing his job.

"Sheesh. Guess I'll live vicariously through you," I say to Cis as I hand him the pack back, "Cigarettes will give us plenty of time with you. It's a fair trade. Enjoy the smoke." I see Jamal still watching me suspiciously.

"Isn't your shift over?" I ask him.

"Almost. Almost," he slowly says then slowly turns around and heads back to his lookout spot.

The door swings open, and Angie appears. As she sees us, she lets out a big sigh. She runs giddily over and gives Cis a big sideways hug.

"Hey! Put space between you! Don't make me come back over there!" Jamal yells from the corner.

"Well, I just feel exuberant now," she says as she smiles really big at Cis. "I thought you ran off and left us behind."

"You'd all be slaughtered without your tank," Cis says to her. "And exuberant?"

"Yeah, and I feel even more exuberant for using that word. It's a great word," she says, then settles down on the bench. "I do owe you both an apology, though. I had no idea about the food situation here or the sticklers. I've seen Intervention a few times on TV and thought it'd be more like that."

"Nothing to be sorry for," Cis says, "It's so bad it's comical. And hell, it gives Brey plenty of material for a book when we break free of here." I nod and smile. It's true, the unfortunate events I've been through have always stayed more vividly in my memories.

Cis lights his cigarette and takes a slow pull off it.

"Oh shit," he says.

"Is it helping the anxiety?" I ask him.

"No. Now I'm anxious and high," he says.

"Quiet now," Angie whispers, "Jamal may hear ya and dissect all of your smokes."

"Did anyone else think the brothers were going to be those big-teddy-bear types of easy going people? I did." I say.

"Absolutely—turns out they're just miserable pricks like the lot of us," Cis says with the cigarette hanging out of his mouth. His eyes squint as the smoke drifts straight up into his eyes. The air is very stagnant here.

"Let's talk about this so-called pond behind us," Angie says, "This should be classified as a bog. Or a swamp. There are definitely gators in there waiting for a patient to dare an escape through the murky waters."

"How many victims do you think so far?" I ask her. I scan my eyes across the entirety of the waters.

"Give me an advantage roll, please," she says as she turns to face Cis. Through the cloud of smoke, Cis struggles to get his hand in his pocket. He stands up, shakes his pants down a little, and retrieves the cube of destiny.

"You can do the honor," he says as he starts to hand Angie the die but quickly pulls it back and sits down.

"NO SHARING…sheesh. Don't you know the rules?" Angie asks, clearly mocking Jamal.

"I know…I almost lost you, my little buddy," he says as he looks down at his cupped hands.

He gives it a little shake when Jamal isn't looking, then reveals the first number to Angie. Jamal looks back to make sure we're being good. Cis pulls the cigarette from his mouth with the hand that holds the die. He waves with his other hand to Jamal and gives him a friendly smile. It's disregarded, and while Jamal looks away again, he passes along the second number.

"Whoa! Okay." Angie pauses for a moment to think. "There are an estimated three victims that were caught on camera after security was put in.

The rumor is that number is in the upper fifties. One guy, goes anonymously by Joe C., swears he saw four people disappear in a single day. They were flirting with the idea of racing across the muddy waters. Due to strict HIPAA laws, the clinic neither confirmed nor denied that those victims were ever even here."

"Where were Jamal and Micah through all of this?" I ask her.

"Ohhh…they were hired right after this incident. The guard on duty that day was slapped by threats over NDAs he signed upon employment. After threatening to unseal the truth, the poor guy came down with a sickness and passed away forty-eight hours later."

"Damn, so we'll never know the truth," I say.

"Does it matter? We're already all dead inside anyways," Cis says as he takes a final drag off his cigarette. He stands up and puts the cigarette out in the ashtray. He turns back to us and says, "Time to face the demons."

We follow him back inside and accompany him as he puts some food in his stomach.

CHAPTER 8

~ First Session ~

Imposter syndrome is kicking in as I make my way to the first therapy session. As I walk into my assigned room, I realize I'm the first to arrive. There are several chairs in a circle and a box of tissues sitting in the middle. A woman stands by a table with her back to me. I'm fairly certain she's dwarven based on size. She spins around and lightens up when she sees me.

"Welcome, welcome! Take any seat!" the boisterous woman announces loudly. I'm fairly certain the smile was fake but well-rehearsed.

"Okay, thanks," I say as I plop down into a seat facing the door. There's chatter as everyone makes their way down the hallway to the sessions.

James and Steve come around the corner. They give me a smile then spread out among the other seats. Following behind are a few faces I saw in the cafeteria but haven't met. James' legs start tapping frantically the moment he sits down.

"Welcome back, everyone! We have a new member of our group today," she says as she turns to me. "Could you please state your name as first name and last initial and what you're here for. For instance, I'd say, 'Carol M., alcoholic.'"

"Brey A., alcoholic."

"Hi, Brey!" everyone says together.

"Welcome again to the group! Today, I have a queue for our conversation," Carol says as she passes out a sheet of paper and pen to each of us.

There are a few questions. The first one reads: "If you got locked up tomorrow, what activity would you miss most?" I'm not sure if "shitting in private" is appropriate, so I dig a little deeper into my thoughts. I hear they have programming classes in prison along with writing materials—so the main two things are accounted for. I write down, "making money."

Jumping down to the second question, it reads: "If you were hospitalized tomorrow, who would be by your side the most?" Good question. I'm actually not sure. My family thinks I'm still on a road trip, so I'd probably go with Cis. However, Angie would probably stop him as he needs to be in rehab, so Angie. I don't want to make things weird, so I just write "a friend."

Onto the third and final prompt: "If you die tomorrow and there's life after death, who would be the most disappointed with you on the other side?" Sheesh. My grandfather would probably be there to greet me then give me a slap on the back of the head. It'd be great to see him again, but not at the cost of so many years.

I put my pen down and look around the room. A few people have finished, and a few seem deep in thought.

"Two more minutes," Carol says. The time passes quickly, and it's time to go around the room. I volunteer to go first as I hate going last. I'm not a fan of public speaking and my nerves just get exponentially worse the longer I wait.

"Great! So what would you miss most about freedom if you were jailed tomorrow?" Carol asks. I now have the full attention of several people I don't really know.

"Making money," I say, knowing that it'll take some explaining.

"That's it?" a surfer-looking girl says from across the room.

"Ultimately, yeah."

"You don't have any hobbies?" she asked.

"I do. I write code as both a career and a hobby. They allow some level of it on the inside. However, I wouldn't get paid for the work I'm doing," I pause for a moment then continue, "I also write. Assuming I don't go in for a violent crime where I can't be trusted with a pencil, I'd probably be cleared to do that."

"So you only do hobbies for money?" she added.

"Amanda, remember, to each their own," Carol says.

"It's okay. I've never been in jail before, but I was broke for much longer than I care to admit. That's not freedom," I explain, "You can't do whatever you want because most things in this world cost money. I chose to not live that way anymore."

"You're in a place full of poor people. How does that make you look?" she asks.

"To each their own, Amanda," I say with extra emphasis on her name.

There are a couple cackles in the group, but they're quickly shushed by Carol. Based on the feeling in the room, I can tell she's a bit of a snotty bitch. Her questioning is fair, though. I'd be turned off by someone like me, too, if I was still trapped in my broke-and-limited phase.

"Why don't you go next?" Carol says to Amanda. Everyone shifts a little in their seats to focus on her.

"I'd miss hanging with my community," Amanda says, "We have a large group of people that hit the beaches every night. We surf until the sun goes down. I don't feel trapped when I'm there." She makes eye contact with me and says, "Money doesn't buy that experience."

"You've mentioned before that this is the group that you did drugs with," Carol says, "Have you thought about how your sobriety may change that atmosphere, or vice versa?"

Carol sits back and explains to everyone that a similar environment will bring similar patterns. It was imperative that we make sacrifices for the sake of our sobriety. A saddened look appears on Amanda's face as she sinks into her thoughts. I do feel bad for her. I'm the only patient in this room that isn't making sacrifices. Perhaps I am the asshole with the "money" answer.

"James, would you like to go next?" Carol asks. His flapping leg slows down for a moment as he's caught off guard. He sits up a bit in his chair.

"I'm a junkie. I don't have freedom," James says straight-faced. It's apparent that he's struggling with withdrawals.

"How are you feeling?" she asks him.

"Fucking awful. The suboxone just isn't enough. All I can think about is my next high," James says with a shaky voice, "The only thing I'd probably miss is the open market. I can find dope on any street corner. But real talk though, can you talk to them about my dose?"

"The decisions around medication are not in my hands," Carol says, "Coming off drugs isn't supposed to be easy. If the suboxone levels are raised to the point of no withdrawal symptoms, you're really just changing your addiction to suboxone. It's meant to be a transitional step to sobriety."

"Sorry if it's rude of me to ask, but how many days are you in?" I ask him.

"This is my eighth day one," he says. His voice breaks a bit. It seems genuine that he's losing hope for his own future. I think the therapists are all trained to assume it's just manipulative behavior to get more drugs. I suppose both could be true. What's worse is I have no doubt that insurance would deny further payments even if he felt the same in a month's time.

"Juan, would you like to go next?" Carol says, cutting off our side conversation. She fully shifts her body to look at him.

"My family gatherings," Juan says softly. His eyes focus on a specific spot of the carpet in the middle of the room.

"Could you elaborate?" Carol asks.

"I have a large family. We get together on the weekends, eat, and play in the lake," Juan explains.

"That sounds nice. Do you have kids?" Carol asks Juan.

"No, not me. I have a lot of nieces and nephews. Then my brothers, sisters come. Also, uncles, aunties…it's a big family," he says with a bit of light shining through his eyes.

"You've mentioned in previous sessions that people drink during these gatherings," Carol sets her question up, "How do you think it'll affect your sobriety? Are your family members willing to forego the drinking?"

"They don't have problems with alcohol, I do," Juan says as his eyes finally leave the floor to look at Carol.

"I'm worried you'd feel left out and relapse," Carol says, "Does that make sense?" Her final words came out like she was talking to a child. She seems to have a bit of a condescending edge to how she presents herself and speaks to others.

"It makes sense," he says. He shrugs in a way that hints he has no intentions of avoiding those events. I don't blame him.

"It's something to think about while you're still here," Carol tells them, "Destiny, what about you?" The Hawaiian girl has been identified. Now heaven help me to remember all of their names. The lanyards only work when they're properly facing away from the body—an achievement I haven't figured out yet.

"It's not an activity per se, but similar to others, I'd miss my grandmother," Destiny says. The other patients nod in unison. She turns to look at me, "I mentioned yesterday how she essentially raised me. She's been my rock. And she's aging, so I already feel bad being here instead of being with her."

"I'm sure you'll be forgiven," I say, "It'll make those days after that much better." She smiles.

"Thanks, Destiny," Carol says, "Family is important through this journey. I'm sure she's proud of you for wanting to become healthy."

"I hope so," Destiny says.

"Okay, last but not least, Steve! What would you miss?" Carol says as she arrives at the last answer to the first question.

"Playing guitar with my band," Steve says, "Coincidentally, it's also the thing I'm most worried about." He gives a playful forced smile.

"Why's that?" Carol asks him.

"It's not exactly a sober-friendly environment," he says as he chuckles a bit. He's clearly having some vivid memories flashing through his head.

"What's your band name?" I ask out of curiosity.

"Pop Rocks," he says. The confidence in his voice tells me he knows it's a bit ridiculous.

"Like the candy that feels like gunfire in the mouth?" I waggle my fingers at my mouth while making popping noises.

"Yes, but 'pop' is an acronym. It stands for 'particles of poo,'" he says with a childish smile.

"Genre?" It has to be punk.

"Punk."

"Fitting, although you don't dress the part," I say. He's wearing a band t-shirt that looks pretty casual with jeans.

"They turned away my spikes at the door," he says with a wink. "Just kidding. You're right. We dress a little of the part when we perform, but otherwise, we're just some kids who like to play loud music."

Carol has us go through the next two questions in the same format. The rounds make sense as it allows us to talk among ourselves and open up. I imagine she's priming us up to becoming our most vulnerable selves. It is a bit disturbing, though that she's getting paid to basically babysit us. Her actual involvement with this circle is lacking in both content and sincerity. After all, I'm pretty sure she just keeps regurgitating the same lines from her script.

Noise picks up in the halls, which is comparable to the hallways between classes in high school. As I start to walk out, I meet Cis at the door. He looks anxious, so I follow him toward the door to go outside. There's a new recruit slumped over the desk as the staff of nurses and doctors flock around her. They look like they've never treated a patient before. The girl's hair is dyed blonde with black roots and it covers her face. She has on a loose hoodie that hides the rest of her. Poor girl.

The staff try to build a bit of a human wall for privacy. We continue down the hall to the exit. A cigarette is lodged in Cis's mouth with a lighter in his hand. He lights it the second his feet touch the outside patio.

"Good session?" I ask him.

"There's something icky about that guy," he says.

"Icky?" I ask. He just nods, and we sit in silence for a moment in case he has something to add.

"How was everyone else?"

"Not bad," Cis says through his cloud of smoke, "We have Sarah in our group. She talks the same amount of time as everyone else combined. To be fair, though, I'd listen to her read the fucking Bible out loud before I wanna hear Frank read an excerpt from a Dr. Seuss book. I mean, he's like a shrieking weasel. And he has this creep vibe to him."

I just laugh it off.

"What about your group?" he asks.

"It'll be interesting—that's for sure. Carol is a boisterous woman. She's like a bubbly, racist coke head and I feel as though she follows a script without giving a shit about our actual lives."

"Maybe Angie got luckier," he says to me.

Sirens get louder as an ambulance comes around the corner and pulls up to the front door of the clinic.

"Christ, did they kill her?" Cis asks.

"I'm surprised she's not gator food," I say as I look over my shoulder to make sure I'm not being preyed on.

"Or maybe she ate the food."

We watch the front door as they enter with a stretcher and then carry her out on it. They pause by the ambulance as they strap her up to a vitals machine and give her oxygen.

"Makes you wonder if she took advantage of that 'last day' or someone just dropped her off in this state," I say as I just stare without purpose.

"Makes you wonder if she'll actually know, if and when she comes to," Cis says. I notice that the distraction has calmed him down a little.

As the ambulance packs her in and pulls away, another car pulls up to the front door. It's like a drive-thru of fucked up people today. A woman gets out of the driver's side and walks around to the back of the car.

"At least this one is walking in on their own," I say.

The woman grabs a large duffel bag from the trunk and then walks inside with it. Before we have time to comment, the doors swing back open, and she comes back out with a security guard. This guard is tall and hefty like the twins but a bit bulkier in muscle and less in fat. A nurse trails behind them.

They walk to the back door of the car and open it. With a little assistance from the guard, a slightly heavy white guy stumbles out of the back. I assume this is what bears look like when they leave their cave after hibernation for the first time. The light shines bright on his neon blue thinned-out hair. My first thought is I didn't know drugs lead to hair loss. His clothes are baggy like he just left a rave or grunge concert, but he seems a decade or two too old for that. Drugs are wild.

This guy is clearly claiming the nickname 'Big Blue,' and I'll be using it immediately. It is a recycled nickname that I liked as it rolled off the tongue nicely. The former target was my warlock's voidwalker from World of Warcraft. I cheered for 'Big Blue' before, and I hope to seize the opportunity to do it again. Carpe diem!

"It makes you wonder what these other folks looked like when they walked through the front door," I say to Cis, who's still staring at the empty car. I nudge him and tell him, "You better not be thinking about stealing that."

He grins and stays silent with his cigarette.

CHAPTER 9

~ Insomnia ~

After dinner, they host an AA meeting in the building. One of the guards named, Earl speaks about his trouble with addiction. He's an older man, probably in his late seventies. I'm not sure what he'd do to protect us as he's a bit frail, but he has a way of herding us with kindness.

Cis stayed quiet and became squirmish the longer the meeting went on. On a normal day, he would be drunk right now. I can tell by his tense jaw that he's fully realizing that he's sleeping sober tonight. Personally, I'm looking forward to a good night's sleep, even if I have the cameras on me.

Angie seems to have hit it off with a girl named Amelia in her therapy group. She occasionally looks over and smiles at me and Cis, but we give her space to do her thing. As things wrap up, Cis slips away to his room.

There's a meditation group that's optional. The ultimatum is to go to meditation or go to bed. The latter seems far better, but I want to check on Cis first. As I walk down the hallway, I notice the meditation group is sitting cross-legged on hard plastic chairs under fluorescent lights. What a bizarre, non-relaxing setup. I overhear Janette lecturing them that the lights have to stay on. Janette needs to get laid.

Cis sits awake and alone in his room; his roommate is likely in meditation. He rests with the Big Book against his chest.

"Hey man, how ya doing?" I whisper to Cis from the entrance.

He says as he sits up a bit to see me. "Oh, hey. Seen better nights."

"Who's the roommate?" I ask him as I try to look for anything identifying from the door.

"Big Blue," he says.

"Big Blue!" I happily exclaim. I hear a shush from next door. It's probably best I don't piss anyone off. I lean back in and tell Cis, "If you need anything, just come wake me up. I'm in the same room as last night!"

Cis nods and says "goodnight." He puts the book down on the side table and stirs in bed a bit. As I'm walking away, the sounds of his shuffling around seize. I assume he found a comfortable position.

As I pass by the women's bathroom, Angie appears in front of me.

"Hey!" I happily greet her. A large smile grows on her face.

"Hey, back! How are you?" she asks as she uses her towel to dry her dripping hair. Before I answer, she says, "The showers aren't that bad! I actually had hot water at a decent pressure all of the way through!" I guess she found the secret—shower when no one else is.

"I'm doing okay. Just stopped by to see Cis," I say.

"How is he?" She sounds quite optimistic.

"He's uncomfortable but hanging in there!"

"Oh, good." Her smile grows big.

"Been meaning to ask, how was your session earlier?" I ask, assuming her therapist was as miserable as ours.

"Quite good, actually. Alan reminds me of my father. He's a bit of a softy," she tells me.

"Wow, you got lucky. Can't say the same for ours," I tell her and give her a quick run down on Carol and Frank.

"Yeah, Alan is that good Catholic type," she says, "He's sweet, sympathetic, understanding, and genuinely wants people to heal and live their best lives. Perhaps it comes with a little naivety that that's possible." She shrugs as she runs the towel through her hair. Even with the generic shampoo and conditioners we're given here, Angie still emits the best smells.

"I'm happy for you," I tell her, "It's been a pretty wild day overall."

We wish each other a good night and move back to our rooms to get some rest.

*

I suddenly wake up to some chatter in the hallway. It sounds like Cis, so I arise and head out to the bathroom as my cover story. It is Cis arguing with a nurse at the station.

"I can't fucking sleep with Big Blue in there choking over his tongue!" Cis says as he imitates the horrendous sounds coming from his roommate, "I just want to sleep! I need a different room!"

"I understand, but we can't change rooms in the middle of the night. We're not equipped to do so, and it would disturb other patients," the nurse says sternly. Cis sees me and turns to explain it to me.

"This guy's snoring is beyond anything I can sleep through! It starts like your everyday loud snoring. Then it sounds like the ooze that created the Ninja Turtles gets released into his sinus cavity. He starts to gag and choke over the ooze," Cis says as he's using his hands to emphasize the intensity of it. He continues, "He wheezes as he coughs it up bit-by-bit, clearly a last-ditch effort not to die from the shit! And then about two seconds of silence. Then it repeats like a broken fucking record."

"Fuck, man. That sounds awful," I say. I hold back my laughter as I'm sure we'll be able to see the hilarity in it when it's over.

Cis turns back to the nurse behind the counter.

"I'm going to sit out here on the couch until that sloppy sleeper wakes up," he tells him, "I'll be missing all of the morning routines again. And if they ask why, you can explain your bullshit policies to them."

Cis nods to me and then walks over to the couches. The couches serve as a place for people to kill time during the day, but their bigger role is a place for people to make their personal phone calls. Nothing is private in this place, so this allows the staff to eavesdrop on all conversations. Cis leans back on the couch and closes his eyes.

"No sleeping on the couches," Micah says.

"Fuck off," Cis says under his breath as he sits forward. He looks up and asks, "Do you all train to make this place as uncomfortable as possible, or is it just natural incompetencies in the hospitality field?" The staff ignores his question.

Beyond hospitality, I'm not sure anyone here is actually good in their field. In the short time we've been here, I've already heard of multiple patients who didn't have their medications available. One patient self-catheterizes, and the nurse offered Vaseline in place of the normal lubrication. They couldn't comprehend the difference between fat-soluble and water-soluble. Idiots. And I basically saw them let that poor girl just rot on the desk before the ambulance took her away. So, the medical program here is broken.

Most of the security guards here couldn't catch a toddler. They don't have any tools besides a flashlight on their belts, which means the only thing they could potentially slay at is some flashlight tag. Nobody trusts the younger guards enough to give any information to them, and the older guards are too weak to do anything with tip-offs. So it's really just the patients looking out for each other.

As for the therapists, it appears not all are bad based on Angie's review. She has a good judge of character, so I only wish we had more Alan's to work with. To play devil's advocate, it's probably really tough working with addicts when they're just starting the withdrawal process. Despite how good or bad the therapy is, the disease is better, and it could all be for nothing. Still, though, they need to put their best foot forward or get out of the way.

The food speaks for itself. It'd be five-star quality if we were on a raw diet. I'm not sure why I'm personally sticking with this. Maybe I do. I suppose a place like this will deter people from having to return. I'm counting the days to be out of here. At least I don't have Big Blue as a roommate.

"Did you need something?" the nurse behind the counter asks.

I tiredly stretch my neck to the side before turning to look at the nurse. "Nah, just zoning out over here. Going to continue along my way now." I wave as I head to the bathroom.

As I return a few minutes later, I catch the back of Cis's foot as he goes back into his room. Out of curiosity, I walk by the door slowly. It sounds like Jabba the Hutt choking on diarrhea of the mouth. I'm not sure what that means exactly, but it's fucking revolting.

My roommate is a guy named Pete, I think, from Angie's group. I haven't met him. His name is written on the door. One of us has been sleeping when the other is awake, but I couldn't have asked for a better situation. I walk into my room, and I'm overwhelmingly thankful for the silence.

*

My sleep is disturbed again by a ruckus going on in the hallway. I glance over at our decades-old alarm clock, and it's half past four in the morning. I lift my head off my pillow and listen in on the conversation.

"The best I can do is move you out of monitoring tomorrow night," the nurse says.

"Is everything alright?" I hear Angie say.

"We have everything under control here," Micah says, "Please go back to bed."

"You clearly don't. You have a patient here who's simply asking to sleep, and you're not enabling him to do so. In turn, many of us are waking up, and we're all becoming increasingly irritated," Angie says.

"Ma'am, I only see you being awake," the nurse says. Not a moment later, a couple doors open. Out of curiosity, I get up and open our door. I look down the hallway and see Cis, who's pretty bent out of shape at this point. He's squatting with his back against the wall. His head hangs in his hands.

Of the four or five open doors, Angie's friend Amelia and another guy from Cis's group are now in the hall as well. I believe I caught his name to be Jonah, but my confidence level is low. He seems to be everyone's extroverted friend.

"Dang man, you're still awake?" I ask Cis as I walk toward him. He just nods without looking up. I look over at the nurse and tell him, "Listen, give him my bed."

"No, we can't do that," the nurse says, "and besides, we have some empty beds, but it's against protocol to move beds in the middle of the night."

"Is it protocol to keep patients up all night?" I ask.

"No, he has a bed he can be sleeping in right now," the nurse is clearly oblivious to Big Blue or is just a useless prick.

"You all are something," Angie says, "Guess we're left with no choice. Smoke 'em if you got 'em." She herds us together, and we walk out to the patio. While it's also against policy, the nurse nods to Micah and Jamal, permitting our action. Jamal follows us to continue his normal watch.

The pond is even sketchier at night. Small movements in the water give me goosebumps. I don't have any guesses as to what's making the noise. I only have wishes of what I hope it's not. We sit at a table close to the door just to be safe.

"Hey, we haven't met yet. I'm Brey," I say to Amelia and Jonah.

"Hey Brey, I'm Josiah," he reaches out to shake my hand. I reach out to meet him halfway as I try to update that memory register in my head. My eavesdropping skills aren't very strong in a crowd.

"And I'm Amelia."

I give her a gentle shake as she doesn't come off as being a handshaker.

"Sorry for all of the disturbance," Cis says as he ruffles in his pocket for his lighter.

"Nah, I heard those heinous sounds. I'm not sure I've heard anything like that before," I tell him as a shiver of disgust runs through my body.

"I have an uncle who put a lot of shit up his nose," Amelia says as she imitates the motion. "I'm sure it's related to that."

"I didn't actually hear anything. I just woke up per my norm and decided to join the revolution," Josiah says quietly with a grin. "Fuck the police!" We all chuckle as it's becoming true even on the first day, we're in this together. Our struggles are shared. To some, the struggles are simply overcoming their own addictions. To everyone, it's finding reasons to smile while navigating through this place.

"It's nice seeing you sober at night," Angie says with a big smile aimed in Cis's direction.

"It's nice being seen," Cis says as he looks up at Josiah, "Did I get that right?"

"You did, my friend," Josiah defiantly says. "Be the victor, not the victim!"

"Carry the message, not the mess?" Amelia adds in. We all have a soft laugh.

One thing I've picked up on about meetings, AA or NA, is you have to learn to be uncomfortable. This obviously applies to oversharing personal information. It also less obviously applies to always being in someone's cloud of smoke outside of those meetings.

"We've completed day one of this forty-two-day journey," Angie says to Cis, "I'm proud of us."

"I heard they're able to pencil in some sleep for day three," I jokingly say to Cis.

"Fuck that if it's not switched before tomorrow. I mean, tonight, I'll smother the blue fuck with his pillow," Cis says, looking in the direction of the door. He catches eyes with Jamal and yells to him, "Hey, Jamal! Could you fill us in on what your 'Stand Your Ground' policy entails? Any clauses about snorers?"

This one finally got a chuckle out of Jamal. Perhaps he's a likable guy if you remove him from this place. He probably likes the cool air this time of morning as well.

*

Several conversations and a few cigarettes later, we've reached our watering time! We make our way into the cafeteria and observe the brewing of the decaf coffee. Micah is in charge of this morning's duty and we all love him a little extra because of it. We cheer for him from our front-row seats and give a standing ovation once we hear those first drops of the fresh brew.

It may only have a smidge of caffeine, but it's really my only withdrawal at the moment. I salivate to the smell of it as it fills the otherwise neglected air. Time is short. I approach the cabinet area where the coffee maker is to grab the largest mug available.

No mugs stick out to me, but I do see a label for 'cups.' It's on a dispenser for Dixie cups. Yes, those cups designed for bathrooms that hold two or three ounces. Are we birds? Who drinks two to three ounces of decaf coffee and thinks, "Oh boy, any more, and I'll overdo it." I grab five cups and line them up next to the coffee maker because I'm a full-sized human.

"This shit is embarrassing. This place must have a huge profit margin!" I say to Micah as he babysits the process.

"Sure as shit ain't seeing my pocket," he says back to me.

"You should join our revolution. You can be our inside man!" Josiah says a bit loudly.

"Shh. Y'all gonna git me fire with talk like that," Micah says as he shakes his head. These twins are probably a hoot outside of these walls. It's a shame we met under this condition.

The coffee maker blows out compressed air, marking the crossing of the finish line. Micah looks relieved as he drops his guard and moves back to the hallway.

"OH, thanks," Cis says as he goes to grab one of the five cups I pulled out.

"OH hell no," I say as I pull the cup away, "This is my serving size. Get your own."

I carefully fill my five cups two-thirds of the way to the top. I add some creamer to each and now I have five flimsy hot cups all filled to the brim.

"At least severe burns don't interact with medications," I mumble under my breath as I transport my cups out in two trips to the picnic tables outside.

Cis joins me after getting his coffee, but the others decide to wash up as they enjoy their cups.

"Congrats on making it this far—it really does mean a lot," I tell him.

"Yeah, I keep hearing all of these people talk about halfway homes and how going back to our old ways will just cause us to relapse," Cis says quite coherently, considering he hasn't slept. Maybe it's the part of the program where they really break you down.

"What do you want to do after this?" I ask him.

"Go back to our apartment. I'm living with strangers now, and it fucking sucks."

It's hard to blame him on that.

"Whatever you choose to do, you've got my full support. I mean, I'm in fucking rehab with you drinking decaf coffee out of Dixie cups. I have nothing left to further demonstrate that," I say.

"I know, I owe you," he says as he holds out his fist for a bump. I touch my knuckles lightly against his.

"Angie was actually behind this. I've also just been along for the ride," I say.

"Yeah. What's up with Angie? Is she a fucking angel or something?"

"I think so," I say. The things she does definitely aren't human-like.

"Guess I'll owe her when I get out of here."

"I actually have an idea, just not sure how to execute it. Time will tell!" I say. I raise one of my cups and down it like a shot. I yell, "Another!" and knock back another cup.

I see Big Blue pass by the glass door and point him out to Cis.

"Finally, my queue to sleep. See ya in a few hours," he says as he gets up from the table. I follow him inside as he lets the nurse know he's going to sleep until lunchtime. Of course, they're not happy about it, but they do approve of it and mark his door as "do not wake up."

After all, they have forty-one more days to help him. It's a marathon, not a race.

CHAPTER 10
~ Rotating Door ~

As I await for breakfast to start, I sit in the lobby, rustling through the collection of papers I have so far. I sip on my refilled cups of coffee, but I reduced my Dixie cup footprint to two cups. I hated taking multiple trips to change locations.

I see Shelly make her way to the door. Before she gets there, that girl from yesterday comes through it, half stumbling in the way hungover people do. She looks ill and carries a black eye and split lip. She's definitely alive, though. It must have been a night worth forgetting! Shelly certainly has her sweetness turned up an extra notch, knowing this girl must be hurting.

"Welcome back, Dakota," Shelly says enthusiastically, "I hope they took good care of you at the hospital!"

"I hope so too. I don't remember," Dakota says sarcastically under her breath.

I'm trying to picture what she's like without the road rash, dyed hair, and hungover energy. My imagination paints her as a good student with a good family and manners. Unfortunately, she fell for the wrong person. Her past likely outshines her present, but with a proper recovery, she'll bounce back. Then again, my imagination is far superior to my guessing abilities.

"We already have your belongings collected and stored in your room," Shelly tells her, "I know the first day can be a bit daunting, so take your time adjusting. Any immediate questions?"

"Yeah, who brought me here?"

"A taxi just brought you back from the hospital," Shelly explains with a strange look on her face. Perhaps she thinks Dakota is dealing with amnesia.

"No, before that. The hospital said they picked me up here."

"Oh yes, your sister brought you in," Shelly explains. Dakota sighs out of relief.

"Was there anyone else with her?" Dakota nervously asks.

"I don't believe so," Shelly lowers her eyebrows as she answers her, "Is there something we need to know about?"

"No. Could you just deny that I'm here if anyone calls looking for me?"

"We neither confirm nor deny the presence of any patient here, regardless of who's calling."

"How about just deny?" Dakota asks. She leans towards Shelly in the hopes they can find a compromise.

"No, we can't do that. We need to avoid the possibility of legal liabilities." Dakota just nods slowly as her shoulders slump down. She's learning quickly how inept this staff is.

"Any other questions?" Shelly asks.

"Just to speed things up so I can go ice my eye, what are you programmed to answer?" Dakota asks.

"Probably nothing of interest to you," Shelly says with a light tone, "Let's knock out a couple forms, and I'll show you to your room."

Shelly slides over the typical forms, which Dakota blindly signs like the rest of us. It's remarkable that consent isn't considered authentic when a person is under the influence. However, if you're at your rock bottom, it's as true as the profits they're making.

"Okay, perfect," Shelly says as she confirms the forms, "If you'd like to follow me, I can show you down the hall right here to your room." As they walk down the hall, I can hear the same script that I heard.

As they disappear and the hall gets quiet, Angie appears.

"Well, hello!" I say to Angie.

"Hi back! How are you doing?" she asks.

"I'm well—ready for day two?"

Angie rests her hands on her hips. "I am—not sure if it's ready for me, though," she says with a smile. "Is Cis finally sleeping?"

"Yeah, thank God. The majority of the staff here sure have shit for brains. I think they spend too much time in the sun," I say as I look around to see who I might be offending. There are a couple people, but they don't appear to be paying attention.

"Careful what you say. You might get a pillow over the face while you sleep," Angie tells me, "I think breakfast hour is starting momentarily. Shall we migrate over there?"

"I would love some breakfast—need to soak up all of this decaf!"

I toss my papers back in my folder and hold it under my arm as we move into the cafeteria. It's not an elaborate breakfast, but it'd be tough to screw it up. Today's menu is scrambled eggs, some boiled potatoes they're calling home fries, bacon, and some sliced melon.

"I'm impressed. Everything looks cooked!" I say to the server. He's the same guy who's here for every meal, at least all that I've witnessed. It's not clear if he's responsible for the preparations, though, or if he's just the delivery guy. He doesn't seem to care what I'm saying, or his English is broken. Honestly, I kind of hope for the latter for the amount of shit he probably hears here.

"Good morning, Jessie!" Angie says to the redhead starting off the line.

"Oh hey, how'd you sleep?" Jessie turns and asks Angie in a very soft, gentle voice. Also, he apparently slept through the noise if he needed to ask.

"Decently! How are the beds over on your side?" she asks him.

"They're slightly better, but they pale in comparison to my bed at home," Jessie says as he makes eye contact with me.

"Hi, I'm Brey," I reach out to shake his hand. He met my hand, but it was more of a quick grab than a shake.

"Nice to meet you, Brey. I'm Jessie. I'm in Angie's group for our sessions," he shyly explains. His otherwise pale complexion turns slightly red as though he's embarrassed feeling on the spot. I'm interested in learning his drug of choice because I doubt he's ever experimented with anything beyond whole milk.

"What do you do for work?" I ask him. Maybe it'll give me the clues I need to come up with a theory.

"I do administrative work for my church," he says. That doesn't help. He then asks me, "How about you?"

"I mainly write code," I say.

"And he's working on a novel!" Angie happily adds in.

"Oh! What's your book about?" Jessie asks me.

"I've chosen not to talk about it, but happy to send you a copy when it's finished," I tell him.

"Why don't you want to talk about it?" he asks in a nasally voice.

"Typically, when I work on something, I share the idea with everyone. Then I never actually finish it," I start to explain, "I read somewhere that when you do that, you're celebrating the project as though it is already finished. In the end, the projects are less likely to actually finish as you already marked off the win for it."

"Interesting," he says.

"I probably shouldn't have shared my passion project then!" Angie says as her eyes get wide.

"I don't think it applies to everyone, but I do have a problem finishing out projects. I'm hoping this one doesn't fall to the wayside like past projects," I say.

"I have faith. And I have to keep pushing you to practice as you're writing that first review for me," she winks as she gives me a reminder.

Food is served to us on our trays as we make it down the line. With a small detour to collect drinks, we sit down at the first table by the windows. Even if we can't freely roam outside, it's nice to pretend we have the liberty to do so.

"I'll be right back," Angie says as she walks down the hall.

A moment after she disappears, the front desk tech comes into the cafeteria and says that Angie has a phone call from her father. I let her know she'd be right back, and I'll inform her.

"I'll be right back as well," I say as I have a successful roll on stealth and sneak toward the phones. There's only one phone off the hook, so I pick it up.

"Hello? Is this Angie's dad?" I ask into the phone.

"Uh, yeah," he says and pauses for a moment, "Is everything okay with her?"

"Yes, everything is perfect. She'll be right here! I actually wanted to say hi," I say to him.

"Hi," he simply says back, "What's your name?"

"I'm Brey."

"Ah yes, I've heard of you. I hope you're taking care of her there! I never knew she had a problem," he says sheepishly.

"We can fill you in on everything once we get out," I tell him quietly so people don't notice I intercepted the phone call, "I was hoping to ask you about something in private. May I call you later?"

"Of course," he says. I collect his phone number and vow to call him later tonight or tomorrow. It all depended on when I'd be able to have alone time.

I wish him the best, quietly put down the phone, and sneak back to the cafeteria. As I get out of sight of the phone, I hear the front desk tech see Angie in the hall and inform her about the phone call.

As the tech works her way back to her desk, something dawns on me. She's the only one in this building with a heritage based out of Asia. Those cultures must really have their shit together!

I scarf down some food to avoid any suspicion from Angie when she comes back. Jessie makes some looks in my direction, but I trust he won't say anything. He's the type to smile when he's 'in the know' but hates confrontations, so won't put himself in any weird situations.

The talk goes longer than I expected, so I manage to finish my plate before Angie shows back up. She walks in with an awkward look on her face. Being on the inside, I realize it must be hard to tell a worrying parent that you're actually fine over a restricted call from inside a rehabilitation clinic.

"Everything okay?" I ask her.

"As okay as it's going to be for a bit," she says with half of a grin. "Poor guy just fell asleep on the couch last night when I left a message. He woke up to that, and then the clinic told him to call back during visiting hours." She laughs and says, "I think I got his nerves down to a six, maybe."

"Out of ten?" I ask to clarify.

"Out of seven," she says back to me.

"So what now?"

"I eat my cold eggs and congealed bacon," she says, "Then we head to the next session."

"Oh, joy."

*

As usual, I'm early. However, I'm not eager for this session. It's different from the smaller groups yesterday. It looks like everyone will be in this large room together. The chairs all face one direction with the exception of a perimeter of chairs on the outside aimed inward. It's as though they couldn't decide if they wanted a circle or a presentation layout, so they incorporated both.

I sit on the perimeter near the back left.

James comes in a couple moments later and sits next to me.

"How ya feeling today, bud?" I ask him.

"It's not getting any easier," he tells me.

"Did they give any guidelines on how many days or weeks before you should start feeling better?"

"Nope. They want to start cutting the suboxone after day ten, but it's not even enough now," he tells me.

"Sorry to hear that. I hope it gets easier for ya," I tell James.

Before my very own eyes, Big Blue comes walking in, looking like he has a grudge against the air he breathes. There's a thud as he drops his weight into a chair. He snorts incredibly loudly as I make brief eye contact with him. I see closer up how ridiculous his hair looks. It's like he glued some blue spikes onto a bald head. I look down at my folder and pretend to be busy with it.

I greet other familiar faces as they come and take their seats. Angie comes in with Amelia, and they sit about two feet in front of me in one of the last rows, looking forward. The rest of the larger group arrives with the exceptions of Cis and Dakota, who are probably sleeping. This includes all of the therapists as well.

Carol sits up front and appears to be the host.

"Okay, welcome all to another session of 'clear the air,'" Carol says loudly with her rotten, untrustworthy smile. "For those new, this is an open floor meeting where people can share grievances. These grievances can be with the facilities, the staff, or even fellow patients. We ask you to be kind and respectful when sharing. Would anyone like to start?"

Juan raises his hand.

"Yes, Juan. The floor is yours," Carol tells him.

"I would appreciate it if we could dedicate the lobby for phone use only," he softly says, "I was on a phone call last night, and I couldn't hear anything they were saying."

"Tell them to speak louder. Next!" Big Blue says over the crowd. All eyes turn to the jerk in blue.

"Please be respectful when others are speaking," Carol tells Big Blue.

"Why? Nobody cares! The staff doesn't give a shit about you or your phone calls. And I think I speak for the rest of us that we don't give a shit either!"

"What a dick," I mumble under my breath.

"I care about your calls," Angie says to Juan. Juan gives an embarrassed nod of appreciation.

"Why?" Big Blue continues, "What exactly do you get from him making phone calls?"

"Okay. That's enough," Carol says, "Please leave the room." She points at Big Blue then toward the hallway.

He snorts in his revolting fashion and loudly says, "Gladly!" As he walks away from the crowd, you can faintly hear him say, "fucking losers."

"Nice guy," I say out loud. I get a few chuckles, but most people are speechless.

They try to make patients feel psychologically safe in order to enable them to open up about their feelings. I imagine for those on the fence about it, this just pushed them in the wrong direction.

"Fuck that guy. Juan," Angie says, and Juan looks up to make eye contact. "I completely agree with you. Our time to communicate with family is limited while we're here. I believe we should reserve that area for phone users during those allocated times."

"I'm sorry, Juan. I think I started it all by playing the guitar over there," Steve says apologetically. "I'll take it outside or at least the far side of the cafeteria next time. Sorry again."

"Thank you. The music is nice, too," Juan says and smiles.

"Okay, any opposing thoughts?" Carol says. She looks around the room for several seconds. She continues, "Then we have it! We expect this rule to be followed now, and we will revisit it in one week."

"Rules are made that easily?" I ask Carol.

"Yes, sir!" she says proudly.

I stand up and announce, "Then I'd like to have regular coffee available in the mornings and afternoons, with decaf all day."

"I'm afraid that's against policy, we can't vote on that," she says. I sit back down as I hear some grumbles throughout the room. At least the pain is shared on this topic.

"Nice try," Angie says as she slides me a low fist bump.

A girl in the middle raises her hand.

"Yes, Lilly," Carol says as she looks over the front rows, "What would you like to share?"

"Is there any update on the poor quality of food? Our food was raw yesterday," Lilly says.

"The report has been made to the provider, and they're going to look into what went wrong," Frank says from the other side of the room.

"That's not a proper answer for something like this. When will we know the outcome?" Lilly turns and asks him.

"I don't think there's a follow-up scheduled with them," he says.

"Then I'd like to move that all staff needs to eat the same food as the patients. I don't see a world where any action will be taken until you have to shove raw worm-infested hamburg into your guts," she says.

"I second that!" I say quickly.

"Thank you," she turns to say to me.

"That's ag—" Frank starts to say.

"Against policy," I finish his sentence and continue on, "It seems policies are all designed to protect you and to fuck the patients. And since HIPAA is one of those things, we can't even bring in people to witness it or use our phones to get proof of the bullshit you sell here."

"Let's keep the topics on things we can act on," Carol says as she tries to shush the conversation.

"Let me get this right," Josiah says, "So you want us to self-manage by adding rules to the existing unchangeable policies to further micromanage our day-to-day activities and behavior."

"More or less," Frank responds.

"Then why are you all here? It seems unnecessary," Josiah asks in an irritated tone.

"We're here to moderate," Frank says back to him.

"Right," Josiah says with an annoyed laugh. He folds his arms then looks around to see who's next to speak.

"Anyone else?" Carol asks. She looks slowly across the crowd, making eye contact with several people. After clearing the crowd, she says, "Okay, we can stop there for the day. Enjoy your break time!"

*

This binder is slowly filling up with excerpts for my new novel. My passions have changed a bit since this journey began. I don't want to completely dismiss my previous novel, but I feel like I'd be doing a disservice to the story that's been handed to me on a silver platter. Similar to prison, there are no policies here against writing while trapped in this place.

I tell people I'm a writer because it's a passion of mine, but it's always been short poems, lyrics for songs, or short stories for assignments. They rarely got seen by anyone other than me and maybe a teacher. Immersing oneself in anything can be very therapeutic and meditative. There are exceptions like drugs and alcohol, which are good for an escape, but they only come with costs.

As I'm stashing away another written memory, Cis comes walking down the hall like a zombie.

"Ahoy," I say to him as I give a sharp wave. "You didn't sleep very long!"

"I woke up to pee, and now I'm hungry," he tells me, "So I'm going to suppress the urge and smoke a cigarette. Then I'll head back to bed!"

"Sounds like a good plan. I'll join ya."

I follow Cis outside to the tables. The heat is turned up today, so we hide away at the corner table—the only one lucky enough to have some shade.

"What have you been up to?" he asks me.

"Had breakfast, a shit-show of a meeting, then just did some writing. Oh yeah!" I missed out some key information.

"Oh?" Cis perks up as he lights his cigarette and turns his head to look at me.

"First, the dead girl isn't dead. She's back, and her name is Dakota," I tell him.

"That's good—probably in rough shape?"

"Absolutely. The normal expected 'rough shape,' but her face is pretty bashed up."

"Yikes," he says.

"And the banger of gossip—" I start to say something as the front doors shoot open.

Big Blue comes running through the doors like he's in a race. Jamal is typically outside monitoring illegal cigarette exchanges, but he must be inside at the moment as it's nearing the end of his and Micah's shift. Big Blue is really moving. He was probably alerted to some local delivery of blow.

Running about six seconds behind, Jamal and Micah both come out, completely huffing it. The effort is there, but they move at a fraction of Blue's speed. Cis energetically jumps up on the table.

"Run, Big Blue!" he giddily yells out. "They're right behind you! Don't stop!" He pumps his fist in the air several times.

"Sad to see him go?" I ask Cis sarcastically.

"Fuck no!" he says loudly with emphasis. "Also glad to sleep tonight! Fuck Big Blue!"

"You'll have to catch him first!"

Angie peeks her head out the side door as she probably hears Cis's yelling from inside.

"Did you all see that?" she yells out to us.

"Did I see that!?" Cis starts doing some poorly performed dance moves on the table in celebration. Angie laughs as she works her way over to us, keeping her head turned toward the area where Big Blue ran.

"Think the twins caught up to him?" she asks as she tries to locate them through the trees.

"It was like a tortoise chasing a hare. The only way that'll happen is if he stops to take a nap," Cis explains, "And the hare had several seconds of top speeds before the tortoise even entered the race. Sorry, tortoises."

"I feel like we should be able to see a small field of blue bopping through the trees," I say. I climb up on the table with Cis as I try different angles to see Big Blue.

There's no sign of any of them. And just like that, the twins appear on the road behind some trees with their heads hung low. They're sweaty and huffing away as they dig deep for the will to get back inside to the air conditioning.

"Did you see him?" Cis yells at them. Their heads lift just enough to see who is making the noise. And just as quickly, their heads dip back down.

"What a day," I say as I sit back down on the table.

"Think he'll come back?" Angie asks us.

"I hope not," I say.

"Yeah. That's fair. He's a bit of a prick, huh?" Angie says.

"You all met him?" Cis asks.

"Not directly. He was a prick at the session you missed. He didn't like the fact that Juan wanted to be able to talk to his family in peace," I say.

The door slowly opens. I'm expecting to see Jamal or his replacement, but Dakota walks casually out.

"You all got an extra smoke?" she asks.

"Yeah, picked up this pack yesterday after years of not smoking," Cis says as he hands her a cigarette. Luckily, the guards are all occupied at the moment, so it's a successful exchange.

"I also haven't smoked in years," she says as Cis holds out his lighter.

"For what it's worth, they have smokes in the vending machine over there," Cis points to the machine just inside the doors.

"I noticed that. I love my sister, who brought me here. I wish she had brought my wallet as well," she says in a disappointed voice.

"Here, no one should be without in here," I say as I slide her a twenty dollar bill.

"Are you sure?" she asks, "I really don't want to become a charity case here."

I laugh and tell her, "We're all charity cases here. I'll deny it, though, if the guards ask. They have strong 'every person for themselves' policies."

She smiles and thanks me again.

"I'm Cis, by the way," Cis reaches out and shakes Dakota's hand.

"Nice to meet you. I'm Dakota. Also, thanks for the smoke and money. I feel like I made a good banging choice coming out here."

"I'm Brey."

"I'm Angie."

"Nice to meet you," Dakota says with a smile. As her lips extend, though, she moans and grabs her lip. We all grimace a little as we know that unfortunate misfortune of opening the scab of a split lip.

"What brings you into this four-star facility?" Cis asks, "For me, it's alcohol."

"Same, and pills," she says, "Unfortunately, this is the shit I wake up to." She points at her lip and eye.

"Looks like it hurts like a bitch," Cis tells her as he stares at her eye, "No witnesses?"

"My boyfriend is usually around. He was under the influence as well but thinks it's from when I fell and smashed my head on this old rocking chair we have."

"Why isn't he here with you?" Cis asks.

"He's a bit of a douche," she says, "My sister apparently stuffed me in her car and brought me here. I don't think he knows where I am. He may not even know I'm gone."

"Is that a good thing?" Angie asks. Dakota just nods in response. I get the vibe she's in a pretty toxic relationship.

"Well, I'm for one excited to have someone to smoke with," Cis says as he cheers her with their cigarettes.

"I think lunch should be served any minute," I say as I stand up. "We unfortunately don't all have appetite suppressants."

"Tobacco is better for the health at this place," Angie says as she stands up, too. "I'll join you."

"See ya in there," Cis says as he gives us a single wave.

As we start walking toward the door, I notice Dakota sitting on top of the table next to Cis. I don't know anything about her past, but they seem to share the trait of overdoing things. Hopefully, they can put an end to each other's madness.

"He gets to sleep tonight AND gets a new friend?" Angie says quietly to me. "I bet we'll see a brand new Francis Freighton tomorrow!"

CHAPTER 11

~ Unwelcomed Guest ~

The meals continue to be garbage, but I'm happy to see Cis and Dakota have been kicking it off. They're sharing laughs, stories, and secondary smoke. Cis seems to be on a new comfort level. While we love him, and he certainly loves us, given the scenario, he needs someone who's truly there with him in that state of mind.

I walk with Angie to the internal AA meeting. They host them in this building, but once we get to the next phase of rehabilitation, we start taking buses to external locations. I hear a downtown location is considered one of the OGs of meeting places. It will be interesting to see how they differ from place to place.

There's a man chatting with Janette. He's got the traditional biker look—certainly someone I wouldn't want to get into a fight with. After the crowd arrives, he introduces himself as 'Jacob L.' and leads the Serenity Prayer to kick off the meeting.

His story is pretty action-packed, but most cocaine stories are. It ended in a body cast after someone hit him purposely with their car. He admits that his group set out that night to fight. They weren't discriminating by any means. First group they saw, they were going to attack. For that reason, no charges were pressed. I guess he fucked around and found out.

The story keeps our attention locked tight. We roll into the traditional AA finale of the Lord's Prayer. The prayer has been familiar to me for a long time, but I believe it's mostly due to it being referenced in movies. I couldn't recite any of it on my own, but I do know there's some daily bread involved. Sourdough or bust.

I'm always impressed by people who do public speaking, especially when they don't get compensated for it. I make sure to thank the guy for coming before everyone disperses from the room.

As I'm saying bye to him, there's some ruckus happening down the hall by the entryway. It's strange, considering everyone was supposedly in the room for this meeting.

"Get your hands off me!" a male voice yells, "Dakota! Where you at? It's time to go, sweetie."

"I said you can't be in here!" Earl, the older security guard, yells.

"I'm just here for Dakota, and then I'll leave. Touch me and find out what happens," he says as his voice gets steadily louder. We hear his footsteps coming down the hall, and all get a bit nervous. Where are Jamal and Micah when you actually need them?

Dakota takes a seat a few rows behind people who are standing. It seems she's trying to hide from him. As he makes it around the corner, he shifts back and forth a bit, looking through the small crowd.

"Aha, there you are," he says to her. She doesn't move or turn to look at him. He tells her, "Let's go. People are waiting for us."

This guy looks straight out of some heroin tales. His clothes are both expensive looking and raggedy. His hair is somehow both super short and unkempt, as though it had a rare opportunity to be both. He also has classic prison tattoos randomly placed across his arms and neck. I imagine he's high now, given the thick white saliva bubbles in the corners of his mouth. He looks like he's rabid.

As he starts to work through the crowd, Josiah and Steve are the first to get in his way. Even Jacob L. steps in behind them.

"Real fucking heroes," he tells them as he involuntarily spits as he talks, "Dakota—I'm not waiting any longer." Dakota just stays quiet like it's some hallucination that will go away on its own.

"She's where she needs to be," Cis says as he joins the human wall.

"Seth, go home," Dakota finally says, and she stands up to face him.

"You're coming with me," he tries to force his way through the wall.

"The fuck she is," Steve says as he and Josiah grab him by the shirt and hold him back.

"You all fucked up big time," Seth says, "I'll be back and I'll burn this place to the ground!"

Cis moves in behind Seth, and bear hugs him around the waist. Steve and Josiah grab onto his arms and they carry him down the hall like he's Jesus being carried on the cross. He continues to threaten everyone in the building as he's being forced out the front door. With his frantically kicking legs, I'm sure Cis will have some bruised-up shins tomorrow. I follow close behind to assist if needed. I suppose we could also hold him down and call the cops, but this seems like the best form of de-escalation at the moment.

Raye arrives with the larger security guard. As he walks by, I catch a glimpse of his name tag, which reads 'Anthony.'

"Welcome to the party, Anthony," Josiah says sarcastically over his shoulder as they put Seth down off of the clinic's property. They all hold their arms up to keep some distance from him in case he tries anything. Anthony stands ground a few feet back. I imagine he needs a little reaction time, as his speed probably doesn't match his strength, but his focus is absolutely sharp. In American football terms, he's much more of a defensive tackle than a cornerback.

"You think you can just take my girl from me?" Seth says with much panic in his voice. As he speaks, some of the drool bubbles dislodge from the corners of his mouth and fly out at different trajectories. He paces back and forth a few times, frantically rubbing the top of his shaved head.

At this point, we take a couple of steps back but watch for his erratic behavior.

"Police are on their way," Earl says from the back as he walks up to join us.

"This isn't over," Seth says as he jumps into his car, "You best send her home, or I'll be back."

I'm a bit taken aback by his ride, as I was expecting him to either walk or jump into a complete shit box. Instead, it's a newer muscle car, and his peel-out is actually quite impressive. I'm not a car person, but I'd guess it's a Mustang or Camaro based on the looks. Regardless of the car's make, it's far better than what that guy deserves.

Steve, Josiah, and Cis give each other knuckles as they sigh in relief that it's over. I give Cis a pat on the back.

"How the shin's doing?" I ask him.

"Ask me when the adrenaline wears off," he says over his shoulder to me.

"That was something," Josiah says, "Does this happen a lot?" He turns around and looks at Anthony and Earl.

"Not in my days," Anthony says as he keeps his eyes on the road.

We hear sirens in the distance.

"I'll talk to the police," Earl says, "Please head back inside and stay available. They may need to talk to you all."

As we come through the door, there are several heads watching us from down the hall. Cis leads the pack as I trail behind. I don't want to take the glory as I was just a benched player.

We round the corner into the large room and see Carol and Alan sitting close to Dakota. Alan seems worried about her well-being and the road ahead of her. Carol seems worried about herself and what further danger could be in store.

Typically, I'd expect them to pluck people from the crowd before grilling them for potentially private information. It seems we're past that, though.

"What else should we know about Seth?" Carol asks her.

"He's just a loser junkie," Dakota says, "He comes from money, so he has an endless supply."

"What about his circle?" Carol continues to drill.

"I mean, he's an endless source of drugs, and this city has an endless source of junkies," she says, "He doesn't run a gang or anything like that, but his group is desperate for his supply."

"And you didn't think this was important to us?" Carol asks.

Tears start to form in the corner of Dakota's eyes. This past day is probably the first time she's felt safe, and now those walls may be crumbling down. Carol's tone is definitely not what she needs at this moment. It sounds an awful lot like she's about to feed Dakota to the wolves.

"Sorry, sweetheart," Carol says, "That came out wrong." Carol sits back and takes a deep breath to recollect herself. For someone that's high strung in her normal state, I think this event has finally caused her to have a stack overflow and become human.

"The police are almost here," Anthony says as he turns into the room, "Stay in this room until things are cleared up."

Cis walks over and sits near Dakota.

"You okay?" he asks her. She begins to cry and shakes her head. He grabs a box of tissues on the floor and hands them to her. It's a violation of one of the therapy policies, but I don't think anyone is going to raise a flag over it. They want people to learn to help themselves, so we're told to slide the box over in front of them, but we shouldn't actually hand it to them. Perhaps it makes sense for people who can't get out of their own way—it's a baby step toward doing so.

"Dakota Mearl?" an officer asks as he enters the room.

Cis points to Dakota. Her feet rest on her chair and her head is resting between her knees. She looks up at the officer, and he looks thrown off by the black eye.

"Could you come with me for a moment, ma'am? We just have a few questions to ask you," the officer asks Dakota. He has a bit of the Southern charm to him and at least treated her respectfully. She follows him into one of the rooms reserved for the visiting doctors. Another officer, Carol and Janette join them as well.

The room is completely quiet due to both shock and eavesdropping. The officer's words are muffled by the walls, so we can't catch what's going on there. We do get an occasional laugh when the officer loudly and clearly talks over Carol and asks her to take a deep breath. I'm not sure she's the perfect candidate for being there. Maybe they should tag her out for Alan.

I walk over to Angie and Amelia, who are lingering in the back corner.

"How are you two doing?" I ask them.

"We're fine," Angie asks and nods in Cis's direction. He's bent over, fidgeting with a tissue in his hands. I nod to Angie as I take her hint and move back over to sit next to Cis.

"Hey man," I say quietly as I crouch down next to him.

"Hey," he says.

"Quite the fucking whirlwind it's been," I say and look over at him.

"Just another Tuesday…Wednesday…fuck, I don't even know what day it is," he says as he shakes his head.

"It's just another day. Who cares what label people put on it? What can I do to help you?"

"Get me outside?" he asks.

It's not a yes or no question. It's a question of how I'm going to accomplish it. Alan, Frank and now Raye are all in the room with us.

"Follow me," I say as I get up, and Cis follows closely behind.

"Excuse me, you need to stay in the room," Frank says to us as we start to leave.

"We need to talk to an officer about something," I say as I start walking a few more steps forward.

"What do you need to ask?" Frank says as he starts to get in our way.

"Sorry, I'd tell you, but it's against the policy," I wedge my body through the opening that's left and then drag Cis behind me.

"Gentlemen, you're going to get in trouble if you keep walking," Frank says to our backs.

"Yeah? Then who's going to protect you when that fucker comes back?" Josiah says as he also follows behind. Steve sees his new muscle pack leaving and quickly gains ground to fall in. As the four of us walk down the hall toward the front door, I nudge Cis and give him a wink. I feel like we just accomplished some major heist.

There are two officers watching out front as the other two interview Dakota. I look at the other guys, and they all look at me as if I'm about to say something. I tilt my head toward the door in a gesture for them to follow me.

"Good evening, officers," I say as I come through the door, "We had two requests." I look at the badge of the officers. It's Officer Jenkins and Officer Lore. There's a joke in there somewhere.

"And that is?" Officer Jenkins looks at me quizzically.

"First," I request, "Could you let us know if that guy who was here is diseased in any manner? As you probably know, he made it inside and across the building. We're the four that carried him out."

"Heh," Jenkins said, "Took four of you? I heard he was pretty scrawny."

The officer has a sense of humor. It's actually both true and funny. The four of us laugh along with the officers.

"To be fair," Steve says, "It was really the three of us. He was just cheerleading from behind."

"Ah, okay," Officer Lore says. "As usual, thee who does the least asks for the most." I nod. True again.

"What's the second request?" Officer Jenkins asks.

"Could my buddy here smoke a cigarette? The side doors are locked, and even if there was a guard out there with us, we've seen how effective they are," I ask him.

"Oh yeah," Officer Jenkins says, "And in regards to the first request, once we find him and identify him, we'll let the clinic know if there's anything to be worried about. I'm sure they'll take good care of ya." We all laugh again as we look at each other in amusement.

"May I ask what brought all of you to this point?" Officer Lore asks.

"The silent beast, addiction," Josiah says to him.

"You're all hiding it quite well. I hope you all stay on the path of sobriety," Officer Lore says, "I'm fourteen years sober. The beast is strong, but it has no power if you put a fucking muzzle over its snout."

"Dang man, congrats," Cis says, "This is just day two for me, and so far, life has become far more chaotic than I've ever seen before. And I work full time in the kitchen."

"I hear it settles down after year twelve," Officer Jenkins says with a wink, "Just kidding. We've seen people come and go with places like this. It's really a crap shoot on what their outcome will be, be it a year or ten years down the road."

"Yeah, you gotta look out for each other on the outside," Officer Lore says, "Some of you will be jumping back into situations where your odds of success are so low that you might as well go straight to jail after this."

"Or worse, the grave," Officer Jenkins says.

"We're aware," I tell them as I put my hand on Cis's shoulder. "This guy, our friend Angie, and I all checked in together. Hopefully, it'll help keep us afloat."

"Just don't give up on each other," Officer Lore says, "Odds are someone will slip. Help them back up."

"I appreciate the words," I tell them.

"By the way," Officer Jenkins says, then pauses to collect his thoughts, "Would you all be willing to point this guy out from a lineup?"

"Yes, are you able to get us out of here to do that?" Steve asks.

"Don't have to. We can do a lineup with mugshots," Officer Jenkins says.

"Oh, cool, count me in," Steve says.

"I appreciate it," Officer Jenkins says.

"Yeah, I think we're all in," Cis says. He looks at Josiah and myself and we both nod in agreement. Cis finishes his cigarette and puts it out in the ashtray.

"One last favor," I ask the officers.

"I can't give penicillin shots. Ask the doctor," Officer Lore says.

"Could one of you bring us back to the room and thank us for the information?" I ask them, "It'd get these therapists off our back."

"I imagine if I had come to a place like this, I'd be walking in your shoes," Officer Jenkins says, "Always glad to serve and protect those willing to serve and protect themselves."

"Excellent," I say with a large smile.

We open the doors and start walking down the halls with Officer Jenkins. The wall is quiet until we're about twenty feet from the room.

"Thanks again for the information! It's a huge help!" he says with great enthusiasm. "And give our station a call if something else comes up or if you change locations for whatever reason. We definitely will check back in the next day or two if we need you for the lineups. Thanks again!"

He stops with a smile and gives us fist bumps as we pile back into the room. Officer Jenkins scans the room and finds the staff huddled together.

"Thanks for letting me steal your patients for a few," he yells over to them before disappearing back outside. Some police officers are simply amazing. We need more people manning our streets like Officer Jenkins and Officer Lore.

The door opens down the hall. Carol walks out first, with Dakota behind her. The officers are a few steps behind but turn the other way to go join Officers Jenkins and Lore out front. No words are spoken as they make their way back down the hallway. Dakota looks both concerned and emotionally drained.

"How'd things go in there?" Cis asks her as she comes up to us.

"Fine," she says, "Want to grab a smoke?"

"Yes, I do," Cis says.

He gives me a nod. Cis leads Dakota down the hall to replay the same game plan to get back outside.

Steve and Josiah wander off to chat with some of their other buddies. Angie sees I've been deserted and comes up to me.

"You and Cis are a couple of heroes tonight. And all this time, I've just been trying to figure out when I can take a shower." She softly laughs to herself.

"It's about time the two of us carry our weight," I tell her, "Neither of us has forgotten your role in this."

"Anything for my new best friends," she says and smiles at me.

"Life's going to be so different after we go home," I tell her, "We probably won't be seeing you as much."

She cuts me off, "Why wouldn't you be seeing me?"

"Because we won't be visiting the bar anymore. I honestly don't see how I could even casually drink with Cis as my roommate."

"I called it in last night," she says with her head hung low. She looks at me as she lifts her head back up with a big smile on it, "I no longer work in the bar."

My eyes widen as I exclaim, "What!?" Then I realize I'm being super loud and go back to a whisper level. I say, "Well, congrats! Where's our favorite bartender going next?"

"I have no idea, but I don't want to be a hypocrite—sliding a shot across the bar as I suggest they should try a new life of sobriety."

"Yeah, I do wonder what Cis will do after this," I ponder.

"I imagine there are at least some kitchens with healthy environments out there that could use his help."

"Hopefully, or I'll have to get back to coding quickly so I can hire him as my private chef," I say.

"I heard it pays well," Angie says.

"Yeah, they've always taken good care of me. And I enjoy it as well," I tell her with all honesty.

"What's the endgame for you? Rise up the corporate ladder?"

"I don't think so," I say slowly, "I enjoy the coding aspect of my coding job. I know that sounds obvious. But when you enter management and rise up, you get further and further away from coding. Yes, there are other things to solve, but while my title and pay would go up, my love of the job would go down."

"So, just coast where you are?" she asks.

"I wouldn't call it coasting."

"Well, I didn't mean it like that," she adds.

"I know. I definitely feel like I'm forever growing in my position. This feels like the 'good ole days,' and I don't want to pass it by," I say. I've definitely been in my head a lot about this exact topic. It seems objectively wrong not to want a promotion.

"Makes sense. If you're happy, you're happy."

"Let's not get carried away now," I say as we both laugh. "Writing has always been something I've enjoyed. I couldn't tell you if I'm good at it or awful at it, but I enjoy it. The novel is sort of my endgame there. Whether it publishes and sells a couple books, or it never sees the light of day, I want to say I wrote a book."

"So you're like the dormant volcano that secretly dug a tunnel underground to blow out from a second volcano?"

"I like the analogy. I hope I don't burn anyone with the book."

An officer comes in and pulls Janette aside. The room gets quiet again as we try to be subtle in our eavesdropping. It's unsuccessful, though, as they finish speaking and all I caught were mumbles.

"Okay, here's the situation," Janette says, then pauses for the final whispers to end. "Due to the incident tonight, we're going to have all doors locked externally until further notice. We will have our security detail patrol a bit around the building before and during breaks. You can still go outside on the patio, but there needs to be a security guard in your presence at all times. Please be respectful of their time and other duties. And, of course, if you see anything out of the ordinary, please tell a staff member immediately. Thank you for your cooperation. You can carry on for now."

In any other place, I'm sure there'd be a lot of questions about a junkie who just broke in and threatened everyone. To us, he'll probably just be another patient someday if he doesn't meet his ancestors first.

CHAPTER 12
~ The Calm ~

As I walk by the cafeteria right before dinner, I notice the menu is already posted. They're serving ribs, potato salad, and corn! It's as though we're finally being rewarded after a long and testing day. I have to share the news! I run out to the patio where my new small group has formed. Both security guards are outside as well and on high alert.

"You guys!" I say to the group. "You won't believe what my guardian angel brought for me today."

"A sense of humor?" Cis asks, followed by some snickering.

"A third storyline for your book," Angie asks.

"Damn, you all have tight guardian angels. Mine brings me a packet of ramen with a lukewarm cup of water to soak it in," Steve says with furled eyebrows.

"Ribs!" I exclaim, "They're serving ribs for dinner!" I let out a bit of a cheer.

"I was expecting a lot more, but ribs? That's a surprise," Cis says, "I hope they're cooking them correctly."

"Something tells me they aren't," Angie says. She distorts her face into a fake smile.

"Well, you non-believers, I believe they've finally decided that they owe us a break," I say as I stand tall with my hands on my hips like a superhero.

"Regardless of the outcome, this needs to become a song." Steve points his finger at me. "We're collaborating on it."

"With me?" I ask just to make sure he hasn't confused my back story with someone cool.

"Yes, you. I've heard that you've written some words in the past. I'll cover the tune side of it," he says. He wrings his hands together out of excitement.

"You can call it the PP Song," Angie says with a giggle.

"The PP Song by the Particles of Poo Rock," I say as my eyebrows raise with joy. "It'd be shameful to walk away from that. I guess we have to do it now."

"It's seriously my calling." Steve bows his head without losing eye contact with me.

"I did choir in school," Amelia softly says.

"We've got ourselves a party!" Steve holds his hands out wide.

I knew Steve was punk rock, but I didn't know this level of energy could be achieved during rehab.

"How do you have so much energy?" Cis says with a bit of envy resonating in his voice.

"He probably sleeps," I tell him.

"Cloud Number Nine!" he says over me.

"The what?" Angie asks.

"Cloud Number Nine!" he repeats.

"Oh good, that clears it up," Angie says as she rolls her eyes.

"You'll hear about it soon enough. It's the week or so after you finally make it through the initial withdrawal symptoms," Josiah clarifies, "You have a level of freedom and energy you haven't had since the addictions started. So you feel like you're floating on a cloud. They warn you that people feel 'cured' at this point. It passes, but being an addict does not."

"Sounds lovely!" Angie nods in Cis's direction, knowing he's the only one in our trio who'll experience this.

A few thuds and controlled crashes come from the cafeteria.

"Ribs!" I exclaim as I run to be first in line. My friends are less thrilled as they aren't behind me once I stake my claim. The server is still setting things up. The hotel pans of the food in the serving table have their lids in place. I bend down and move side to side in hopes of catching a glimpse of the splendid meat.

"I don't have much of an appetite," Dakota says as she sneaks up behind me, "But I think karma should be good to you. I hope they meet your needs!"

"And I came to witness the disappointment," Cis follows behind her.

The server finishes getting the hotbox turned on and matching utensils to each of the pans.

"Drum roll!" Steve says as he and Josiah show up in line with a handful of other people.

The server's blank face starts wearing down my hope. Are they slow-cooked? Did they ruin them and boil them? The suspense is killing me. The server sees my stare. He starts to lift the back of the lid off of the ribs but quickly puts it back down and turns around.

I let out an involuntary moan. The server turns around again with a smirk on his face. Without further hesitation, he lifts the lids off of the ribs and corn.

"What the hell? Those aren't ribs; they're patties!" I say in shock. Cis starts laughing uncontrollably.

"Those are," Cis tries speaking. "Those are—" He lets the laughing win.

I turn to look at Cis and say, "Well? What the fuck are those things?"

He bursts out in harder laughter as he says, "Processed meat!"

I turn back to the server and say, "You're telling me someone had the nerve to prepare processed meat and sell it as 'ribs?'"

"Looks like it," the server says. He probably takes a lot of shit from patients, so he's going to take the most out of this incident.

"Is tomorrow canned ham disguised as spiral honey ham?" I ask him.

"So, you going to get some food or just chat up the server all night?" Josiah says.

"I'll take the processed meat, shriveled-up corn, and a scoop of those hydrated salt and vinegar chips," I tell the server. I exaggerate a bit in my phrasing to hopefully come off as half playful and half incredibly disappointed and disgusted.

"I think you should give him a side of apology, too," Dakota says.

"I like her," I say, then turn back. "Hey, Angie!"

"Yeah?" Angie says from halfway back in the line.

"Dakota is replacing Cis in our trio. He's dead to me. Us. He's dead to us."

"Okay. Can you grab your tray and skedaddle? You're holding up the line!" Angie grunts back.

"It may just be the two of us," I quietly say to Dakota, then move off the line.

My stomach curdles a bit as I look at the food about to enter it. I skip the generic sugar-loaded drinks and go to the safe choice of water. It's probably the only thing with a positive nutritional fact sheet.

Dakota sits across from me at the table. She seems more indifferent about the food than me.

"I'm planning to call my sister tomorrow," she says, "I'm going to have her wire some money over."

"That's good," I tell her, "It certainly helps as I pray to the vending gods at least three times a day."

"Yeah, but I meant I can pay you back."

I pulled out my best Southern Grandma voice and told her, "For what? Giving money is a clear violation of the rules here, and I am embarrassed you would accuse me of such actions!"

I shift back to my normal voice and say, "No, but seriously, I don't want or need it back. How about this: once you get that money, I'll stop giving." I slide another twenty under her tray.

"I feel like there are strings attached to it," she says as she lays her hand on top of it.

"Not the strings you think," I say, "More a potential favor."

She stirs in her seat and asks, "What's this favor?"

"Cis has been my best friend for a very long time," I say, "He was the catalyst to the three of us coming. I can go into details when we have more time later, but I just ask that if you see him being distracted by the outside…you know…like he's falling off the recovery tracks, please tell me or Angie."

"That's it?" Dakota asks. "I don't need to be paid for that." She begins to slide the money back.

"Please keep it," I say, "It's important we all stay in the game. We're a team."

"Well, would you accept my ribs as repayment?"

"I hate you," I tell her, "But I'm still glad you're here."

"Me too."

"Oh yeah! Me three!" Cis says as he plops down on the seat next to Dakota. He looks between us and asks, "What'd I sign up for?"

"We're having a processed meat competition," Dakota makes up a quick lie, "I'm going to see if I can fit this entire rib in my mouth."

"That seems like a horrible idea with your lip," Cis tells her.

"Don't make excuses for me," Dakota tells him. "If you're too chicken to try, just back down." I'm impressed by her commitment. I'm less impressed by the lie.

Before I have a chance to talk my way out of this, Dakota stabs her ribs and brings it up to her mouth. Realizing brute force was required for this job, she pulls the rib off her fork and uses both hands to shove every last piece into her mouth.

"Holy shit. This is actually happening," I say. I look down at the blob on my tray and hope the barbecue sauce is at least decent. I dive right in and two-hand it right into my mouth. There's so much mushy meat in my mouth. I don't actually know what I'm supposed to chew. Do I just swallow? Now I understand why cats are such assholes. This is awful.

As my saliva struggles to break it down, I look up at Dakota, having the same issue. We both turn our heads simultaneously to Cis, who clearly isn't ready to back down. He bends down and meets the meat halfway. Dakota and I both start laughing hysterically as Cis dry heaves a bit on the food.

Heads have all turned to us at this point. We probably look like some wild boars who haven't eaten in days. Dakota has the genius idea of cupping her hand over her mouth. I believe she's letting a little food out so she can regain control of what remains. She shoves the rest back in her mouth and finishes it. Cis and I, both impressed, do the same.

"What is happening over here?" Janette walks up and asks us, "Are you a bunch of wild dogs?"

"What else do you serve dog food to?" I ask her. She looks unimpressed with my question.

"Old corn is more of a pig food," Cis says to me.

"I stand corrected," I say as I look up to Janette. "Other than pigs, what else do you serve dog food to?"

"This is not dog food," Janette says, "Have you considered the cooks who prepared this for you? How do you think they feel?"

"If they have to eat it, they are probably sick to their stomachs," I say.

"Do you have their numbers? I recommend a shot of apple cider vinegar," Cis brings up his home remedy again.

"If you don't drop these defense mechanisms, you're going to let them get in the way of your recoveries," Janette tells us.

"If we keep eating this food, we'll probably need two recoveries," Josiah says as he and Steve join us at the table.

"Oh, the things you all take for granted," Janette says with a sigh as she turns around and walks across the cafeteria.

Dakota picks up her corn, snorts like a pig a few times, then finishes off her corn cob in a single attempt. To be fair, the kernels were about ten percent their normal size. I get the feeling they cooked the corn and then let it cool in the fridge. Once the kernels lost their last bit of life, they microwaved them and brought them here.

"I don't know if I can stomach another one of your challenges," Cis says to Dakota. He uses his fork to prod at his corn.

"Dead on arrival," Steve says.

"Have we all commented on this 'potato salad' yet?" Angie says as she and Amelia finally make it to the table. "If not, I'd like to start."

"Besides an earlier reference to rehydrated salt and vinegar chips, it's open for business," Dakota tells her.

"That's all I had," Angie says as she sits down.

"I have something to say," Dakota says as she looks up from her food.

"Floor is yours," Angie says.

"I appreciate what you all did today," she tells the table. "I've never had anyone stand up for me before." We nod in support as she thinks of her next words. She says, "Seth and I have a long history. The drugs used to be recreational and not habits. But soon after we hooked up, he told me to stop working as we had an endless supply of money from his parents. He's a trust fund horror. The drugs soon became our full-time jobs. He quickly became what he is today, and I missed my early chances to get away. It's not a good place to be where you're afraid of the person who claims to protect you."

"I'm sorry you had to deal with that," Angie tells her, then corrects herself, "'Have to,' not 'had to.'"

"What about your sister? Can't go with her?" Cis asks.

"She's a decade younger than me. She's doing the college thing, living on campus. I don't want to interfere with that."

"That's fair. How do you feel about Boston?" Angie asks her.

"I hear it's cold. Otherwise, no opinion."

"Come check the place out when we're done with here. It's got plenty of room for good people," Angie says with a smile. Cis perks up a bit with the idea and looks at me. He smiles and then looks back at Dakota.

"Is that what I am?" Dakota says with a soft giggle, "I'll consider it."

"Good," Angie says and leaves it at that.

"Okay," Steve says as he stands up and looks at me, "Let's go write the PP Song."

CHAPTER 13

~ The Eye ~

The mood is lifting across the group at this point. As I look around meditation, I can see beautiful bonds that are forming among the patients. Even the staff seems to have lightened up a bit too. I don't think anyone wants to ruin the mood though by asking to turn the lights off. Nor would we push boundaries by asking to sit on the floor. We'll just sit cross-legged on these hard plastic chairs and appreciate that we're sober and kind of happy.

Micah and Jamal are back on shift. I can faintly hear them as they discuss the incident in a room down the hall. Their tones are more clear than their words. At a minimum, I would say they're taken back by it. I'm glad they're at the front door now. If someone shows up with bad intentions, I think they would turn away after seeing those guys. That's assuming they haven't previously witnessed the twins running. You can out-maneuver a gator, but good luck getting out of their jaws.

As our meditation is ending, Micah and Jamal arrive in the room to the beginning of some light chatter.

"We're going to open up the patio for the next hour," Jamal says.

"You're what?" Amilia asks. Everyone seems caught off guard of a schedule change.

"We figured y'all could use a little more chill time." Jamal nods to Micah, who starts walking towards the exit door.

"Hells yeah!" Steve says and he starts jogging down the hall toward the reception.

"Where ya going? Door is this way!" Jamal chuckles and shakes his head.

Steve comes running back down the hall with the guitar in his right hand. He holds it high as he looks at me like it's his first Christmas morning. I suppose we need to work on our song if it's set to hit shelves never.

"Let's go!" Steve says as he runs past me out the door.

"Come on, superstar. Let's go." I turn around and see Angie smiling at me. Her hand dismisses me towards the door. As I playfully swat her hand down, our hands clasp for a short moment. She winks at me and pushes me softly towards the door.

I find a seat next to Steve as people fill in around us. As he starts strumming the guitar to find the right tune, I can't help but notice James. He seems relaxed and is part of the crowd tonight. His leg is also tapping to the beat of the song and not the heart rate of a jackrabbit.

"Brey." Steve steals back my attention then starts a new strumming pattern.

"That's gold," I say.

Amelia begins singing.

I am a PP Patient.
Don't try to fuck with me.
We are the PP Patients.
We do our own security.

As she sings security, I look at Jamal and Micah to get their reactions. They grin at each other as their thumbs keep the beat on their pant legs. The crowd sings along with Ameilia as they repeat the chorus. It begins feeling like a genuine concert as the fog effects kick in, supplied for free from Dakota and Cis's cigarettes.

In the past, I've written down thousands of lines of lyrics for all types of genres. Never did I expect to hear any of those words come out of someone else's mouth, though. Even if they're a bit juvenile, it feels good.

I slip inside to grab some water. As the door shuts behind me, it almost immediately opens again. I look over my shoulder to see Angie following behind me.

"Walking away from your own show?" She smiles as she tucks her hair behind her ear.

"I did my part. Now I've gotta let the band shine."

"They are definitely shining out there!"

As we walk down the hall towards the cafeteria, I can't help but think of all that has unfolded since the roll of those dice. Life just feels better in so many ways.

"How do you think Cis is holding up?" Angie says quietly to me.

"Quite well, considering he's been awake for almost the entire time we've been here." I grab two red plastic cups from the stack next to the water cooler. I fill one and offer it to Angie.

She accepts the cup then pauses. "You know him better than anyone. What do you think of the Dakota situation?"

"I think she's a good distraction from any side effects he's feeling." I take a sip from my freshly poured cup of water. It's amazing how these cups always smell like dirty dish water.

"And if it ends badly?" Angie takes a sip from her water. She seems less distracted by the smell.

"We can cross that bridge if we get to it. I'm sure there'll be plenty of opportunities for him to get tempted back into drinking. My plan is to just remain available and to help wherever I can." Angie nods to me. It's probably not the concrete answer she was hoping for, but I'd rather stay optimistic that everyone will just work out.

To avoid suspicion of the staff, we make our way back to the patio. The group is sharing a lot of laughter over the PP Song. Cis and Dakota have wandered off to the viewpoint by the water.

"Hello!" Cis yells across the water.

I look over to see who he's yelling at. There's a little movement in the shrubbery across the pond, but no signs of life.

"Yelling at the squirrels?" I yell up to Cis.

"Nah, there was definitely a person over there." Dakota says down to me as Cis focuses his eyes on the darkness.

Jamal and Micah walk to the edge of the water to look across. After a few moments, they shrug and come back to the crowd.

"Ok, we're going to call it here." Jamal tells us as Micah walks over to open the door.

While the noise of the crowd doesn't settle, they do begin to disperse in pairs down the hallway. Jamal and Micah lock the place down behind us. The front of the parade breaks apart into the bathrooms as everyone begins their preparation for bed.

As Angie and I get close to parting ways, she slyly holds my hand with her index finger and gives it a light squeeze.

"Goodnight," she says with a smile.

"Goodnight," I tell her as she releases my hand and continues down the hall.

CHAPTER 14
~ The Clouds ~

There are ducks forming in the hall, and they need a leader. A boulder comes crashing down.

BOOM!

My eyes open, and it's dark, very dark. I lift my head up off the pillow and try to focus. I realize now I was still in dreamland. As I look around the room, I recognize it and lay my head back down. My bladder decides I've got one more thing to do first.

I quietly sneak across the room and open the door. Shelly and Daymond are talking to a new patient. It seems like an every night affair at this point, so I just turn my back to them and stumble down to the bathroom. As I do my business, I reminisce on the night before. It turns out this place isn't so bad.

As I leave the bathroom and start walking back down the hall, I see the person crouched over in a chair, going through the typical onboarding routine. They seem fairly calm and collected compared to the ones I've heard about or seen, including myself.

With one hand on my door, I hesitate to walk back in when I recognize the voice. I don't usually mean to be nosy, but sometimes I absolutely do. I let go of the door and walk toward the desk for a better view of this person. Shelly notices me but stays on her script.

Her script actually sounds a bit different as I get close enough to fully hear it.

"You're starting with two strikes," Shelly says, "There's going to be a lot of angst with you here. I hope you're serious about getting help. If you instigate any issues, though, we won't be able to keep you here."

"Absolutely, I want the help," he says. My goodness, is that Big Blue? Cis is going to be pissed! I move in range so the desk's privacy wall reveals the body behind it.

It's Seth.

Yes, that lunatic junkie who had to be carried out of here. This is when you know the only focus here is profit.

I look up at Jamal and Micah, who also seem to be in disbelief as well, but maintain their composure. I have no idea how they could admit him. It's clear Seth's intentions aren't to actually get help. Nobody changes that quickly.

My words are forming in my head when Jamal comes over to me.

"We'll talk about it in the morning. Please just get some sleep for now," he tells me. His tone at least seems sympathetic and he's definitely not in a position that would get commission for this move. I'm flabbergasted. I think he is too.

*

The door to my room slowly opens as I sit up quickly in bed. It's Micah. And it's a lot sunnier than usual when I wake up. I look at the clock and realize I overslept. It makes sense, as it took quite a while to clear my head and fall back to sleep last night.

"We're having a mandatory meeting this morning in fifteen minutes," he tells me.

"Yeah, okay. No problem," I say as I lift the blankets off of me. There's certainly no question about what we'll be discussing.

I expedite my morning routine then make my way to the main room. Angie and Cis are with Dakota and look to be in good spirits. I may be the only one that knows the news so far. Jamal catches my attention and gestures for me not to say anything.

"Good morning, soldier," Cis says. He smirks at my unusual tardiness.

"Had a problem with the alarm this morning?" Angie asks.

"Yeah…something like that." I make an effort to restrain my grumble.

"Something wrong?" Angie has a concerned look on her face as she looks at me.

"A lot of things," I tell her.

"Bad dreams? I mean, what could go wrong during sleep time?" Cis asks.

"You'll see," I tell him, "You'll definitely see."

"Yikes," Angie says. She shrugs it off and continues some small talk she had going on with Dakota.

"I had an idea for a verse," Steve says as he plops down next to me.

"Oh, we'll have plenty of ideas momentarily," I tell him.

"Wait," Dakota says, "What do you know?" She squints at me in a playful way. I now have the attention of everyone around me.

"Jamal, get them out here now, or I'm telling everyone," I tell him.

"They'll be here soon," he says directly to me. His body language suggests he's also worn out by everything.

"Fuck that," I say as I stand up.

"Don't you dare," he says as he points a finger at me.

"I dare," I say as I look him in the eyes. "I'm sorry, Dakota. These lowlives admitted Seth in here last night. I woke up in the middle of the night and saw them onboarding him." Jamal is clearly disappointed in my action, but mostly shrugs it off.

Gasps fill the room, and all eyes turn to Dakota.

"Brey, sit down," Janette says as she enters the room, "You were told we wanted to handle this. It was very clear."

"Janette, I owe you nothing," I say as I sit down again. I turn to Dakota to see how she's doing. All eyes remain on her.

"This is fucked up." Dakota appears confused as she's trying to process the news. "When someone breaks into your house, do you invite them to spend the night?"

"This is a place for second chances," Janette says as she works her way to the front of the room.

"What about my fucking second chance? You think I can recover with that monster in here?" Dakota's voice gets louder with each word.

"There's room for everyone," Janette says.

"Where is he?" Cis asks.

"He's sleeping. He'll join us sometime in the afternoon." Janette appears unaffected by our response.

"Can we relocate his bed to the gator pond out there?" Josiah asks.

"We don't condone violence here," Janette says to him.

"You literally condoned violence when you allowed him in here," I tell her, "Perhaps you can use some of the profits to invest in a community dictionary."

"That's enough, man." Jamal seems to be running extra low on patience. "Just be quiet and listen."

"This is going to be a challenging day or two for everyone," Janette tells the group, "I sincerely think he's here to better himself just like the rest of you are. We need to give him a chance. Because of the events yesterday, he's starting on two strikes. We'll keep a close eye on his actions and step in if necessary."

I look over at Dakota, and she seems lost and confused. Cis cups his hand over hers and gives a gentle squeeze to show his support. He pulls his hand away before Jamal or Janette has the chance to piss and moan about it.

"Hey," Angie says softly to me. "We'll keep an eye on her. Remember the reason we're here. Don't do anything stupid."

"How does anyone stay sober in here?" I whisper back.

"Why are you all so invested in Dakota?" Amanda says from the front of the room, "Aren't we told to let people take care of themselves?"

"She has a good point," Janette says, "It's better if Dakota and Seth resolve issues on their own. If we interfere—"

"Y'all're crazy!" Amy cuts her off and raises her clenched fist in the air, "If we were back home, his ass woulda caught a beatin'."

"Again," Janette corrects Amy, "We don't condone violence here."

"I ain't condoning nothing," Amy says, "I'm just saying, his ass woulda caught one. Be walkin' sideways like a crab for a week."

"Has there been consideration in increasing our security for the next week?" Sarah asks.

"There has been talk about that, but as of now, nothing is set in stone," Janette answers her.

"It's not like the guy is armed," Amanda says, "He's just an addict like the rest of us."

"Amanda," I say, "Before saying that, did you ever consider not saying it? You're like the wart on the bottom of my foot—easy to ignore, but still…so fucking annoying." It's hard to imagine how someone can lack such empathy.

"Okay, we're way off topic," Janette waves a hand in the air, "Let's break and have breakfast now. Depending how the day goes, we may reconvene this afternoon. Until then, please just be kind to one another."

A slow clap starts behind me. I swing my head around to see Josiah giving it. After several claps, he gives Janette a double thumbs up.

"We believe in you," he says, "Keep on keeping on!"

Janette rolls her eyes and disappears back down the hall. Everyone slowly migrates down the hall to the cafeteria, where I'm sure they're serving another epic meal.

"Every time I think this place is getting better, they find a way to hit a new low," Cis says.

*

Carol knows I won't be in therapy today. I can't conform to being a perfect patient. I want to be there for people in my group, especially Steve and James, but my stress levels wouldn't make this session productive for anyone.

This is a good time to sit in a quiet corner and write. My general notes, ideas, and character-building have slowly begun, but I feel like if I don't just start writing, this book will never get done. I can always spend an eternity afterward fixing the rough draft—if I ever get that far.

I've decided my working title is going to be 'Bonds from Addiction.' Everyone is familiar with the bonds of addiction—the hold the disease has on you. This book will be more focused on the friendships that form because of it. From what I'm witnessing, the bonds seem to release from the drugs and transfer to the people in your support system. Perhaps it's part of the 'trading addiction for addiction' logic. Like any bonds though, they must be handled with plenty of care in their infancy.

In my book, everyone will have some type of addiction. There will be no sex addiction, though. While it certainly exists, it's not something I'm ready to romanticize. Drugs, alcohol, food, people, money—those are all fair game.

I align with the last one. I enjoy coding, but part of that enjoyment is the high salary. It enables me to jump on a hiatus and live life for some time, if that's what you call this trip. It gives me a skill that I can carry from workplace to workplace. While some skills reset in new places, the ability to code only gets further enhanced by new experiences. And the more you switch jobs, the more money you tend to make. It's a viciously beautiful cycle.

Come to think of it, I may align with the 'people' addiction, too. When I find someone I connect with, I have no problem being with them all of the time. Thinking back, there are several people I've been addicted to. I'm fairly confident the addiction part was always one-way, but at least they put up with me.

Cis will be the inspiration for my main character. He's handled different types of hardships through work and love. None of them were so severe they could be blamed for 'putting him over the edge' though. However, the constant pattern of disappointment dragged him deeper and deeper into his love of alcohol.

I don't know where Angie would fall into my book. Her biggest shortfall is that she doesn't seem to have any shortfalls, which, while lovely, may not make a very exciting character arc. Perhaps she's just the catalyst that saves the world.

Of course, if I'm talking about addiction, you can't leave out the infrastructure within our country that is designed to assist in recovery. It's not well defined because it's also not well supported. More importantly, though,

I'll talk about clinics like this one that are solely focused on profits. This doesn't seem like a place where they find the most qualified for the job. They look for the lowest bidder. In the pamphlets, they're advertised as selling paths toward sobriety. In reality, it's more of a gauntlet of tests.

I fell into another rabbit hole in this writing session. My focus really needs to find some focus. The more I try to lose myself in my story, the more I get sucked back into the realities of today. Maybe another day!

*

The monster has crawled out of the abyss. The security guards are changing shifts earlier than usual today, so Janette, Jamal, and Earl pull Seth aside for a discussion. Now that he's had some sleep, I imagine they want to repeat the same two-strike policy they mentioned earlier.

As they finish up their conversation, word quickly spreads that they want to reconvene with everybody. I imagine it'll be another one of Carol's 'clear the air' bullshit type of meeting. Perhaps Seth wants to make a big fake apology to everyone. Buy himself some type of alibi or brownie points with staff.

"Hey, stranger," Angie says as she walks up behind me in the hall. She puts her hands on my shoulders and rubs them gently.

"Hey—how was your session?" I turn my head to ask her.

"We found out Seth will be joining our group, so there's that."

"I wouldn't worry too much about that. I doubt he'll make it to tomorrow," I tell her. The small group therapy sessions are between breakfast and lunch. He slept through today's session, at least.

"I've seen stranger things!"

"Me too! And hey," I turn around to look at her, "if things are looking better in a week or two, do you have any interest in bouncing out of here with me? I was thinking of checking another place or two off our road trip list."

She smiles at me and just stares into my eyes. For several seconds, I feel hypnotized. I actually started to forget that I even asked a question. Angie then replies, "Yes. I'd love to."

I find myself putting a hand on each of her shoulders with outstretched arms, saying "excellent" in my monotone voice. I have no idea why I did that, but it sliced through that serious moment. Mission accomplished. We walk side-by-side to the main room to hear what that scumbag has to say.

Seth sits front and center, facing a few staff members. The quartet of security guards is spread out in the crowd. Patients come in, but the room remains quiet beyond the whispers occurring within small groups. There's a funny gradient of moods as you move back in the room. They seem all cool and collected in the front. As you move back, there are emotions of anger and fear. Our group sits in the far back to create the most space between us.

As Angie sits down next to Dakota, she gently rests her hand on Dakota's shaking forearm.

"You hanging in there?" she asks her.

"It's all a bit surreal at the moment," Dakota says.

Janette stands up and moves to the center of the room as if to stand behind an invisible podium. She looks across the room to assess it.

"Thank you all for coming," she recites to the group. "I want to start today with a clean slate across the group. An incident happened yesterday that we need to let go of. Our judgments over a single action will only act as obstacles toward our own journeys to sobriety."

Janette clasps her hands together and looks around the room. Her pause quickly turns from dramatic to annoyingly uncomfortable. Is a stripper supposed to pop out of a cake or something? Is there supposed to be a cake? So much is missing at this moment.

"Okay," Janette finally says, "Seth has agreed to say something to the group. It takes a lot to stand and speak to a large group like this. I expect you all to be respectful."

Seth quickly rises from his chair and turns to face the crowd. His hands peck at each other like a cock fight. He continuously steps side to side as his focus moves between the ceiling and the floor, completely missing the dozens of people in front of him. Earlier in the lobby, Seth seemed to have it together. Perhaps he dropped something right before walking in, or he found a way to smuggle his dope inside. Either way, I have a hard time believing he's anything but high right now.

"Floor is yours," Janette says with anticipation.

"Yeah…it is…" he says as he struggles to look across the room. He finally locks in on Dakota, only she's refusing to look up at him. She has her one leg crossed on top of the other and she's picking at her shoe.

"I'm sorry," he says, "It won't happen again."

Promptly after finishing, he sits back down in his chair. The room stays silent as he looks over his shoulder a few times in hopes that Dakota notices him. She finally looks up at Janette to clarify she wasn't planning to respond to him. Janette takes the floor again.

"Okay, sweet and simple," Janette says as the other staff smile. They all just sit around this place, giving each other head under the table, hypothetically of course. The pleasure they all feel is one of artificial power and dominance. It's strange, as the bar they actually set is incredibly low. I would much rather put Cis's care in the hands of the patients.

"If you're stuck on using alliteration, I think you mean pithy and pathetic," I tell her over the heads of everyone else.

"That's incredibly rude," Janette says, "I appreciate you getting up in front of everyone, Seth. You're all dismissed. Please carry on with your regular schedule."

"Pithy?" Steve asks, "Never heard of that word."

"It's like the opposite of verbose," I tell him.

"Ah, nice. I'll keep that in my back pocket," he says.

As we start to flock to the outdoor patio, Janette pulls me aside.

"Brey, I don't appreciate your hostile behaviors," Janette tells me, "They need to stop immediately."

"Yep, okay," I say as I turn and walk away. I decide there's no point in arguing with them. Considering my plan, I probably shouldn't have said anything. Cats are silent when moving in on their prey.

"I'm serious, Brey," she says from behind me.

"Me too, Janette."

Angie stops and turns around. She waits for me to catch up.

"I know," I tell Angie, "Stay in our lane."

"I was going to say you took the words right out of my mouth," Angie says, "And his sincerity? That really brought it home for me."

"No kidding."

"Hey, Brey," Dakota says as she walks up to us, "I appreciate all of the support you've given me. I think this is going to be an uphill battle with him. You're all in your own personal wars already. I'd hate to see you lose those because you weren't on the battlefield."

"Great analogy!" I tell her, "Don't worry about the two of us. Our wars are on auto-pilot."

"Agreed," Angie says, "You and Cis have us in your corner. That's the most important thing for us now."

"Okay," Dakota says, "Please don't burn out! We like having you around."

"Thanks, Dakota. I like being around."

As she runs ahead to catch back up to Cis and Josiah, I catch a glimpse of Seth through the crowd. He's clearly keeping a close eye on her, an eye that is now on me. His ominous stare is piercing. It gives me goosebumps as I've never had someone loathe me quite like this before. I just stare back without intent or purpose.

His attention turns back to Dakota as she's walking by. The guy is a grade-A creep, for sure.

"Can we talk?" he quietly asks her.

"No," she simply tells him and keeps walking. His face is completely indifferent to the answer. It's as though he already knew it.

Seth does, however, follow us outside. He walks to the side of the permanent dock structure and starts tossing rocks in. We can only hope a gator is actually in there and does the job. Unfortunately, the only movement in the water comes from the rings from the rocks.

Jamal and Micah are both staying out on the patio tonight. They should probably keep Seth on one of those leashes they created for young kids.

There's no guitar this evening. There's not a lot of laughter, either.

"Yo, Steve," Josiah says and waits for his attention. "If you could share the stage with someone, alive or dead, who would it be?"

"Probably Janis Joplin," he responds.

"Yeah? I was thinking you'd say the Sex Pistols or Ramones," Josiah says.

- 180 -

"Apples and oranges are both great. Let's say I'm an everyday gala apple. Why would I want to match up with a Honeycrisp? I would taste boring next to it. I'd rather get paired with a delicious sumo citrus. It would outshine me still, but I wouldn't immediately become compost."

"Why the analogy?" Josiah says as he looks confused by it.

"I'm in the same genre as Sex Pistols, Clash, Ramones, etc. If I play next to those greats, I will look, sound and smell horrendous."

"Smell?" Cis asks.

"I don't think rich people ever smell bad. No matter how much they're sweating," Steve tells him.

"I'd like to hear you with Kelly Clarkson," Angie tells him.

"Why her?" I ask.

"Have you heard her duet with people? She always sounds amazing and is able to elevate whomever she is paired up with," Angie explains, "I think she's one of the greats that'll be remembered for a very long time."

"I do like her. She has a bunch of those 'fuck you, I don't need you' songs. They're a mood I can thrive in," I say.

"Right!? I've definitely binged her music at least a dozen times before hard conversations," Angie says. She smiles and sighs, "I miss music."

"Hey!" Steve, our local musician, says.

Angie laughs and tells him, "We all love your music, Steve. Just saying, I miss having the ability to play songs that fit my mood."

"That's fair. I'm not a very good jukebox," Steve says.

"Just need to get into a PP mood, and there'll be a natural match," I say. Steve points to me as though I made a solid point.

"What do you think he's doing over there?" Cis asks us. We all turn to look at Seth, who's crouched over by the shore. I'm surprised Jamal and

Micah haven't called him back from the water. I also shouldn't be surprised anymore around here.

"Maybe he's rubbing one out?" Josiah suggests.

"He's probably starting to withdraw," Dakota says.

Seth stands up and turns toward us. He stares at Dakota for a brief few seconds, then walks back inside. This prompts Micah to move his guard to the inside of the building.

Jamal comes over to the table we're sitting at.

"Brey and Cis, we're moving you into 12A and B," Jamal says.

"Isn't that James' room? Is he okay?" I asked him.

"Yes, sir. He's moving onto the apartments."

"Oh yeah? Good for him!" I say. In the back of my mind, I wonder how that'll work out for him. He seems most likely to sneak away for a fix.

"And you," Jamal tells Angie, "You'll be moving into 18A."

"Yay!" Amelia energetically says, "Welcome, new bunkmate!" She bounces over to Angie and gives her a quick hug from behind.

"Isn't this early for your shift? Or are you and Micah doing doubles now?" Cis asks him.

"Due to the recent events, they have added two more temp security guards for the early morning duty. They want to make sure we're on top of our game," he explains to us.

"For a place that preaches schedules, they sure like to shake them up," I say.

He shrugs and says, "I don't mind getting some extra sleep."

"Touché," Cis says.

*

As I eat my dinner, which is slightly better than the last, I can't help but notice Seth is just picking at his food. He's kept to himself for the most part, so perhaps he deserves a bit of a break.

"Tell me more about Boston," Dakota says to our table.

"It's an older city with a generally younger population," Angie says.

"She's basically saying there's a lot of amazing architecture with people who don't quite appreciate it," Cis says.

"How are the people?" Dakota asks.

"I mean," I say as I try to gather my words, "it's not Portland. If you've visited there. People can be tough. Rideshare drivers can be rude, people will honk at you, but…"

"But?" she asks.

"They're just the older people angry that the younger people don't appreciate the architecture," Cis says.

"I mean, I'm willing to appreciate it," Dakota says.

"Then you'll fit right in," Cis tells her, "Does that mean you're considering the move?"

"More like preemptive considerations. My sister lives in town here, so I'll talk to her whenever she gets around to visiting."

"That's fair," Cis says, looking slightly disappointed not to be hearing 'yes.'

"I also don't know how I'd make it there," she says, clearly still planning it out in her head.

"My car is a couple blocks away," I say with a shrug.

"Perhaps we trade it in for some plane tickets," Angie winks at me.

"I imagine the street value won't get us too far, maybe to Orlando?" I suggest.

"We should at least head north," Cis says.

"There's magic in Orlando."

"I don't think it's real," Angie tells me. It breaks my heart to learn she's a non-believer.

"You have my vote," Dakota says, "I don't have a lot of good memories from there."

"Let's take a step back," I say, "I'm happy to go to Orlando, but we don't need to sell the car to get there. It's, like, two hours away?"

"Almost exactly. Cis looks like he could use some magic," Dakota says.

"I think an edible plate of food would seem like magic at this point," Cis says as he prods his food a little.

Seth rises from his table and walks away from his abandoned tray of food. As he walks in our direction, he stares at the back of Dakota's head. It's the same stare I witnessed earlier. He sure has a lot of hate in him for a rich junkie. I would expect him to just buy a bag and try to forget her. Rinse and repeat. You don't even need to be rich for that.

He continues walking toward our table when I would've expected him to turn to leave the cafeteria. My heart starts racing a little as he stays on course. I'm too focused on him to know if anyone else is alerted at our table. His jaw is clenched. His hands are alternating which is clenched and which is in a full stretch.

I stand up as his encounter gets less than ten feet. I put both hands on the table and one foot on the bench behind me. It may be time for this jaguar to pounce.

He cuts his distance in half. Micah coughs as he enters the cafeteria. Seth immediately takes a sharp right and then a left to zigzag around our table. His focus turns to me as he wears an evil grin under his dead eyes. He walks up to a new guy we haven't met yet and whispers something in his ear. The guy nods, and then Seth promptly turns around and heads back to his table.

After Seth passes our table, I use hand gestures to quietly get Dakota's attention from across the table.

I lean into the middle of the table and say quietly, "Do you know the guy behind me that Seth just approached?"

She nods and says softly back, "Yeah. It's Sam, one of Seth's junkies."

"Oh?"

"Yeah, I'm not sure how he feels about Seth, but I do know how he feels about the dope that Seth supplies."

I ponder a moment and ask, "You think he's desperate enough to do something stupid in here?"

"I don't see why else he'd be here."

*

Seth is spending more time skipping stones in the pond than anything else. Sam seems like he's in a euphoric state, just chain-smoking cigarettes in the corner. He hardly looks up or acknowledges the dozen people around him. It worries me that they're acting like they don't know each other. I keep my paranoia to myself, though, as I don't want to cause anxiety to the people actually here for recovery.

Everyone is calling it a night at this point, though. As Jamal grabs the door to hold it, Sam makes a short trip to Seth by the water. Seth counts the number of skips his final stone does, then challenges Sam to beat it. He then hands a flat stone to Sam and takes a step back.

Dunk! The stone leaves Sam's hand and sinks immediately as it touches the water. That was embarrassingly bad, but I don't know if these two have enough emotions left in their bodies to feel that.

Jamal calls for them to come inside, and they execute his order immediately. If nothing else, they're better subordinates than me.

I get to bed and rest my head, knowing that Cis is safe with me, Angie is safe with Amelia and Dakota, and Seth and Sam are all in monitored rooms. Assuming these assholes watch the cameras, it'd be quite a feat to pull someone off at night.

CHAPTER 15

~ The Storm ~

I wake up suddenly to the sound of shouting in the lobby. This place feels more like prison each night. Cis's heavy breathing suggests he's far too exhausted to be awakened by something simple like loud voices. I'm not going to ruin that for him.

Flinging the blankets off me, I reveal my body to the cold air. My curiosity drags me to the door and down the hall.

Sam stands with a fire extinguisher by the phone area and aims it at the security guards. They stand guard in front of the desk to protect the nursing staff.

"Put down the extinguisher and go back to bed," one of the security guards instructs him to do.

"We can get a doctor on the phone if it's meds you need," the other security guard tries to negotiate with him, "If you spray that in here, you'll have to say goodbye to your sobriety. This is your chance to do the right thing."

"The right thing?" Sam asks. "I'm a fucking junkie. Since when do junkies have the judgment to know what that is?"

I see Raye standing several feet behind the desk. I try to stay undetected so I can make a move later if needed to protect my friends. For now, I silently cheer for the security guards to drop Sam, who appears high.

I'm under the impression that withdrawals look different based on my short time with James. However, Sam just got here, so maybe that's the difference?

"Say hello to my little friend," Sam says as he raises the extinguisher head and aims it toward the first guard. The guards turn to speed away as a forceful cloud gets released. He sprays back and forth toward each guard as they each get out of reach of it.

Raye seems to be frozen with fright as Sam makes eye contact with her. A large smile appears on his face as he takes a few steps closer to her. He turns the extinguisher and begins to aim it at her. I quickly move in, grab her wrist, and pull her down the hall where I was hiding.

"What the fuck is happening?" she asks rhetorically as her body just stiffens up.

"Fucking junkies, right?" I'm strangely calm in an amped up way.

A loud crashing sound comes from the desk area. I can hear broken glass scattering across the tiled floor. Based on the sounds, Sam is going to town on the desk and equipment. Then I hear a loud grunt as I believe a security guard has finally engaged with Sam.

I walk down a bit and poke my head around the corner. Sam used the extinguisher to smash pretty much anything electronic. The second guard makes it back down the hall to help hold down Sam as he violently shakes and screams like a madman.

Raye comes slowly down the hall, looking to see if it's safe.

"Raye! Call the police!" the guards yell as they do their best to restrict his movements.

As she struggles to find a phone in its original state, it dawns on me that Sam just destroyed any view of the monitored rooms. He also successfully gained the attention of these two guards.

I run down the hall and see that Dakota's door is ajar. I carefully push the door open, trying to prepare myself for the worst. The room is empty. I hear a cry from the next room over.

This is beginning to feel far more premeditated than I gave those fucks. I cautiously open the door and see Dakota lying on the floor, clearly hurt and crying.

"Fuck," I say. We let her down. I attempt to take another step toward her. I feel a large hand grab my head, and WHAM!

Pain pierces through my right temple as I make a hard impact with the door frame. The pain then disperses throughout my body, quickly like a drop of blood diluting in a glass of water. I find myself lying sideways on the ground. Three masked men step over my aching body. Two of them pick up Dakota—one holding under the armpits and the other on the legs. Ironically, it looks more like they're rescuing her in their approach.

The third and smallest man turns around and squats next to me.

"You should learn to mind your own fucking business," Seth's voice comes from behind the mask.

He stands up and kicks me twice in the stomach. I watch as he leads the other two out of the door. They turn away from the lobby where Sam is still being detained and are headed to an emergency exit.

I want to chase after them, but this piercing pain is making it difficult to rise, so I wither and try to squirm my way there. The image of them gets smaller and smaller as they get further down the hall.

"Please stop," I try to yell, but it only comes out as a whisper.

I can hear the door swing open as the larger masked man backs his way into it. The light above the door shines down on him and Dakota. I get an unsettling feeling that this is the last we'll see of her. I should have woken up Cis. He'd know what to do right now.

As the small masked man holding her legs starts to see the light upon his head, some object comes quickly into view. The sound it makes as it smashes over the large man's head is identifying. It was a fucking terracotta pot from the patio. The large man drops faster than the plant from the pot.

Josiah lets out a noise that can only be described as a war cry. I can see him catch Dakota's head before it hits the hard concrete. The leg man pulls out a taser from his back pocket. He lunges at Josiah and gives him a zap. Josiah falls backward but is able to scurry away before a prolonged shock.

The leg man says some words I can't make out as he gets closer to Josiah, who's still on the ground.

TWANG! Steve comes from behind the door and smashes the guitar over the man's head. It's a clean shot. Steve just earned himself a gold plaque and deserves to be on stage with the greats!

Seth sees the two hit the ground and pulls a gun from his belt. He points it at Steve and Josiah and has them move away from the door. Seth walks up and picks up Dakota by her hair. She screams in pain as he does so.

"I warned you, didn't I?" Seth screams into her face. "You think the black eye is bad? Wait until we get home."

"You did this, you asshole?" she asks him. I imagine she had suspicions, but he's an addict, and addicts are pretty good liars.

"You're so fucking gullible. That's why I love you," Seth tells her, then starts to pull Dakota around the building. I've officially lost Dakota's war. I see nothing. I hear nothing.

I'm able to pull myself off the ground. I struggle as I drag myself toward the door.

BOOM!

A gunshot goes off and then I hear some struggling outside. I take step after step, focusing on my balance. Angie comes around the door and sees me. She runs down the hall to me.

"I'm so sorry, I fucked up," I tell her, "I really did try to help her." My eyes start to well up.

Over Angie's shoulder, I see Josiah and Steve run toward where Seth presumably is. There's additional struggling and screaming, but it sounds like Seth's voice.

"Please help me over there," I asked Angie. We make it through the lit-up doorway and turn right.

Seth is on the ground, holding his head. Blood flows from his nose as he rolls intensely around. Like a scene straight out of Hollywood, Cis stands above him with the gun. As he hears sirens in the distance, he unloads the clip, empties the chamber, and tosses the pieces into the wooded area. Josiah and Steve rush over to sit on Seth to avoid an escape.

Angie and I hurry over to Cis, who has Dakota cuddled in his arms. She's shaking and crying into Cis's shirt. She's conscious, though. Dakota looks up at me and reaches out a hand. I hold her fingers and give a gentle squeeze.

"You okay?" she asks.

"Yeah," I say, "I'll make it. How are you?"

"I'll make it."

As I pull my hand back, I notice blood smeared across it. Dakota's hand is clean, so I retrace my motions. I turn to Angie to inspect her and see blood pooling on her upper sleeve, running down her right arm.

"Oh shit, you got shot!" I tell her as I lift her sleeve to inspect.

"Yeah, I'm getting slow in my old age, I guess," she says jokingly, "I already looked at it. It has a clean exit. It'll heal."

I pull off my shirt and wrap it around her arm tightly. I look up at her, and she seems unfazed by it.

"That's kind of badass," Dakota says.

"There's nothing badass about bleeding out," I say as I continue to apply pressure.

"You wouldn't understand," Dakota says to me as she tries to sit up while holding Cis's hand. "You aren't girl strong."

"I'm certainly not," I say. I take a moment to breathe and look across the faces of our friends outside. I tell them, "You all are amazing. I thought these fuckers got the last laugh."

"We came out as we saw you were talking with Raye," Angie informs me, "It was Josiah's idea to split up and cover the exits."

"Steve, what about the guitar?" I ask.

"There'll always be another guitar," he tells me, "Friends are harder to replace."

"How'd you get it?"

Steve laughs and says, "Honestly, I'm surprised you didn't hear us. We ran through the lobby, grabbed it, and ran out through the patio door. Josiah grabbed the lovely perennial on the way through."

"I'm not sure it'll be returning next year, though," Josiah says.

"I hope we aren't either," Cis says.

Police sirens get louder as they once again quickly approach the Pond Point facility. I move closer to Josiah and Steve and squat down. Seth uses his last bit of energy to try to squirm free.

"You should really learn to mind your fucking hands," I tell him. I stand up and give him a solid kick to the side. As much as I'd like to leave him looking like Dakota, I choose to slow the bleeding for Angie instead.

Police radios get louder as at least one officer comes down the hall. The door was left ajar by an unconscious masked man.

"Police!" Officer Jenkins says as he comes quickly outside with his firearm drawn. Officer Lore follows closely behind, looking in the opposite direction.

"Don't shoot," I say as I hold up a hand.

"Aren't you all supposed to be the patients?" Officer Lore asks.

The officers have ambulances move in as they handcuff Seth, Sam, and two mystery junkies that Dakota didn't recognize. We're brought through the building, where the lobby area is trashed and covered with a fine powder from the extinguishers.

Steve and Josiah show no sign of injury, so they stay back. Not knowing our future, as we're likely not coming back to this clinic, we exchange numbers. We give farewell hugs and then jump into the back of the ambulances. I ride with Angie in one, and Cis rides with Dakota in the other.

"I probably should've checked out the Yelp reviews of that place," Angie tells me as the paramedic patches up her arm with bandage and gauze.

"I think we were exactly where we needed to be," I say. I hold her hand as we traverse the streets.

*

We all breathe a sigh of relief as we're unloaded from the ambulance. Dakota and Angie ride on gurneys as Cis, and I walk alongside each of them. We make it into the ER and opt to share an available double room. While Cis appears unscathed, the staff is determined to check all four of us out anyway. Like any ER visit, though, it begins with waiting.

"How ya feeling, Cis?" Angie asks.

"I should be much worse," he says as he nods to Angie.

"Why should you be?" I ask him.

Cis looks at Angie and tells her, "I think the world deserves to know that bullet was meant for me."

"Wait, what?" I ask.

"We were sneaking around the building just as Seth came around the corner with Dakota. I was against the wall, and she was slightly behind me to the right." He uses hand gestures to show approximately where the wall and each of them was located. "When he saw us, that gun was pointed at my chest. This ninja grabbed the barrel and pulled it away from me. Had the gun shot off any earlier, she may not be here as its aim went across her chest."

"Next time, I'll wear Kevlar," she says.

"Let's not have a next time," I tell her.

"Agreed," Cis and Dakota say at the same time.

Cis continues his story, "I got a decent shot in—probably broke his nose. Then she comes back with the gun and pistol whips his sorry ass. It was amazing."

"Yeah, you deserve to have a movie made about you," Dakota says.

"I don't need any more evidence. You're clearing my guardian angel," Cis says.

"Has this happened before?" Dakota asks him with hesitation in her voice.

"Not exactly," Cis says, "This can't be spoken outside of this group, but these two aren't alcoholics."

"I knew it," she said, "They seem way too focused on our problems."

"Like I said, guardian angels."

"Angie gets full credit for putting all of that in motion, but we won't blame her for the outcome of it all," I tell her.

"Blame my sister for that. She brought the horror," Dakota says.

*

The ER doctor believes I have a concussion, so I'll be woken up every two hours tonight. They want to keep me overnight as we technically don't have a place to go to currently.

Angie is getting some stitches and an arm sling to keep her arm in place during the initial healing. She's going to be discharged but is allowed to stay with me as a guest. There's currently a one-guest limit for overnight guests. They've offered to bring bedding for the night, so hopefully, we get some rest.

Dakota's stay is optional as they'd like to get the swelling down in her eye and give her some antibiotics to avoid possible infections. She opted in, and since Cis is fine, he'll be staying as Dakota's guest. This allows all four of us to stay together. It feels like our luck is changing a bit.

KNOCK KNOCK.

Someone is knocking on our slowly opening door.

"Y'all decent in here?" a voice says from behind the door.

"Jamal?" I say.

"That's me," Jamal says as he opens the door the rest of the way. He walks in, followed by Micah. They're carrying all of our belongings that we checked in with.

"I heard everything that happened," Jamal says, then lets out a big sigh. "I'm sorry things turned out how they did. They've got some issues to work out in that place."

"I'd say a lot of issues," I tell him. "We appreciate you coming by, though. So much for that extra sleep?"

"Heh, I guess it wasn't meant to be."

"He was probably just playing video games instead of sleeping anyway," Micah says.

"We talked to Janette before coming over here. They're moving everyone from phase one into the apartments as they clean up that building and add more security," Jamal explains.

"Sounds like there are different plans for us if you're dropping off our luggage?" I ask him.

"This was my decision," Jamal says, "I can understand you all not wanting to go back to that place. They've agreed not to charge your insurance for anything for those first few days. This means you shouldn't have issues starting fresh somewhere new. They also have several affiliated clinics, run by completely different people, that they can make calls to on your behalf."

"Dang, I appreciate that, but I don't think Angie and I are looking to go anywhere at this point. I'll let them speak for themselves, as they may be interested," I tell him.

"Yeah, I'm interested. I've heard good things about Portland and Colorado. If you have information about those, I'd love to hear it," Cis says. He turns to look at Dakota and asks, "You in?"

"Absolutely," she says as she rests her hand on top of his.

"Excellent, we can go do some digging and get back atcha," Jamal says.

"We appreciate it," Angie says, "But don't you both need some rest before your next shift?"

Jamal and Micah look at each other and laugh. He turns back to me and says, "As I said, we had some words with Janette. We made it clear we're going to spend the next week making sure you all get settled properly to hopefully avoid a lawsuit. It may even turn into two weeks, as we'll probably run into some issues. It's usually the case when working with troublemakers like yourselves."

"But just for the record, we don't give a shit if you sue," Micah says, and they both start giggling.

"Sounds like you've got some time to fill," I tell them, "Good for you."

"Now, we're going to get started right away, and then we'll swing back in an hour or so," Jamal says, "Y'all need anything?"

"How about some of dem raw burgers?" Micah asks with a cackle. Cis pretends to dry heave over the thought of it.

"I want a tasting menu before we decide on a venue for our next rehab," Cis says.

"I'll see what I can do," Jamal laughs.

"It's not for me. I'm fine with raw burgers and processed meat. Dakota here has made the demands clear to me."

"That's correct. And if I can't get fine dining, I'm going to demand that I don't get beat up anymore," she says.

"Aww," Angie says, "Girl, you're breaking my heart."

"Mine too," Jamal says, "Be safe. Get some rest. We'll see you in an hour or so."

CHAPTER 16
~ Factory Reset ~

Dakota's sister Jade comes to the hospital when she hears everything that went down.

"Oh my God, please tell me Seth is put away for good?" Jade says as she runs up and hugs Dakota tightly.

"We haven't had any updates, but he was at least in cuffs when we left him," Dakota responds.

"Are you headed back to rehab after you are discharged from here?"

"Here's the thing——" Dakota starts to say.

"Please tell me you're serious about getting clean. You all need to help me get my sister back!" Jade's eyes start to well up.

"Oh my love, I'm going to get clean. We're thinking of going to either Colorado or Portland, though, which is so far away fro——"

Jade cuts her off, "No. No excuses. Go tonight."

Dakota is caught off guard and gives out a forced laugh, "Wow, didn't realize I was such trouble to you."

"You're not. You're trouble to yourself," Jade says, "You're my amazing big sister with a big heart, a big brain, and a big addiction. One's gotta go, and I vote for the addiction."

"I second that," Cis says.

"We're making sure Cis and Dakota both get into a clinic and settle in with their recoveries before we turn our eyes away from them," Angie says.

"No offense, but you were shot. I'm not sure how valuable your word is," Jade says sarcastically to Angie.

"She's our guardian angel. Her word is gold," I tell her.

"Yeah, she's pretty badass," Dakota says as she cups her hands together over her heart.

"Okay, then, I appreciate you all for looking out for her. She hasn't had a good circle in years," Jade says.

"If you'd like to visit them, I can send you a plane ticket," I tell her, "I'm sure shrinking that distance between you two will help everyone. Just promise me you'll send me a full report."

Jade smiles wide and nods to me. She becomes excited and hugs Dakota tightly.

Jamal and Micah arrive back in the room with a pile of pamphlets and information for the two of them. As we all pass around the info, the clinics all appear to be four star resorts compared to the last place. One even has the opportunity for patients to cook for themselves. It's to give patients some new skills that they can focus on once they're on their own. Cis sees it as a good opportunity to show off.

"I'm really liking this Mile High clinic. It's got everything from kitchens to horseback riding to rock climbing. There's even a trivia night in case we begin to feel too confident," Cis says as he points some things out in the pamphlet to Dakota.

"Do you think that's too extravagant compared to our real lives? Wouldn't it make reality suck after leaving there?" Dakota asks.

Jade tells her, "Considering where you've been, the bar has been set pretty low. Plus, I think you could use a little pampering to see what life should be like."

"Agreed. Let's go big, then we'll go home and make that big too," Cis says.

"We've actually had some friends move out to Denver. Remember Billy and Mags?" Micah asks Jamal.

"Oh yeah, I caught up with them a few weeks back. They likin' it out there," Jamal tells Micah.

"What do you think?" Cis holds Dakota's hand as she looks over the pamphlet closely.

Dakota looks at her sister for a few seconds. She turns and looks back at Cis.

"I'm in," she says. Jade immediately gives her a tackling hug and cries happily into her shoulder.

"We'll be right back then," Jamal says. The twins pull their phones out of their pockets and head into the hallway.

After a few moments, Micah pokes his back in the door and asks, "The plan is to discharge tomorrow?" We all nod in response.

Jamal comes in about five minutes later. He looks proud of his achievements as he fights back a smile.

"Okay, here's what's in the making. Tomorrow at lunchtime, two tickets to Denver for the two of you and two tickets for the two of us to make sure you make it there without issue. The clinic also has a six-week schedule that they can squeeze you in on," Jamal explains to us.

"What about the cost?" Cis asks.

"Hey now, you're embarrassing me," Jamal says, "Of course I'll cover that. Y'all never seen my negotiation skills. It's a free ride for the two of you if the four of you are willing to sign NDAs and some contracts that state you won't sue."

"Whoa!" Angie exclaims, "That's huge!"

"Not even through insurance?" Cis asks.

"No insurance. All free," Jamal says.

"Yeah, of course, we'll sign it!" I say. I turn to Cis and Dakota and tell him, "This is a huge opportunity. I'm incredibly happy for you both."

"There are some other more sobering details I want to share with you about things that transpired since last night," Micah says, "They found notes and traces of drugs by the water line where Seth was hanging out, throwing rocks. The police went back and carefully watched our security footage, and there was a whirring noise that happens a few times in the middle of the night. The thought is he had people on the outside using drones or RC boats of some sort to drop things off."

"What'd the notes say?" I ask him.

"They were essentially instructions. The fuckers had a list of things, and depending on where and how many stones he threw in, they would react accordingly," Jamal says, "Honestly, it's a lot smarter than I considered their operation to be. It also means someone was watching."

"Should we continue to be worried?" Cis asks.

"I don't think so. The police have them in custody, so I think it's a wait-and-see situation," Micah says.

"Yeah, I didn't want to alarm you with the news, but wanted you to know for your own safety," Jamal says.

"I'm sorry. I really don't know what he wants from me," Dakota says. She stares down at the foot of the bed. Her tired look feels like she wants to just throw in the towel to get a break from it all.

"You may be thinking there's no way we're gonna win this war," I tell her. "Reality is, there's no way he's gonna win this war."

"Damn straight," Cis says.

I turn to look at Jamal and Micah and ask, "Is there any possible way they'd be able to track them to Colorado?"

"Only if Janette is part of it," Jamal says.

I tell them, "I couldn't bribe her to let me sit on the floor during meditation. I'm fairly confident she's not helping him. On purpose, at least. It is possible, however, that he's got eyes on the hospital."

Cis speaks up, "I mean, they have him on gun charges at least. I can't imagine he's orchestrating everyone from prison."

"Uh, what?" Micah asks.

"In this short time, he probably only had a single call," he says.

"No, I mean about the gun. Police haven't recorded anything about a gun," Micah tells us.

"Ah fuck. I tossed it into the woods to avoid any accidental discharges," Cis says, "I don't think they know about it."

"Micah, go give Janette a call and let them know there's a gun out there. Cis, where exactly is it?"

"If you walk outside the emergency exit where everything went down and turn right, I threw it from that corner. It should be in that tiny forest area."

Micah nods and disappears into the hallway to make the call.

"Well shit," Cis says, shaking his head.

"Don't worry, they'll find it," Angie tells him.

We sit anxiously for Micah's return. All of the possibilities are flooding through my head now. I try to stick to the happy path where they find the gun, match his prints, and lock him up for a long time for a slew of felonies.

Micah comes walking in with a disappointed look on his face. He's tapping his phone into the palm of his hand. After some hesitation, he looks up at us.

"There's no gun." Micah's head slowly shakes back and forth. "There are footprints but no guns."

Angie lets out a disappointed sigh. "Someone cleaned up after him."

"What does that mean for the case?" Cis asks.

"It means he's already been bailed out under the claim that he had a manic moment due to withdrawals," Micah says.

"Unbelievable," Dakota says. Disgust echoes in her voice as she hangs her head for a long breath. "This is just more reason we have to get far away from this area. It's plagued with his scum."

"A minute ago, I'd say this is my paranoia, but I think we need a plan to get out of here safely," I tell everyone. This is all becoming a bit surreal. It feels like we're suddenly part of a movie.

"We can catch a lift directly to the airport from here," Jamal says.

"That could work, but my car is still a couple blocks from the clinic," I say.

"Get it towed?" Angie asks.

"That's not a bad idea, but I should just go pick it up tonight. Then, at least, I can tell if I'm being followed?" I ask. I'm not confident with that plan though.

"Or the two of us can pick it up and bring it to the airport?" Jamal suggests.

I say, "That's also not a bad idea. I think if you can get the car to the airport and you all leave immediately after with a layover somewhere, it'll be nearly impossible for them to properly track you. Then Angie and I will take the car and drive it out there."

"Let's plan on that then," Micah says in agreement.

What an ongoing nightmare this continues to be. I still find it hard to comprehend how a junkie has the attention span to pull all of this off. In another world, he probably would've made a great software engineer. He's definitely covered all of the edge cases. You know, except for the fact that our team is better.

"Okay, write down your license plate and approximately where it is. We'll run home, pack, and get some sleep. In the morning, we'll grab the car and meet you at the airport around lunchtime?" Jamal asks.

"Yeah, that sounds good," Angie says. We all toss in a "yeah" or "yep."

"We should probably all get some sleep, too, considering the nurses will be waking you up every two hours," Dakota tells me.

"It's not just me. She'll be taking your vitals as well!" I say back to her.

"The joy of hospitals," Angie says.

Taking turns, we all get ready for bed. The staff brings in the promised sheets, blankets, and pillows. Luckily for the non-patients Angie and Cis, there are rather comfortable benches on either side of the room. While we don't have any special security for our room, we feel rather safe here as we're all together.

"Okay, friends," Angie says as she turns off the lights, "sleep well."

CHAPTER 17

~ New Day ~

The morning came, then it came again. It came several times.

I have a tender egg where my head connected with the door frame, but I'm otherwise doing fine. Dakota and I are semi-conscious based on how often we were woken up for various things. Angie waking up was a side effect of all of the commotion. I'm not surprised to hear that Cis was able to sleep through the night, though.

Cis steps outside to catch a smoke break while the girls get their things prepared before discharge. Dakota takes a decorated, bleached denim jacket out of her bag and tries it on in front of the mirror.

"Oh my, Dakota!" Angie says with excitement.

"What's that?" Dakota asks as she turns to look at Angie.

"That jacket! It's so fun!"

"It's comfortable, too. Try it!"

Dakota removes her jacket and hands it to Angie. She promptly puts it on and poses in front of the mirror.

"I need to get one of these! Where'd you get it?" Angie asks Dakota.

"It was a gift from scumbag. I should probably ditch it."

"Oh God, no. You paid the dues, now you get the lovely jacket!"

Dakota pauses and looks at Angie for a bit. She tells her, "You hold onto the jacket."

"I couldn't possibly!" Angie tells her.

"You can and you will. I expect it back, though, so now you can't disappear on us while we're away," she says, smiling at Angie.

Angie walks to Dakota and hugs her tightly. She tells her, "There's no way we'd ever desert you! And okay. I'll keep a close eye on the jacket and make sure nothing happens to it!" She turns and poses again in front of the mirror.

"What do you think, Brey?" Dakota asks me about Angie.

"Stunning as usual. I'll be honest, though. I'm a little intimidated by the jacket. It's going to completely outshine my coolness."

"Perhaps you just need a stunning jacket of your own," Dakota says.

"Perhaps I do!"

Cis comes walking back into the room with four coffees and a bag from the bakery down the road. I'm not sure what's in the bag, but it smells absolutely delicious.

"Breakfast of champions!" he says as he hands out some breakfast sandwiches and pastries.

Angie raises her coffee as a toast and says, "Cis, you're amazing. Bad timing, though. Brey's starting a streak of looking bad."

"That's not the coffee doing that. It's his lack of personality," Cis responds.

"Yikes. What is this hospital doing to my friends? Tough crowd this morning," I say as I lazily raise my cup up. "Thanks anyway for the goods!"

I admire Angie from afar. There really is no outfit that could look bad on her. This is the first piece of apparel that I've seen her excited about, though.

"I need to make some calls. I'll be back!" I say as I head down the hall with my coffee and delicious Danish.

It felt like I was only gone for ten minutes, but now that I'm back, everyone is packed up and ready to go. The first caffeinated coffee in days probably plays a role in their haste.

"Everything good?" Angie asks me.

"Always." She smiles at me. I feel like she is genuinely happy when I'm happy. She's definitely the empathic cleric in this group.

"Oh hey," Cis says as he walks over to us. "I want you to put this to good use while I'm in Colorado." He hands me his twelve-sided die.

"Are you sure?" I ask him as I continue to hold the die out in front of me. "What if you need it to make the clinic more interesting?"

"Not this time. This sobriety thing is starting to grow on me. I'm going to play it straight." He smiles and gives us each a hug. As he's squeezing me, he whispers "thank you" into my ear.

My phone rings.

"Hello?"

"Hey, still aiming to meet early?" Jamal says from the other end of the line.

I'm a bit nervous to set these next steps in motion, but it's exactly what needs to be done. "Yep. We're working toward discharge currently and will head over after," I inform him.

"Good. See you." I begin to say bye, but the phone disconnects before I get a chance to.

On a positive note, when doctors know you're heading to the airport to get to rehab, they accelerate the discharge process. What would be a couple of hours gets completed in fifteen minutes. Perhaps this is a trick I can hold onto for a rainy day.

I tell the group, "Okay, Jamal and Micah are headed down, and we're going to meet up for an airport meal before we part ways."

"Where are we headed?" Angie asks me.

"I hope you're okay with surprises because it's a surprise." She shrugs and nods in agreement. It appears I've gained enough trust for this.

I look around and make sure we don't forget any of our belongings, which is typically a toothbrush or phone charger. This group is on top of their game, as it appears nothing was left behind. I can't blame them for wanting to get out of this city.

Our ride to the airport is quiet. I think back to when we first drove to the clinic and had our car party. Everything felt so complicated at the time, but our outlook was positive. We held onto a dream that life was about to be simplified. I can't help but have the same thoughts now. Part of it worries me that fate isn't being too supportive in Cis's journey of becoming dry. I also worry that the drama with Seth follows them out there.

We discuss a plan for the next six weeks. I have a surprise to fulfill first, but then Angie and I will do a temporary rental in Denver for the remaining portion of the six weeks. We'll communicate with them daily by phone and then during any in-person visits. Planning around this ahead of time is insane. Based on this past week, though, I know nothing about the world we live in today.

Jamal and Micah beat us to the airport and are waiting for us by the check in counters. We get Dakota and Cis processed and ticketed.

Dakota looks down in shock and asks, "First class?!"

"Whoa!" Cis says as he inspects the ticket further.

"He told ya to respect his deal-makin' skills!" Micah says with a laugh.

"Yes, sir!" Jamal says as he polishes his knuckles with his shirt.

"Y'all are too good to us," Dakota says as she gives the twins each a hug.

"Shall we?" I ask rhetorically.

I begin walking down the hall, and everyone follows me without question. They probably assume we're headed to a restaurant. I suppose that's mostly true. I guide them straight to the security gates.

"Oh, I guess this is goodbye for now?" Dakota asks with furled eyebrows.

I turn to Angie and ask, "Got your ID ready?"

Angie blinks a few times. She's clearly confused about what's happening. Like the good sport she is, though, she removes her ID from her wallet and holds it up for me.

"Coming to Colorado?" Cis asks me.

"No, the destination is a surprise for now. But we leave about twenty minutes after your flight."

"You're a man of great suspense," Cis says to me.

"The suspense won't last long. The gate will give it all away. And if that doesn't, the overhead speakers will," I say with a shrug. "But I'll keep it going as long as I can."

"I'm down for a surprise," Angie says, "Let's keep it going."

We get through security, and the TSA is friendly enough to not reveal where we're going to Angie. I find a restaurant where we can all sit down and relax for a while. Puddles of drool form on my menu. It's mind-blowing how little time we actually spent at Pond Point, but how long it felt. I completely blame the food and lack of coffee. A single meal felt like a lifetime of depression.

"Oh yeah, before I forget," Jamal says as he pulls the car key out of his pocket.

"Hang on to it? I heard you two complaining about your car when we were first checking in," I tell Jamal and Micah. "It's nothing fancy, but it's reliable. And it's yours if you want it."

"I'm pretty sure this would be against policy," Micah says.

"They don't go to Pond Point," Jamal says.

"And it's a sale, not a gift," I tell them. They look at me when I mention the word sale. I say, "It's only a dollar, but a sale is a sale." They both look relieved.

"I think this process takes a bit more than just gifting a key," Jamal says to me.

"I'll send a bill of sale and the signed-over title when we get back home. As long as you're insured, you should be good to go."

"Well, damn, man. This is quite huge," Micah tells me.

"We still owe you for not catching Big Blue." Cis lifts his head just long enough to tell him. "What a miserable night that was!"

"Big Blue?" Jamal asks.

"Mark something, I think—the guy with the bright blue spiked hair?"

Jamal and Micah both laugh as they shake their heads at the table. They clearly had similar conversations regarding his choice of hairstyle.

I pull the die out of my pocket, "Shall we roll to see how good we can eat?"

"Fuck off—put that away," Cis says without looking up from the menu. Angie just looks at me and slowly shakes her head.

"Roll me a zero," Dakota says, "I couldn't pull myself to ask my sister for money. So I'm here for the free stuff!"

"Don't be silly. Pick something good," Cis says.

"Yeah, if it doesn't excite you, we're going to keep adding food in front of you until you are," I tell her.

"I feel like a money-sucking leech," Dakota says.

"Then act like an actual leech and suck away," Cis says, then follows up quickly, "That came out wrong. But yeah, order something good."

Dakota blushes slightly as she giggles and starts looking at the menu.

Our taste buds find the food to be two stars better than its modest Yelp rating. It feels like a normal meal out with friends for most of it. Then, it dawned on me that no one ordered alcohol. I'm pretty sure that's a first in my group. Thinking through today's outing, the talks and laughs feel similar, but they feel genuine. I can certainly get used to it.

"What the fuck?" Dakota reads her phone that just buzzed.

"What happened?" Cis asks. She shows her phone to the table. A text message from a private number reads, "You can run…"

"Check your phone locator apps," I advise her. Instead, she just hands me the phone. Seth had turned it on in her phone, so he was probably watching her every move.

Angie tells her, "I'm glad he messaged you now and not after he saw you in Colorado."

"I have no idea how to get this guy to just off himself," Dakota says, "He's beyond repair."

"I'm still not sure how he's walking free," Cis says with a tone of disbelief.

"Money," Dakota says, "Endless amounts of money. Rich people don't get in trouble for poor people crimes."

I fidget around with the phone then give it back.

"You should be good now," I tell her, "I'm not seeing any other obvious red flags."

"Thanks," she says as she looks down at her phone suspiciously.

"I'm starting a group chat with all six of us. If anyone sees or hears anything off, please message the group immediately," I tell everyone. I hit send on my message and verify everyone's phone dings.

"Should we just change our tickets to Colorado?" Angie asks me.

"No, no. We've got this. Do your thing, and we'll see you when you get there," Cis tells her.

The time comes for the four of them to catch their flight, so Angie and I walk with them. The mood is pretty somber since the text arrived on Dakota's phone. I still think this is the right move and we'll just fix problems as they arise.

I pull Cis aside and tell him, "Hey man, are you good with all of this?"

"Yes, of course," Cis says.

"Okay, because it's undeniably a lot. I still think we're doing the right thing, but I want to make sure you're getting what you need."

"If I have any issues, I'll fire over an SOS to the group chat."

I nod and give him a hug. As I release from the hug, I hold his shoulders and tell him, "I'm proud of you, man. You've got this."

I let him go and give Dakota a hug. She seems lost. I quietly tell her, "I think we're past the hard parts. Just hang in there. Lean on Cis. He's a pretty sturdy dude." She nods as a tear rolls down her cheek.

We finish the rounds by saying bye to Jamal and Micah. We thank them feverishly for all of the help they've been over the last twenty-four hours. It is seriously clutch to have them helping out with aligning this new location up for Cis and Dakota. And to boot, they're personal bodyguards for the travel over there.

Angie and I begin our walk to our gate, which is luckily only about ten gates away. Halfway there, she spots a baseball cap that she immediately wants to buy.

"I've never seen you wear a hat before," I tell her.

"I usually want to look up," she tells me. As she puts it on, she rides the brim very low. It's apparently to avoid seeing the signs at the gate. She's really invested in helping me keep this secret going.

We grab a couple of waters and hustle over to our gate just in time for boarding. As we approach the gate agent, I have Angie look away. I tell the agent, "This destination is a surprise for her, so I beg you not to spill the secret."

The gate agent looks unphased and steps aside where Angie is looking. She ducks her head to look under the brim to meet eyes with Angie.

"Hi," Angie says as she smiles and waves at the agent.

"You know this guy?" the agent asks her.

"Yes, very much so."

"And you're going voluntarily?"

"Absolutely," Angie says with a little bit of a nervous giggle.

"If you make the call, I can have him shot dead on the spot," the agent says, completely straight-faced.

Angie bursts out into a laugh. She rests her hand on the agent's forearm and tells her, "Oh, please don't do that. I'd really like to see through the surprise!"

The agent nods and comes back to look at my tickets again. She winks at me and guides me through the door.

As we're boarding the plane, I realize the captain tends to state the destination a few times during the flight. I quickly download some videos to watch that aren't using the plane's wifi. This way, I can have her just watch them on my phone during the flight, and it won't be interrupted by announcements.

I stop at row two and turn to Angie. She seems slightly confused why I'm stopping.

"Aisle or window?" I ask her.

"You got us business class?" Angie sounds genuinely surprised. She underestimates her importance in this world.

"Only the best," I tell her.

"I love the window like everyone else, but I'm also happy with—"

"Window it is," I say as I get out of her way. I prefer the aisle, so we both win.

"Honestly," she says, "I hope this is the surprise. I already feel spoiled!"

"We're not even closing in on it yet," I tell her.

*

The flight takes a little finesse with the announcements. We set up a good strategy where we leave the videos playing on headphones. Our conversations can carry on, but when that static sound rips across the speakers, she quickly lifts the headphones to her ears and applies pressure. I then advise her when it's safe to remove the headphones again.

Given the surprise I have lined up, it probably doesn't matter if she knows the destination or not. I just assume that she may not figure it out if she has limited time to process it. Either way, I'm excited to see her reaction, as I believe she's really going to love it.

CHAPTER 18
~ Viva La Vida ~

The initial part of the surprise is revealed as we enter the terminal from the plane. Not too many airports have clusters of slot machines spread throughout them. Only the lovely Las Vegas.

"Vegas!" she exclaims, "You remembered the list!"

"Of course I did. Let's get out of here. The surprise awaits us!"

"What?" she asks, "There's more? When did you have time to set this up?"

I laugh instead of answering. I'd hate to give away my trade secrets. They may be needed again in the future. I like how she stays curious, yet doesn't press for information. It's making the build-up to the surprise much more enjoyable for me because I have no doubt it'll be a highlight of her year.

"So, Mr. Gambler," she says as she flings her hair to the side. "Where we headed?"

"You'll know soon enough," I say. I smile as I see the urge for her to know, peeking through her body language. I tell her, "I'll let you know afterward if it got pulled off properly or not. The one thing I'll share is that I expected this all to happen in a couple of weeks. Those calls this morning were expediting everything to today."

"That's fair," Angie ponders. "What about a hint toward the first destination? Could you give me that?"

"Of course, that's fair," I say, then sit in silence as though I'm thinking. The excitement in Angie is showing in her eyes as she anticipates what I'm going to say. I turn to her and say, "It's the place..."

"Come on, just say it!" Angie says with a pained laugh.

"It's the place where we'll pick up our luggage," I nod as I get it out.

"You're killing me. I get it. I'll wait and see," she says. In my peripheral vision, I can see her glancing back every few seconds. She's under the impression I'm going to break, and while I completely want to, I pretend I don't notice her looks.

We take a pit stop on the way to the baggage carousels for a bathroom break and to grab coffee. The others sent some updates in the chat that they arrived safe and sound. They are stopping for another meal before check-in, just in case the food isn't as good as advertised.

By some miracle, our luggage is on the carousel already when we arrive to pick it up. I order a ride on my phone then we head outside in the dry heat to wait.

Our ride arrives promptly and we ship off to our hotel, which is managing to remain a surprise so far. As we drive around the strip, we point out various fun features to each other. The driver also points out some of his favorite things as well. He'd play a pretty solid tour guide, as he knows a lot of history as well. Or he's a good bullshitter. Either way, it's fun, and I don't care enough to fact-check him.

Angie is so focused out her window that she doesn't notice the hotel next to us until we're almost at a complete stop.

"WHAT!? The Majestic Facade!?" she half screams out of excitement. She turns to me and places her hand on my forearm, "How could you have possibly remembered this?"

"Good stories are easy to remember!"

She gives me a tight, sideways hug and then rushes out to grab her luggage from the trunk. I check in at the front desk. I purposely have her wait with our luggage by the couches in the lobby.

"I should give my dad a call," she tells me, "I'm curious if he remembers the rooms they stayed at."

I smile at her and say, "Yeah—I may have intercepted one of your calls from your dad back at Pond Point."

"So sneaky! How long have you been planning this?" she asked.

"Pretty much since you told us that story. I just didn't know how or when at that point. The first part of the surprise is you'll be staying in the same room your mom did." Almost immediately, Angie starts to well up.

She pauses, then asks, "Are we reenacting the story?"

"Not exactly. Your father's room was already taken. My room is down the hall a ways," I tell her. She seems slightly disappointed but still touched by this gesture.

We get off the elevator and turn left toward her room. Down the hall, an older gentleman sits on the floor.

"Dad!?" Angie screams as she breaks out into a full cry. She runs down the hall as her father, Henry, slowly rises to a stand. He welcomes her embrace with a large grin and open arms.

As her hug ends, she asks him, "Were you part of this scheme?"

Henry shakes his head and tells her, "This was all Brey. That snot wouldn't even let your old man pay for his plane ticket."

"What room are you staying in?" she asks him.

Henry points at the door behind him with a thumb. He says, "The luckiest room I've ever had."

Angie turns back to me and asks, "Room was taken. I see." She shakes her head and smiles at me.

"I'm going to freshen up and grab a bite to eat. Here's your key, and there's your surprise. Now you have a reenactment partner," I say with a smile. "I'm going to work on my book and leave you two at it. You know how to contact me."

"This really means the world," Angie says as she gives me a tight hug.

"And thank you for making the trip out," I say to Henry as I shake his hand, "We can officially meet when we reconvene."

Henry wipes a tear from his cheek and tells me, "No, thank you for this. As Angie said, this means everything." He points to the floor next to Angie's room. There sits an older portrait photo of her mom smiling. As they share another hug with several tears, I disappear to my room.

*

I'm shocked that Henry was willing to jump on a last-minute flight this morning. It meant everything to have this surprise here and waiting upon our arrival. However, seeing their reactions to that moment though, I'm no longer surprised by his eagerness.

While I love socializing with my friends and family, I do need some alone time to reconnect with my creative side. It isn't my intention behind this surprise, but it's certainly a bonus. My brain floods with ideas and thoughts, and writing this novel is my way of opening the gates.

Since their room is viewable from the elevator, I map out the emergency stairwell on the other side of my room. I plan for unnecessary things all of the time. This time, I'm figuring out ways up and down the hotel without interfering with their bonding time. It'd be a lot easier if I could just commit to staying in my room or staying out.

My room is nice. It has the classic Las Vegas feel to it. It's a bit dated, but I think that's what gives it its charm. I'll be honest, though, it feels empty. Even before the road trip started, I still had Cis as a roommate, so my room never felt quite like this. It's kind of like having an empty sandwich. My empty back then was a sandwich roll with nothing in it. Now it's nothing. No roll. No bag. No napkins.

I realize I need some background noise, so I go to the coffee shop that's right off the casino floor. It's enough constant noise that it's not a distraction, but it keeps my annoying inner voice from talking too much. My focus isn't as clear as I was hoping for.

To avoid being a complete disaster, I try to organize my notes into a document to help define my characters, the attributes I want to highlight, and general ideas for their stories. I look over my old notes of my previously planned novel and realize how impersonal it is. The characters were all made up of thin air and quite shallow. My notes have some creative edges to these characters, but their plots didn't do much to showcase them.

There's a man sitting a couple tables over, reading a book. He seems completely engaged in it, so I swing by to distract him.

"Good afternoon, sir," I say.

"Hi," he says. He seems very uninterested in me, but I decide to keep with it.

"Feel free to tell me to go away, but I see you're an impressive reader. I assume you do it often."

"Yeah," he says slowly.

"I'm actually working on my first novel. It's technically my first and second novels as I've begun work on both of them."

"That's fun!" he says.

"Could I give you a five-minute pitch for each book? I'm happy to buy you food, drinks or whatever. And you can completely shit on them. I'm just having a hard time getting either one moving forward, and I was hoping to get some gritty opinions from a stranger," I tell him.

"I have to leave in thirty minutes. You better get started," he says as he puts his bookmark into his book and sets it down.

"You're amazing," I tell him. The first book has a lot of twisted stories that intersect in different parts of the book. I do my best to explain it to him using objects on the table. He asks some good questions to clarify the many plots, so I'm fairly certain he followed along. It took a bit more than my five-minute prediction, so he recommended that we go over the second synopsis.

I watch the clock better this time and actually tell our personal story from the past week. Of course, I use fake names to keep anonymity. His face remains pleasant through both presentations, but it stays static, so it's hard to read his face.

As I finish, I ask him, "Which story, if any, do you think would stand a better chance on paper?"

"Both stories are nice. In this first one, it seemed you were in love with the plot as you came up with all of the storylines," he says. I nod in response. I did have a bit of a war room technique going with it to make sure the plots came together.

"In the second one, you were in love with the characters. It feels much more natural and likely to happen in the real world. I would recommend giving that book a big finish or go back to the first story and give more life to the individual characters. They are the ones living through your book," he tells me.

He talks through some examples of how I could approach both. Ultimately, he says my passion should drive what I write because that's the key to finishing a book. Even with a full outline and character descriptions, it's impossible to write an exciting hundred thousand words on a subject I'm already bored with.

"May I ask what you do for a living? This advice was top quality. I was picturing I'd get an aye-or-nay type response," I say.

"I'm a college professor of literature," he says with a friendly smile.

"Unbelievable. I honestly don't know where my luck comes from sometimes. Can I get you something or compensate you for your time?"

"Oh no. I was just waiting for my daughter to get done with work," he says.

"She works here?"

The man nods and points to the girl behind the counter.

"Then I shall tip her for your services. I really do appreciate the help!" I reach out and shake his hand. I pack up my belongings and swing by the front desk.

I lean in and tell her, "Your dad is incredible. Could you take him out to dinner for me? I think he'd dig it."

As the teenage girl is muttering, "Uh," I slide two hundred dollars under her hand. Her eyes get really wide. I may have spooked her a bit.

"He's given me the deepest and purest inspiration that I've had in a while. It means the world to me. And it'll mean the world to him if you go offer to take him out to dinner. Trust me."

The girl agrees to it. I leave her alone and head out of the coffee shop. I turn around as she runs up to her dad and says something to him out of excitement. The largest smile shines on his face as he gives her a big hug.

He catches a glimpse of me outside the store. He gives me a thumbs up and a silent "thank you." I return the nonverbal thanks and continue down the hall.

This is one of those moments I'd share with my friends, but it won't translate well in text messages. I check my phone and there are messages from the gang. Dakota and Cis are checked in. They have to keep their phones at the front desk, but they're not locked away like Pond Point had them. You can come by and check your phone for fifteen minutes at a time. And they try to limit patients to only a few times per day. The Mile High staff seems to understand today's world. I did inform them that we should all do a video call tomorrow once they're settled.

Jamal and Micah wished them luck in that chat but then started a new group with just Angie and me. They gave us a rundown about how nice the place is. Their friends welcomed them to stay with them for a week or so, so the twins may still be there to hang out when we arrive. It sounds like they're digging Denver. It's younger and more vibrant, for sure. It seems like it's been a solid startover for everyone so far.

My mind does wonder about Steve and Josiah a lot. They did get a bit of a shaft from everything happening over there, considering they're still there. I send them each a longer text message, which I'm sure they won't get for a month or so. I want people to know that they're thought about and have support. They'll be leaving those safe zones soon from drugs and alcohol. The real world doesn't care if you're trying to be sober.

I find myself back in the elevator, heading up to my room. I'm still hungry, but I want to drop off my laptop as it's not the best dining companion. My brain failed my plan, as I ended up getting out on our floor. It didn't dawn on me until I heard Angie down the hall.

It was inevitable, I told myself. My subconscious needed to see the reenactment. I look down the hall, and I see Angie sitting next to her hotel door, hugging her mother's portrait. Her dad is next to his door across the hall. By the hand gestures, I can tell her dad is very engaged in whatever story he's telling. I'm happy that Angie is so occupied by it that neither of them actually notices me getting off the elevator. The plan may not have failed after all.

I look through the hotel guide and find there's a buffet place downstairs. Vegas is certainly famous for these locations. It would be a crime if I didn't go to one, and I'm not sure how Angie and her dad feel about them. I treat myself to a little feast and then call it a night.

CHAPTER 19

~ Full Battery ~

Holy everything-that's-good-in-life! This can be certified as the first morning in a very long time that I wake up feeling refreshed. First, it was a hangover, then a squeaky cot, then a monitored room, then disaster, and finally a beeping room. How did all of that lead to this massive, comfortable bed in a room void of any noise?

I even slept through some text messages from Angie. One came in last night and thanked me for giving her that memory. The other was this morning regarding breakfast. Considering it was thirty minutes ago, I imagine that ship already sailed. I still respond and apologize for my tardiness. It turns out they were just drinking coffee downstairs in that coffee shop awaiting my arrival. I guess I better pull myself together.

As I arrive at the coffee shop, I find them loitering outside, ready to move on to the next place.

"Well, good morning!" Henry says as he catches me in the crowd.

"And a good morning to you too, sir! How'd you all sleep?" I ask them.

"Quite well, except for when I rolled over on my wound," Angie says as she looks down at her fresh gauze.

"I suppose you caught him up on the last week or so?" I ask Angie.

"Ohh yeah, she did. What a train wreck you've all been through. I'm glad you're here and safe now," Henry tells me.

"Me too! Felt like a neverending incident!" I tell him.

"Shall we?" Angie says. She walks between us and loops her arms into the back of our arms. Her cheeriness is contagious. Henry and I smile at each other and swing our arms along with hers.

She asks me, "Any word on how Cis and Dakota are doing?"

"Not yet. My only conversations with them are in that group chat." I put my hand in my pocket to grab my phone. Hopefully I haven't missed any messages.

They must have been listening from afar. Both of our phones start buzzing at the same time. It's a call coming in from Dakota.

"Helllllooo!" Angie says happily as the phone connects.

"Angie! Whoa—where are you?" Dakota asks as she inspects our high ceiling background.

"Vegas!"

"Hey-yo! High rolling? I like the 'surprise!'" Cis says from over Dakota's shoulder. I'm happy to see them both in positive moods.

"Surprise was far more than that," she says as she turns the phone to Henry then back to herself. She says, "Remember the story I told you?"

"I do!" Cis says. "Is that your father?"

"It is! And Brey got us the same hotel rooms from the story!"

"Damn, dude. You just shot yourself in the foot," Cis says.

"Right?" Henry says. He chuckles as he leans into view of the camera. "You don't really top this."

"Exactly, gotta start low with some chocolate or something," Cis says and shares a laugh with Henry.

"How's the jacket holding up?" Dakota says as she notices Angie is still wearing it.

"Amazingly! I fit right in with these fancy folk!" Angie tells Dakota. She does a little spin to show it off to the video.

"Any more messages from Seth since yesterday?" I ask them.

"Just one, it just said 'Marco,'" Dakota says.

"What a sketch ball," I say, "Let us know if things go further, and we can figure out who needs to get involved."

"Will do—I'm pretty sure he just wants me to live in fear," Dakota says, "But this place is so nice, it's hard to think about him or what we left behind." She shrugs it off while fighting off a smile.

"That's great to hear," Angie says.

"And the food?" I ask as I lean in close to the phone. The suspense grows in me.

Cis gives a double chef's kiss gesture from behind Dakota. That's all he had to say.

Angie turns to her dad and says, "I chose a pretty sketch place, but to be fair, the person on the phone painted a completely different picture."

"Stop, Angie," Cis cuts her off as he takes the phone for a closer view. "I'll never be able to repay all that you've done for me. I'll try, though. I'm sober and actually incredibly happy. The journey is always part of it, and I'm glad I had great friends to do it with."

Angie starts to well up a little. Henry grabs her shoulder and gives her a side hug. He's clearly very proud of his daughter, and he absolutely should be.

"So, what's the plan for today?" Dakota asks.

"We're currently headed to breakfast, then may just do some strolling around," Angie tells her.

"Awesome! We'll try giving a call back on our next break. Gonna give my sister a quick call before we have to get back," Dakota says.

"Okay," I say, "I'm glad you're doing well! We'll speak soon!"

We disconnect the phone feeling relieved that things are looking up. The three of us continue our stroll down the enormous hall littered with overpriced stores.

"Where are your friends now?" Henry asks me.

"They're at rehab," I tell him.

"Oh, I know that. I mean, where is the rehab?"

"Denver, Colorado, you been there before?" I ask him.

"Ah yes, I've seen most major cities from my days of being a commercial pilot," Henry says.

"Oh, right! I forgot about that. Decided it wasn't for you?" I ask.

"It's not like that," he says. Angie perks up and looks at him. He looks at her and says, "It's just not good when you have a wife and kiddo back home. We didn't have video calls back then. I didn't want to miss any of those special days with my loved ones. And for what? It was seeing the same sky day after day."

"What'd you do after?" I asked him.

"I was always a tinkerer. I set up a handyman service where I'd travel around the community and help put their homes back together. It made community events far more enjoyable as it was like a reunion of friends each time."

"That sounds wonderful for many reasons! How's the market for that type of work?" I ask him.

"Homeowners always need two things in life: something fixed and a special price. While the money was never quite where I wanted it to be, I felt like it gave me so much more than my heart had ever desired."

"Ever miss piloting?" I ask.

"When her mother was still alive, we wanted to have this exact experience. So, at that time, I missed the compensation. I do wish I could have brought her while she was alive," Henry says, then pauses in his speech. He takes a deep breath and says, "But as life goes, you trade special moments for different special moments. I think this one will live more vividly in Angie's memory for many years to come, so perhaps this is how it was supposed to be."

"I think she was with us last night," Angie says, "So win-win."

"So, how about you," Henry says, "What are your work plans after all of this is said and done? Angie mentioned you were working on a novel?"

"Ah, yes. I'll be picking up a new contract for writing code full time, then hopefully get a book released in the next few months."

"Sounds like you have your hands full!"

"I've actually had a bit of an idea to try to tie everything together," I say. It's not a well thought out plan, so heaven help me if they ask too many questions.

"Oh?" Angie says.

"I enjoy remote work, but sometimes it's nice to be among the living. I was thinking of trying to open a coworking space that's attached to a coffee shop that serves food."

"Don't most remote people just work from coffee shops?" Henry asks.

"That's a fair statement. A lot do. However it doesn't give any quiet places for meetings or tasks that require privacy, so I was thinking of a floor with open seating. It'll be surrounded by soundproof two-person booths. Then probably have some larger conference rooms stashed away in the back for whoever wants to rent them out."

"So, an office for people that don't want an office?" Henry asks. I can't help but laugh. It does sound quite backward.

Angie suggests, "But at least you get to pick who you're working beside. In the traditional office, they pick for you."

"Ah, okay. Well, let me know if you need a handyman," Henry says as he chuckles. "Things are very different from when I was your age."

I nod in agreement. "Things are very different from just five years ago."

"So, what about the food side of your spot? What's the plan for that?" Angie asks me.

"About three weeks ago, the plan entailed just moving Cis and his favorite cooks over to show off whatever they wanted."

"And now?" Angie asks.

"Your dream has grown on me, but…" My voice tampers off as I look at her in a wishful manner.

"But?" Angie squints her eyes and looks at me.

"It would only work with you."

"It would only work with Cis running the kitchen," she adds.

"That sounds an awful lot like a," I say as she cuts me off.

"Yes. Yes. It was a yes," she excitedly says.

"Then we clearly need to start brainstorming when we get back to Colorado, " I say through my big cheesy grin.

"Of course! I look forward to it!" Angie cups her hands together.

*

It's nice being in the land of edible food. I keep reminding myself of the days before me so I can extend this period of not taking certain things for granted. Cloud Number Nine isn't just for sobering addicts, apparently.

We're walking Henry back to his room. He wants to relax a little and catch up on some calls. He's the veteran maintenance man for an apartment complex. While there are other employees, a lot of them are green in the field. So when problems come up, he tends to get the calls and emails to try to diagnose the issues at hand without seeing them. It would probably bother some to work while taking personal time, but he says it gives him purpose. Plus, he doesn't mind a break from all of the noise that comes with Las Vegas.

As we get to the room, Henry requests that I follow him.

He tells me, "Come on in for a minute. I have some old family photos. Little Angie was a hoot. You have to see it." He chuckles to himself.

"We don't really have time righ…just kidding. Absolutely!" I say.

I follow him inside and sit down on the bed next to him. Angie takes off Dakota's jacket and tosses it next to the television. She excuses herself to use the bathroom while we get some laughs at her expense.

"Wait a second, these aren't embarrassing at all!" I tell Henry, "I was hoping for a dodgy haircut, some ridiculous clothes, or huge glasses."

"Angie kind of knew who she was from the start," Henry says, "We didn't have much control over any of that. Honestly, I'm pretty sure we were more like roommates during some stages of her life rather than in charge."

"I don't doubt it. She's certainly a force to be reckoned with."

"Absolutely. I loved having that front-row seat to her life. I miss it every day," he says with a bit of sorrow in his voice.

"It's never too late to skip rows again," I tell him.

"Only if she'll have me. She's not a kid anymore."

"Maybe wait until she comes out of the bathroom before asking?"

We both let out a chuckle as I peruse the remaining pages of this photo album. Angie really looked like a kid from the modern age all throughout her childhood. I was hoping for some bright clothing, crimped hair, nerdy anything. Alas, nothing embarrassing came up.

CHAPTER 20
~ Roll Again ~

Angie and I cut loose in the casino for a bit while Henry gets some rest. One thing I've learned about gambling is to always follow the happy crowds. Now I don't know the rules to some of the fancy games, but things like craps, roulette, blackjack, and poker I can hold my own in.

With that said, I do get easily intimidated in games where it seems like everyone else is a veteran at it. Maybe they are, or maybe the alcohol tells them that. Either way, I try my best to appeal to the crowd while also following my gut. When I'm with someone that naturally boosts my confidence, though, goodbye gambling etiquette. I do what I want.

As we pass each game, I slow down to explain the general concepts and rules. We make our way around to craps, and she immediately attaches to the idea of the dice.

"We clearly need to roll some dice," she says, "In honor of the original trio!"

"For honor!" I say as I pretend to hold up a sword.

Angie leads the way to find a lively table. We belly up to it, and it's a twenty-dollar minimum. I typically stick to the five or ten-dollar minimums based on my amazing ability to lose.

"Right, should we find a lower minimum?" I say, and before I'm done, she's plopped a few hundred down on the table.

The dealer-on-the-stick quickly swaps out her money for chips. Angie tosses one on the pass line, then looks back at me.

"You know the game?" I ask her.

"I know all of the games, even the ones you can't pronounce correctly." She smirks over her shoulder at me.

"Well, aren't I an ass. Why didn't you cut me off back there?" I should never underestimate this woman.

"I heard men involuntarily self-combust when they're cut off prematurely while mansplaining."

"In that case, I appreciate you letting me finish." I grin as I direct my attention back at the table.

The stickperson hands the dice to the roller. She rolls the dice around a bit in her hands while doing some drunken dance. Shake and release.

"Seven!" the crowd yells out as the dice come to a stop.

"Sevens have been good to us," I say close to her ear.

"Amen." Angie turns and winks at me.

She lets it ride. So much for me needing a confidence boost. I'm just going to sit back and see how the closeted professionals do it.

"Seven!" they all scream after another roll. She now backs away her bet a little.

"Are you understanding the game?" I sarcastically ask her closely to her ear.

"Maybe. I think I'm losing," she says loudly back to me. It's always a good sign when you can't hear the person next to you without screaming.

Watching her stack of chips is like watching a triple-leveraged index fund on a good day. It had its dips, but she must be sitting around two thousand now.

"You know, if you just listened to my instructions from earlier, you wouldn't have the burden of all those chips to carry," I tell Angie.

"Think I'll cash out." She casually says as she gestures to the workers. "Let's go see what Pops is up to!"

The stick person gives Angie a chip tray so we can transport them to cash out. Besides not being bulletproof, I need to start keeping track of what she's not amazing at. What is Angie's kryptonite? And where the hell can I fit in and look impressive?

We collect her winnings and start with a trajectory toward the hotel elevators. I pull out my phone to check for messages. Thirty-seven messages and seven missed calls! I suspect it's the group chat going crazy.

Sure enough, it is. I unlock my phone and Angie and I both look on to see what they're chatting about. The first message is from Dakota asking us where we're staying. A screenshot follows of a message she received from a different private number. It's a hand holding up today's newspapers in front of our hotel.

"How the fuck," we both say in bitter tones.

Just then, another video call comes in from Cis, and we pick up immediately.

"Hey man, what the," I start to speak as Cis and Dakota on the other end cut me off.

"Thank God!" they exclaim.

"They fucking followed you guys. I'm so happy you're alright!" Cis says.

"What do they want with us?" Angie asks.

"No idea. The messages keep coming from what appears to be burner phones," Dakota says.

"If it's private, how do you know?" Angie asks her.

"We have the local police involved out here. Unfortunately, they can't help you with your current problem. Can you reach out to someone there?"

"Yeah, we'll give them a call from our room. We're headed up to check on my dad."

"Okay. Please message us along the way so we know you're safe."

The elevators always take an eternity when you're in a rush. Nothing seems out of the ordinary so far, at least.

Angie jogs to his door from the elevator and knocks repeatedly.

We hear Henry's voice from the other side say, "Whoa. I'm coming!" The door opens, and he's standing there with sleepy eyes. He sees Angie then his eyes get wide.

"What happened? It looks like you've seen a ghost!" he tells her.

"Those people I told you about followed us," Angie tells him, "We need to make some calls to the police. Just relax here. Don't open the door for anyone! And set all the locks!"

Henry doesn't seem too panicked, but he follows the orders once the door is closed. We can hear the clicking from the other side. I join Angie in her room, and we start looking up numbers to call.

The non-emergency line picks up quickly, so we avoid the emergency route. Angie explains the overall problem and then gives endless details to the officer on the phone. It feels like a lifetime later when Angie hangs up.

"They're sending someone to come talk with us in person," she tells me. She immediately calls Henry and catches him up. It sounds like she woke him up again, so I'd say he's fine, just hanging in his room for a bit.

"Oh. By the way," I hear Henry say over the call, "you left your jacket over here. Are you cold? Would you like it back?"

"I'm good. I can get it later."

They hang up, and we immediately hear a knock on his door. Angie and I become startled and move quietly to the door to look through the peephole. We don't recognize the two men out there. Henry stays quiet, so they knock again.

"We know you're in there," they say through the door.

"I'm sleeping. Come back later," Henry says.

"We're hotel security," one guy says, "We were asked to come question you about an incident."

Henry opens the door. I assume he wants to help resolve the harassment we're getting. The two guys look a little uneasy when they see an old man by himself.

"The incident included a woman who was associated with this room. Is your daughter with you?"

"No. I'm traveling alone."

"Okay," one of the guys says, "And you don't have any female companions visiting?"

"You mean like prostitutes?" Henry chuckles, "No. I'm afraid not."

"Okay, perhaps it was a different floor. Thanks for your time," one of the guys says.

Henry steps back to close the door.

The other guy sticks his foot in the way and asks, "Then where is that jacket from?" He points to Dakota's jacket by the television.

The two men start to force their way into his room. Henry stiff-arms one guy with his left arm as he takes a modest jab at the other. He connects. The guy's head flings backward, but his body keeps moving forward through it. It's unfortunately not enough to deter someone with meth energy. Henry is overwhelmed by their rabid force.

"Close the door behind me," I tell Angie. I expect her to stop me, but she doesn't. Rather, she helps unlock the door. The door swings open large enough for a body to squeeze out. Angie pushes me aside and runs across the hall. I swing the door open and try following closely behind.

Angie holds an arm out to tell me to stay back. The stiff-armed guy has his body turned somewhat sideways to us as he's trying to maneuver around Henry's steel arm. Angie gives a straight kick to the side of the guy's knee. His body contorts in her direction, and she meets that momentum with a solid headbutt directly to the temple. The guy collapses on the floor as his nap time begins.

Henry grabs the remaining guy by the shirt with both hands. The guy screams threats as he continues to push and push against all odds.

"I don't think so, you little shit," Henry says with a calm, strained voice.

He holds him in place and gives a nod to Angie, who knees him in the right kidney. She comes up with a second knee and connects with his ribs. Henry reaches back, loading up for a full swing. His fist comes shooting back like a bullet. It connects directly with the side of this guy's jaw. He drops like a fly, and Henry uses his falling momentum to fling him head-first into the dresser.

"Ya like the jacket? Go get it."

Angie and I grab the unconscious guy blocking the door and drag him in enough so we can close it.

"It appears your jacket is famous," Henry tells Angie.

She just nods as she stares down at the two dormant men.

"But it may also be cursed," Henry adds.

"It's not my jacket, it's Dakota's," Angie says, "Brey, call nine-one-one and let them know what happened. Dad, see if the hotel security can send up some help in the meantime." Angie is quick and clear with her instructions but more out of urgency than fear.

Angie makes a video call to Dakota.

"Hey, are you good?" Dakota asks.

"We're okay. But do you know these assholes?" Angie asks and aims the phone at the two guys on the floor.

"I feel like I've seen their faces once or twice. They're probably mules of some sort. But being 'okay' doesn't include having two bodies on your floor. Did you talk to the police yet?" Dakota asks.

"The slow fucks are supposedly sending someone to talk to us. Brey is currently calling the emergency line. And my dad is calling the hotel security to hopefully detain these guys while we wait. I hope it all happens before these guys start to multiply," Angie tells her.

"What happened?" Cis says as he comes into view in the call.

"I was just a spectator. I'm here in Vegas with a father-daughter pair of badasses," I yell to him as I cover the microphone on my phone.

"It's clear you didn't do this," Cis says with a smile, "But seriously, I need details."

"Okay, okay," Dakota says as she pulls back the phone, "He can wait on those. You need to focus on more important things! Call us back when the police show up and I'm happy to connect them to the officer here." Dakota pulls back the phone and points it at the officer who's in some sort of office with them.

The emergency number finally picks up. I explain to them how Angie just called the non-emergency line and then move into the fact that there are two unconscious bodies on our floor now. This seems to bring up their scheduling and they tell me a nearby patrolling officer should be over very shortly.

It feels like only a few moments have passed, and there's already knocking on the door. We look through the peephole and verify badges before opening the door.

"Good evening. I'm Officer Hadet, and this is Officer Plead—please step back into the room and make room for us." He turns to the security guards and instructs them to handcuff and inspect the downed men.

"Okay, so we have an officer inspecting the cameras downstairs. We'd like to question each of you individually to figure out what happened here and get some reports filled out," Officer Hadet says.

"We have multiple rooms if it'll help," I tell them, "Angie here is across the hall, and my room is down the hall."

"That would be great, actually," Officer Plead says. He points to one of the security guards and asks, "Could you stay in the hall and keep an eye out there? I'll take them one at a time across the hall for questioning. Everyone else stays here. For everyone's safety, please keep your hands visible at all times. No sudden movements. The typical stuff."

"All of this originated in Florida with our friends. They're now in Colorado working with a local officer there. Is it okay if we loop them in?" Angie asks.

Officer Hadet nods to Angie. "Yeah, that works." He turns to Officer Plead and tells him, "I can get caught up with them over here."

Officer Plead nods and then turns to face me. "Do you want to start while they make that connection?"

"Yeah, let's do this," I say as I grab Angie's room key, and we head across the hall.

I have a pattern of being verbose in my storytelling. This remains true as I explain to Officer Plead every detail I can remember. He cuts off my elaborations in order to keep the report dense with important facts.

"What's your relationship with Angie?" he asks with an accusatory look.

"Friends." I feel it's important to let cops break eye contact. Otherwise they may start making up stories with unintended body language.

"How long have you known her for?"

"I mean, I've known her as my bartender for at least a year now," I say.

"What about as friends?"

I hesitate, as that's a bit murky. I tell him, "I mean, our trip just started about a week ago. This is the first time we've done something outside of the bar."

He lets out a single chuckle as he says, "I wouldn't be surprised if she doesn't want to go on any more trips with you."

I smile and nod. "Yeah. It's a bit of a disaster, right?"

"So, what do you know about Dakota?" Officer Plead asks.

"Dakota showed up to rehab with a beat-up face and needed help. She has a kind heart and a rocky past, it seems."

"If it were just the past, we wouldn't be here right now." He looks up from his notes to see my reaction

"That's fair. Some pasts have a harder time staying there."

"Why did you all choose to stay involved with her after knowing the dangers that come with her presence?" he asks me. It's a fair question. Why didn't we just pack our bags and get out of there?

"I don't know," I tell him, "I suppose this trip has become a soul-seeking journey for all of us. It's hard to learn who we are if we just stay in our comfort zones."

"I understand. I was a guidance counselor once," he tells me, "I decided I needed to turn up the dial a bit."

"Those skills carry over at least."

"Yeah," he says, "They definitely do!"

"Know anything about this Seth guy?" he asks me.

"I know he's a bit of a junkie. His money and drugs hold some influence over his fellow junkies. And he's dangerously hell-bent on trying to get Dakota back."

All in all, this day made me realize how ignorant I really am. Historically speaking, I know nothing of the people I've surrounded myself with. There's this strong magnetic pull, though, that is making me want to know more. When I'm around them, a certain void in my heart goes away.

My conversation with Officer Plead tampers off, so we end it, and I head back across the hall. I am curious what we'll learn back over there as Officer Hadet was conversing with the officer in Colorado. Maybe they already solved the mystery.

Officer Plead and I walk back across the hall. Officer Hadet remains on the phone and is taking continuous notes on his pad. I point at the ground and hold my hands up, silently asking Angie where they went.

"They're being detained downstairs," Angie tells me.

"Did they identify them?" I ask her.

She shakes her head and tells me, "Not yet, but they're going to fingerprint them at the station."

I stare at her for a long moment. There's probably a better time for this, but I ask her, "Where'd you get those moves?"

She smiles and says, "I was a competitive kickboxer for a bit."

"What do you consider a bit?" I ask. I mean, her moves were well rehearsed.

"Fifteen years, was it?" Henry asks her.

"After this is said and done, I have thousands of questions lined up to ask you," I tell her. She smiles and nods.

"We have plenty of time," she tells me.

Officer Plead taps Angie next for questioning across the hall. I sit down close to Officer Hadet, so I can participate in the cross-state video conversation still in progress. There's still a question on who was involved in locating us here. And more importantly, how do we put an end to this harassment and threat?

Henry just lies back on the bed and stares at the wall. He's clearly listening to everything happening around him, but I don't think he knows where he can fit into the mix.

"What's next for you after this, Henry?" I step back to ask him.

The question startles him a bit and he sits up more alert. He hums as he thinks about it. He says, "I was planning to go home, but I'm not going anywhere until there's a resolution."

"Once we have the go-ahead, we're headed to Colorado to stay for a month or so. It'd be great if you could join us," I tell him.

He smiles at me and says, "I'd like that. I appreciate the invitation."

CHAPTER 21
~ Mile High ~

There isn't much success in identifying Henry's attackers. The men don't have records, at least not ones that are linked to their biometrics. We know without a doubt they're attached to Seth somehow and that they were actually coming for Dakota. It's a mystery where the mix-up happened. Maybe some eyes at the airport saw us with Dakota and Cis, then later saw us get on this flight to Vegas. This city is well monitored, so there are several ways they could use footage to track us to our rooms.

The security did confirm that the men did attack Henry unprovoked. We can at least leave this city. There's way too much activity here to know when we're in danger or not. And if we can't enjoy the city, there's no reason to get held up here.

Two undercover officers travel with us to the airport to watch for tails or other suspicious characters. We get cleared to take our flight, and an undercover officer on the Colorado side awaits our arrival. Unfortunately, we didn't get to take business class on this trip. They claimed it could rile up unwanted attention. At least there are three of us, so we're not wedging in with strangers.

Officer Blake is the receiving officer. Based on appearance alone, I'd say he's one of the younger ones in the force. His clean face and shaven blond hair give him a 'fresh out of the military' look, but in a forest ranger-type way.

It certainly doesn't take away from his ability to do the job unless, of course, someone did follow us.

One of the counselors at their rehab clinic was able to secure us a small rental on the outskirts of town. It's only about a ten minute walk to go visit them. The police outfitted the outside of the place with a couple cameras to help watch for suspicious activity. They're pretty confident we left the scumbags behind, though. On special request, the two guys from the hotel haven't been put into the general population, so they probably still think Dakota is in Las Vegas.

The officer drops us off at our rental, and it's cute. It has three bedrooms, two bathrooms, and a nice fenced-in backyard. There's even a flat-top grill for our use. I'm looking forward to finally being able to have some home-cooked meals. Angie and Henry both bragged about each other's cooking, so hopefully, I don't get shamed too badly. After all, I share an apartment with a chef.

After some convincing, Henry accepts the primary bedroom. He goes to bed earlier so at least he can close the door to his private suite and relax. I can stay up late trying to figure out everything about Angie.

I come out of my room after getting my things settled. I ask them, "What's everyone thinking for dinner?"

"I imagine we should stay close to home for at least tonight," Angie says.

"Probably should have gotten groceries on the way here," Henry says as he thinks about what to do.

"There's an app for that. Let's get groceries delivered. Any cravings?" I ask.

"More and more 'in my day' feels like a thousand years ago," Henry says as he chuckles.

"I'm not craving anything particular," Angie says, "What about you?"

"Craving? Nothing special. But I can make us some chicken parmesan with a side salad and garlic bread?" Henry gives an a-okay hand gesture. Looks like we have a winner.

Angie nods and smiles at me. She says, "That'd be lovely."

As we wait for groceries to arrive, I dig through some of the cabinets in the living room. There's an assortment of games and playing cards. I challenge them to a game of Risk. It's not a game I can say I'm great at, but I do have some good memories playing it. I think I'd like to make some more.

Henry isn't feeling up for it and asks to play after dinner. He retires into his bedroom for a nice long nap.

"So, how serious was this kickboxing?" I ask Angie.

"I started young and did it through college. I've actually been state champion a couple times for my weight group."

"Wow—congrats on that! Maybe we should tell Seth to deter anyone else from coming! What stopped you?"

"During my last competitive fight, I was left with a nasty concussion. My dad lost some time at work to care for me. He loved doing it, but I had to decide if I wanted to go professional or give up on it. The latter won."

"Any regrets with your choice?" I ask her.

"Not really. Any regrets I do have are easily outweighed by potential regrets I could have if I did go professional. There's no guarantee of safety or avoiding permanent injury."

"That's fair!"

"I still get to spar from time to time in the gym, but my sight is on the new dream," she says.

"It's always good to have something to strive for," I tell her.

"Absolutely." Angie inspects her nails, clearly processing something in her head. Her face turns serious as she looks up at me. She asks, "Are you really serious about this coworking and cafe place?"

"As long as I get buy-in—I can't do it alone," I tell her.

"What's the minimum buy-in you need?"

"I'd love to see you doing your thing in the front of the house, making it something really special that you can find true joy in. And the same for Cis, only back in the kitchen. I can handle the coworking space where I'll continue doing my coding and writing," I explain.

"I'm all in," Angie says as her face gets excited.

"Also, hoping we can bring your dad into it."

"He'd really like that," she says with a heartwarming grin.

Our conversation spirals into a full business plan. The amount of initial investment really comes down to two things about the location. One part is, of course, the physical location of the building. If we aim for Boston, it's going to be expensive. Very expensive. However, we've expanded our search on our phones for places around Denver. The general rent seems more fair if we're aiming for the suburbs.

The second part is regarding the actual structure that we decided to invest in. It'll probably be easier to find something with a kitchen and an extended dining room. The dining room could easily have some walls thrown up. With wireless, we wouldn't have to worry about getting ethernet wired up either. Either way, both are within Henry and my wheelhouses.

I put Angie in charge of the general infrastructure surrounding the cafe. We decide, though, that we would focus on breakfast and lunch and have similar hours as the nine-to-five workers next door. She's beginning to put together what a rough schedule would look like so we'd know what type of hiring we'd have to do before kick-off.

Angie doesn't want to brainstorm anything related to menus, though, until Cis is signed on and available. We both want him to be an equal partner and committed to it. Together, I'm sure they'll come up with something amazing. And I look forward to indulging in it!

The groceries arrive, so I start prepping for dinner as Angie continues sketching out her ideas. She's been running a bar for a while now, so the operations piece is already known to her.

"How are you feeling about location?" I ask her as I slice up the chicken.

"Honestly? I kind of like the idea of starting somewhere new. It sounds liberating. It would come down to my dad, though, as I don't want to move thousands of miles away from him."

"Perhaps after I'm done with preparing dinner, we can start our web search for potential places in the area then," I tell her.

"That'd be great! And hopefully, we'll be free to check out the city after the police get to the end of this crap," she says as she continues to scribble down some notes.

I lay out two plates and a bowl for breading the chicken.

"Want some help?" Angie asks.

"Yeah, that'd be great. I can get them floured and egged. I'll toss them into the panko. Want to coat them and lay them out on this pan?"

"You got it," she says. She swings by the sink to clean her hands. She looks over her shoulder, "What if everyone agrees to relocate out here?"

"What do you mean?"

"You know," she says, then pauses to gather her thoughts, "We have apartments and stuff back there. We can't just write it off and expect it'll disappear."

"We could get a couple pods and pay to have our stuff brought out. Just fly back for a week or so to take care of things."

"I don't like putting too much energy into things that are up in the air, but I think I want to get excited about this. It feels right." She dries her hands and comes over to finish off the chicken.

"We'll make it happen," I say as I watch her diligently sprinkle the bread crumbs on the chicken.

"Thanks, I hope we do." She leans in and rests her head on my shoulder for a few seconds.

"No sleeping on the job," I jokingly say. She giggles as she lifts her head and moves the finished chicken over to the tray.

There's certainly a pull between us, but I don't want to mislabel it or assume it's more than it is. It naturally feels right, so I'm going to see where it naturally goes.

Angie and I worked together to finish off dinner. We give Henry a little warning so he has time to properly wake up from his rest. I think Cis would be proud of us. The garlic smell is rich, and there's enough butter on the bread to clog city sewers. Even the salad looks like it came out of a magazine picture.

Henry comes out of his bedroom looking fresh.

"Whoa," Henry announces loudly, "I didn't know I had Michelin star chefs staying with me! It smells fantastic!"

"So do you, Henry," I tell him, pointing at him. "So do you!"

We settle down at the six-person dining room table and pass around the food. My stomach senses the food is coming, and it starts crying for help.

"So, Dad," Angie says. She brings her hands together as though she's praying.

Henry clears his throat. "So, Angie," he says back as he glances at her hands.

"How much do you enjoy your life back in Boston?" She begins tapping her fingers in a rolling motion.

"I enjoy it quite a bit, but it's not a unique situation. At the end of the day, I mostly work," he explains to her.

"Remember that place Brey was talking about?" she says and he nods, "We're thinking about going through with it. We'd be combining each of our dreams into one building. And we'd run it as a team."

"A lot happened during my nap," Henry says through his laughter, "Did you already buy a place too?" Angie and I both laugh with him.

"Not quite," I say, "We're considering looking at places around here, but there's one major caveat that would make or break the deal."

"I imagine that's if your friend was interested?" Henry asks.

"No, dad," Angie says.

I jump in and say, "It's if you're in."

"Wow," Henry says and his face turns serious. He starts to well up. Angie puts her arm on his shoulder and rubs it.

"Oh, don't cry! You're going to make me do the same!" Angie says to him as she makes a sad face, too.

"It's just," he says, then pauses to catch his breath, "It's just that it's been a while since I've had someone truly want me to be around."

"I've always wanted you around!" Angie exclaims.

"Well, of course, but people get busy. It's no one's fault. I was busy too," Henry says. He pauses again, then continues, "When I came out here for dinner, it was like I was visiting a life that I miss. I swear in my head. I was wondering how long this would last for. I don't want it to end."

"That's good because we have some ideas that could really use your help!" I say as I point out our napkin sketches of the building. And we have no idea where we'd all be living, but there's guaranteed a bed for you if you want it."

"I mean, I'd be an old fool if I said anything, but 'yes,'" Henry says.

"Just to reiterate, we're hoping in the next day or two to start exploring the city and see if we actually do want to commit to this city. It's really just an idea at this point," Angie tells him.

"Can I bring my lucky mug?" Henry asks.

I laugh and say, "You can bring all of your lucky belongings. We'll be going back to pack and ship stuff out. Again, that's assuming we commit to living here. You'll be with us at least to make that decision."

"Well," Henry says as he tastes the food, "you all made an old man really happy tonight. Thank you."

CHAPTER 22
~ Déjà vu ~

Officer Blake is our chauffeur today as we go in to visit Cis and Dakota. He arrives in an unmarked vehicle and parks a couple streets away. It makes the whole situation feel a bit more real.

"Good morning, Officer!" I say as I let him inside the front door.

"Good morning! Have you come across any suspicious activities since we last met?" Officer Blake removes his hat as he enters the house.

"Nothing on the inside. Hopefully, the same is true for the cameras?" I ask him. Angie and Henry walk from the kitchen to listen in.

"So far, so good," he says.

"Still no word on those Vegas punks?" Henry asks.

"They're still detained. They'll be charged for assault, but neither are speaking," Officer Blake tells him.

"That's unfortunate. Shall we head out?" Angie says as she approaches the door.

"Yeah, let's go see your friends," he says. He walks ahead of us to keep an eye on the surroundings.

As we step outside, it's slightly colder than we expected. While Officer Blake does a walk around the house, we run back inside for extra layers. Henry comes out with a fancy maroon sweater over his button-down shirt. He's bringing out the classy look. Angie has on Dakota's infamous jacket. She's either anxiously wanting to return it or to show off that it's still in its original condition. I'm a fan of the sixty-degree weather, so I opt out of smothering myself with cotton.

The drive through Denver is vastly different than either Boston or Jacksonville. Architecture is new, people are young, and people seem happy on the streets. It feels like a place I could call home. The minor hiccup would be the headache I'm getting from the elevation change, but it's pretty small. It supposedly fades after bodies adapt. We have at least a few weeks to see how true that is.

As we pull up to the clinic, it's absolutely breathtaking. It really does look like a ski resort with its bright wood structure loaded with windows. There are outdoor group activities happening with all smiling faces. Some places like this, choose to hang a carrot in front of you. You're rewarded for your successes. Other places ready a sturdy stick to smack you with it when you fail. I'm thankful for seeing the carrot end of the spectrum here.

Cis and Dakota come jogging down from a side door with these monk-like outfits on. They're white, baggy, and very light in material.

"You're here!" Dakota says as she runs to hug Angie.

"Hey, bud!" Cis runs over and hugs me. He turns to Henry and says, "Hello! You must be Angie's dad! I'm Cis, short for Francis." Cis reaches out and shakes Henry's hand.

"Cis? Never heard of you," Henry says as he starts to chuckle, which makes the rest of us laugh.

"Don't worry about the troublemaker here," I say as I point to Henry.

"We have so much to catch up on," Angie says as she moves from Dakota to Cis with hugs. Dakota moves quickly over to me and gives me a warm embrace.

Officer Blake introduced himself and then asked us, "Could I have you all move inside for now? I'm going to do a little walk around."

Angie and I happily oblige as we're both excited to see what the inside of this place looks like.

"We signed out one of the rooms for visitors," Dakota tells us, "Do you want to grab some coffee on the way?"

"Is it decaf?" I ask suspiciously.

"It's a barista running a full coffee bar. It can be whatever you want it to be," she tells me.

"Coffee!" Angie says. She looks like a kid at a candy store for the first time. Her eyes gaze at every luxurious feature they have available for patients here. As we pass by each thing, she lets out minor squeals and points every tiny thing out to Henry. He's getting an honest preview of living with her.

Angie and I get some fancy coffee drinks that would probably cost a fortune anywhere else. We return to the room and get cozy on their big, puffy leather couches.

"Before Officer Blake gets back, Angie and I have a very futuristic proposal for you," I tell Cis, "And of course, Dakota, you're invited in as well."

"Oh yeah? I hope it's not another road trip," he says through a grin.

"We're going to open a business, which will be a coworking space on one side and a cafe on the other. Angie will operate the front and fulfill the dreams she was previously talking to us about. And then we'd love it if you can own the kitchen operations," I tell him.

"What's the dream?" Dakota asks.

"I'd like to run a menu of drinks and food that are healthy mocks of things like comfort foods, which typically aren't healthy," Angie tells her. Dakota nods and smiles as she listens.

"What's the restriction on the food? How healthy does it have to be?" Cis asks.

"You and I would build the menu from the ground up. I was thinking you could do the menu as you like, and maybe I can have a health section on it?" Angie tells Cis.

"How early are you starting everything?" Cis asks us.

"First, we don't want you to be involved in anything until you're out of here and feeling good. Obviously, your sobriety means the world to us, and that's non-negotiable," I say, and Cis nods, "Secondly, we were going to start looking around and try to see what's available on the market. That alone will take time, even if we find a place tomorrow."

"That's true," Cis says, "Are you flying back to Boston to see the places?"

"Oh, right," Angie says, "Another tidbit we forgot to mention."

Cis raises his eyebrow at us.

I clear my throat and say, "We're actually thinking about checking out this area. It'll be a fresh start for all of us."

"I do like all of the sunshine," Dakota says, "And the people have been super friendly."

"Yeah?" Cis smiles at Dakota and says, "If you're in, I'm in."

"Of course I'm in," Dakota says then starts to speak out of the side of her mouth, "But there's one problem."

"What's that?" Angie asks.

"I don't really have any skills or experience for any of this," she says. "Like none." She holds up a big zero gesture with her hand.

I say to her, "You don't need any skills. You can be a floater and move around wherever you like. Then you can see what you enjoy or don't enjoy."

"Any good with a hammer?" Henry asks, "We'll likely have a lot of walls to put up."

"I'm awful with a hammer, but I'm a great gopher!" She changes her zero gesture to a one.

"Then you're hired!" Henry says with a smile.

"We'll keep in touch as we do our search. I definitely want everyone's buy-in before we commit to a location. Also, Angie, Henry, and I are going to explore the city in general just to make sure it's a place we want to call home," I tell them.

The door opens, and Officer Blake walks in with another officer.

"Hello again," he tells us, "We thought it'd be a good time to do a debrief on everything that's happened. For you guys, this is Officer Sampson. He's the on-site security here."

Dakota's phone vibrates. She pulls out her phone, and her face fades into a lighter shade.

"Private number again?" Officer Sampson asks. Dakota sighs and nods. After a deep breath, she unlocks her phone to reveal the message.

"Oh my God," she says as she drops her phone on the couch.

Cis immediately picks it up and simply says, "Fuck." He turns around the phone to show the rest of us. It's a picture of Officer Blake doing his walk around the clinic.

"They must have tracked my car. Stay in this room and lock it. Officer Sampson, come with me," Officer Blake says as they disappear through the door. I can hear them speaking into their radios as they move down the hall. Angie follows behind them and locks the door.

"I'm really sorry," Dakota says, "Perhaps I need to go back home after this and face the fire. This is going way too far." Her phone buzzes again. Cis turns the phone to Dakota to unlock it with the face recognition feature.

"Sorry, I should've asked. May I?" Cis asks her.

"Yeah, it's as much your nightmare as it is mine at this point," she tells him.

He flips it open and then immediately looks out the window. We move to look over his shoulder and see it's an aerial picture, likely taken by a drone. It's a clear shot into the windows where we're sitting. Dakota is front and center in the picture.

"Shit," I say as I run over to the windows and quickly roll down the blinds. I turn and tell everyone, "Quick! Move to the sides of the room. Expect the worst and take cover."

Cis grabs the tables and sets them on their sides. It'll at least protect us from something like broken glass. We hear Officer Blake come around the outside of the building and tell Officer Sampson by radio that there's an active drone. The walls and windows are pretty thick, but when we're quiet, we hear the buzzing noises of the drone.

POP!

A gunshot blast sounds from outside our window. Everyone jumps and Dakota lets out a small scream. Then, a loud banging sound on the window. It's a similar sound to when a bird flies head-first into a window. We all duck behind the tables, expecting glass to follow.

It's silent. It's way too silent. We can hear some cries of the patients from afar, but all of the nearby buzzing sounds and voices have halted. It feels like eternity since the last noise. Some footsteps walk up to the window then stop. For a sunny city, the unfortunate overcast skies paint a very dull and rounded picture of the person on the shades.

Like a jack in the box, the weasel pops, and those feet scatter rapidly into the woods. The cracking of twigs can be heard getting further and further away. The door to our building swings open, and we hear police radio chatter. Footsteps approach the door.

"Drone is down," Officer Sampson says into the radio.

"Where's Officer Blake?" I ask through the door.

"He had a suspicion on the direction of the drone operator. He moved in on foot," he says.

"Shouldn't you be out there backing him up?" Angie yells at him.

"No. My order is to remain here and keep you all safe. So please stay down and keep the door locked. Our backup should be here shortly."

"Dakota, was Seth part of a larger group?" I ask her. This seems deeper and darker than just some junkie missing his ex. Dakota seems frustrated with the question. Before this goes to a bad place, I tell her, "Sorry, they've probably been drilling you already. It's not my place to question."

"No, it's not that," Dakota says, "I'm frustrated with myself for not really paying attention. People came and went often. To be honest, he said the money he had was from his dad." Dakota pauses for a few then says, "I've never met his dad. I really am naive."

Angie shushes her and says, "Don't be hard on yourself. He's the bad guy, not you. It's nothing you should own."

"So this whole operation could be Seth as the mastermind or as a ground soldier," Cis says.

"Or anywhere in the middle," Dakota says.

"I don't see how we're going to figure this out unless we get our hands on one of these assholes," I say.

Officer Blake makes it back without success in locating the drone operator. Given the quality of the drone, the person could have been a mile away. If they drove off after flying it into the window, they easily could've been five or more miles away by the time he made it there.

They decide it's best if we go back to our rental, and the cops can watch the cameras for activity again. The top theory is that it took this long for them to catch up to us in Colorado, so maybe they'll stick their noses up again soon. An undercover cop will be there in person, too, watching the cameras from inside. The cop will switch out around midnight, and another will finish the night with us.

The same setup is happening here at the clinic for Dakota and Cis. Since there are a lot more patients here, though, a team of three will be monitoring the grounds and cameras.

Officer Blake leads us to his car again. He and Officer Sampson inspect it to look for any possible trackers. Nothing obvious is found, though.

"You think they'd at least start the car before we got in. What if there's an ignition bomb or something?" I ask.

"You watch too many movies. Besides, maybe they think I'm going to steal it," Henry says from the front seat.

"Movies or not, it's so stuffy in here. Can you pull my sleeve?" Angie says. I give her a pull to help her take off the denim jacket.

"This jacket officially yours now?" I ask Angie.

"I tried giving it back. She told me to hang onto it."

Even though this car is unmarked, it's still a police cruiser with child locks on the backseat. So we're at Officer Blake's mercy to get fresh air. He eventually realizes it as he apologizes when he enters the car. I do feel bad for Henry in the front with the button-down and sweater.

We get dropped off at the house, and Officer Blake stays and waits for another officer to get there. He'll be our roommate for the day. He introduces himself as Officer White, who appears to be a quiet older guy who clearly would rather be home with his own family.

It takes no time at all for Officer White and Henry to kick off an extended conversation. The officer is ex-Air Force, so they talk about planes and piloting for a while. Although Henry was on the commercial side of things during his career, he does have a strong passion for fighter jets. They're probably both feeling quite grounded on this day.

Angie and I will make the best of it. We just ordered some more groceries so we can make lunch and dinner for everyone. It feels kind of like a snow day where everyone is trapped inside but healthy.

We hover over my laptop for a while and search the market for buildings we can invest in. We're starting the search with a simple two-part filter. One, it has a kitchen. Two, it's been on the market for a while, so negotiations can be stronger for us. Since we have Henry, it's okay if it needs work. We bookmark a few locations and plan to show Cis in person during our visit tomorrow.

The doorbell rings. It seems about time for the groceries, but Officer White still takes caution as he answers the door. It's someone trying to sell pest control services. We certainly need that. I hope they target humans.

The doorbell rings again. The officer looks at the camera and doesn't see anyone. He quickly rewinds and finds someone flew a drone down and used that to ring it. These creeps are high-tech.

"Please make sure all doors and windows are locked. Put shades in the closed position. We're going to barricade a bit just in case," Officer White says to us. As our party gets smaller, these run-ins keep getting scarier. It's like they want us to know they're watching every move we make.

Officer White calls Officer Blake to return, but there's no answer. After another attempt, he calls the station to see if they can locate him.

"I'm sorry, what happened!?" Officer White says in a panic over the phone. He says a lot of "mhmms" then hangs up.

"What happened? Is he okay?" I ask.

"No," Officer White says as he shakes his head at the floor. "He stopped at that Markdown Market convenience store on his way out of here.

As he went around the back of the building to use their bathroom, some fucking meth heads jumped him."

"What's his status? Can we go see him?" Angie asks.

"They thought there was some brain swelling, and almost put him into a medically-induced coma." Our jaws drop. "Luckily he seems cleared of that though," he tells us. "He's considered stabilized at the moment."

"My god" I say. Shaking my head, I turn and walk away. Angie follows behind with her hand resting on the middle of my back.

I whisper to Angie, "We've gotta end this shit."

She scoffs in disbelief. "Yes, we do."

CHAPTER 23

~ Regroup ~

"I have a theory. Wait here," Angie tells me. She pulls her dad aside, and they talk quietly in his room. He gives her a tight hug before she leaves the room. I continue to act casually, though, as their suspicious behavior is out of sight from Officer White. I meet eyes with Angie and she gestures for me to come into the room.

"Want to join us for a movie?" Henry asks me.

"Yeah, what are you thinking?" I ask him.

"I guess it depends what this rental has to offer!" he says with a forced chuckle.

As I enter the room, Angie has me come into the bathroom with her. I notice the ottoman from the bedroom is sitting under the window. She quietly closes the door. Henry turns on the television at a high volume. The bedroom door opens and closes again.

We hear a kitchen cabinet open and close loudly. Angie immediately unlocks the window after. Then, a second slam almost immediately after. Angie gradually opens the window with great stealth. Clearly, they're communicating in a way only a father and daughter can.

"Hey, White," we hear Henry yelling loudly over the television. "Could you come help an old man out? I can't read this."

A few moments pass, and then we hear smashing glass. Angie pulls me close to her.

She whispers in my ear, "Grab my feet." Then, she lunges her body through the window. I grab her feet as they almost slip by. It slows down her fall just enough that she lands in a handstand on the ground. I release her feet, and she gracefully lands like a perfect cartwheel. Unbelievable. While I sit in awe, she waves at me to hurry up.

I step on the ottoman and start to lean out of the window. Angie comes up and hugs me tightly as she drags my body through the window.

"We've gotta move," she says, and I run with her to the picnic table. We use that to bounce over the fence and disappear into the neighbor's yard.

"Okay, we're off their radar now," Angie says to me quietly, "Let's move a few streets away and call for a ride."

"Where we going?" I ask her.

"To the Markdown Market, with one stop on the way," I'm not sure what the angle is here, considering a police officer was just attacked. I imagine the place is swarming with cops. With or without ambiguity, her plans seem to have solid success rates.

The first stop is a costume store. We're months away from Halloween, so I'm astonished that these things are even open. I can't imagine their business plan expects much inflow of cash during these other fifty weeks of the year.

"What's the game plan?" I ask Angie.

"We're accidentals. They want Dakota."

"So, where do these costumes fit into the plan? Going to turn Dakota into a brunette?" I ask as we walk toward the wigs.

"Close. I'm going to become Dakota," she says.

"Stop," I grab her arm, "This sounds like an awful plan."

"That's because it is an awful plan, but it's all I have," she winks at me and moves into the wigs. As much as this plan scares me for Angie, I go along with it because it may just be the beginning of the end to all of this madness.

Angie tries on several wigs. For some of the outrageous rocker ones, we have to imagine what they'd look like with some hair product. She holds down the metal hair and it actually has the same color patterns as Dakota. Angie walks around the store to find a baseball cap and an oversized hoodie. With her head ducked down, any angle could easily pass for Dakota, especially to some whacked-out meth heads.

We purchase the supplies and get another ride to bring us to Markdown Market. Our ride drops us off a few blocks from the convenience store. Like any cliche, there's a rusty white van about a block away from the convenience store that has a direct view of the unmarked vehicle Officer Blake was using. The van is unmarked and has its engine running. Angie leads us through a path that stays out of sight of the van until we're a building away.

"Promise me, no matter what happens," she says to me. "You'll stay right here."

"You know I can't promise that," I say.

"Then I guess your word will have to do." Angie drops her cap and purposely strolls like a nervous body, trying to look casual. There is no end to her talents.

She looks around as she gets close to the car. Then she quickly reaches through a broken window and grabs for Dakota's jacket in the backseat. As she struggles to grab it, the white van pulls into the convenience store quickly and brakes hard next to her. This cuts off any view I have of Angie. I just hear the door fling open, and then a struggle occurs.

I take a photo of the van's license plate, so I can hopefully track it down later. My heart is racing. My hands are shaking. I hear the door slam shut and then silence. Even my heart appears to have stopped beating.

Then, the moment I was terrified for. The van peels out and pulls out of the parking lot. Is this the last time I'll see Angie? How do I explain this to Henry?

All of a sudden, the van spots me and veers in my direction. Perhaps I won't have the opportunity to explain anything. The van slams its brakes next to me. Only the sliding door doesn't open.

The horn goes off multiple times. I hesitantly bend to look in the passenger window and Angie is driving. Holy shit! She's gesturing for me to hurry the hell up. I jump into the passenger seat, not caring about the consequences.

"Well, okay," I say to Angie. She's wearing Dakota's jacket. Two guys are in the back, unconscious.

She hands me a taser and says, "I don't think they'll be moving on us. But put an end to it if they do."

"Got it, but where'd you get a taser?"

"The guy with the fucked up jaw had it. It was almost a clean shot," Angie says as she pulls up her right pant leg. There's a minor burn mark on her calf.

"Damn, you got zapped?"

"A tiny one. My foot was already touching the top of his mouth by the time he connected," Angie says as she snickers. She looks at me and says, "Something tells me they thought they had it in the bag."

"I sort of did, too," I say. Angie gives me a look like I'm crazy. Perhaps I am. I ask, "So what now?"

"We get some answers," Angie tells me. Her knuckles go white as she grips the steering wheel tightly.

As we're driving, she has me collect the jacket off of the one fallen meth heads.

"Care to fill me in on the rest of this plan of yours?"

"I'd rather you be a victim than an accomplice if this all falls apart. So, no."

A buzz comes from the backseat. I move back and check the guys' pockets. One of their phones has some messages. Luckily he has facial recognition on for another easy unlock. I open the message and it says "Come back. We got her."

"I think they have Dakota," I tell Angie, who immediately looks worried.

"Got a phone number or private call?"

"Phone number."

"Excellent," Angie says as she puts her phone on speakerphone. She gets Henry on the speakerphone and gives him the number.

"Glad to hear you," Henry says, "I'm on it. Love you." Then he hangs up.

"That was short?" I ask Angie. She laughs in response.

She tells me, "My dad always said, 'less talk, more action.'" I see she took it to heart.

It feels like we're driving aimlessly, but perhaps it's part of Angie's plan. I look at the Taser in my hand, the guys in the back, and the puddle of blood forming under an obviously broken jaw. I sit quietly for a bit, though, as thoughts fill my head.

"I'm clearly an accomplice at this point," I tell Angie, "Which, with you, I want to be. Could you please fill me in on at least the next step?"

Just as I finish, Angie's phone buzzes. She looks down at it, smiling, then holds it up for me to see. It's an address.

"How cryptic," I say.

She laughs and says, "My dad has a friend who has some special powers. He was able to trace the cell phone through triangulation."

"How accurate is it?"

"Probably not super useful in a downtown location. Sometimes, it'd give you a neighborhood or cross streets. Given that this is an address, it's probably correct."

"So we're just driving up and knocking on the door?" I ask her.

"Probably not. Going to drop these assholes off first. You mind driving?"

Angie pulls over, and I take over the driving. At least now I have some instruction to work with. We're heading to the police station. Angie's in the back, securing the two guys with zip ties and duct tape. It was nice of them to bring the supplies.

After we park a block away, Angie gets out of the back and then marks the door with a big X, using a hammer to scratch the paint. She empties a backpack that she found in the van and fills it with the zip ties, duct tape, and a hammer. We walk a few blocks away and then she makes an anonymous call using a burner phone they had. She tells the police those guys are responsible for Officer Blake's incident and that we'll step forward with more information soon. Just like the movies, she wipes the phone off of prints then tosses it into a bush.

"Now to the address?" I ask. She nods slowly as she looks down at her phone and calls in a ride for us.

She looks up and says, "It's apparently only fifteen minutes away."

"What happens if these people have guns?" I ask her.

"We take them," she says as she shrugs.

"You make it sound so easy. There's no way I can do what you do."

"Okay, then I take them," she says. She clasps my hand with hers and wraps her other hand around my arm.

Our ride swings by and takes us to our destination, which is a few blocks from our actual destination. It's a very ritzy rural area. The house is huge, with a humongous yard and a fancy gate manned by thugs. Something wasn't right about the house. Seth is from Florida, so it seems weird there's this mansion in Denver that they're at.

I search for the address online and found it's a holiday rental. That kind of ties it all together, but it also means we have no idea how long they'll be here. Or who is actually in there?

Angie guides me onto a neighbor's lawn. We run up to their shed. She removes Dakota's jacket and tosses it inside on a workbench. The door is left slightly ajar.

"Don't want to get it dirty?" I ask her. Seems like it's a bit late for that.

"Yeah. See the opening under the deck?" she asks me.

"I do."

"Please go hide under there. No noises. I'll tell you when to come out. And if anyone shows up, I need you to wedge the same number of fingers through the boards on the second step."

I'm not in a position to argue with Angie. She really is the main character of this story. I jog over to the porch, staying close to the wall to avoid detection. I crawl under the porch and align myself, looking out from the second step. She moves to the side of the shed, then nothing. I suspect she's still over there, but I can never be sure.

A sharp whistle echoes over the wall between the two yards. One of the guards comes over the wall. Given the arch of the jump, he probably got boosted over by another guard. He scopes the place out. His glance passes over the deck I'm under, but I'm fairly certain he didn't see me.

The voice on the other side of the wall tells someone, "We've got company."

As the guy slowly walks up to the shed, I wedge a single finger between the boards. The man pulls a gun from his holster. He raises it up as he reaches for the door with his other hand.

"Aha!" he says as he rips open the shed door. He sees the jacket then looks clearly confused. He lowers his gun.

Angie sneaks around the door and smashes her hammer over top of the guy's head.

WHAM!

Catching his body from falling, she quickly drags him to the deck. I help pull him under the deck. She hands me the backpack with the duct tape and zip ties. As she gets back into position, I make sure this guy won't be leaking any noises. I also still have the taser if the need arises.

"What do you see over there?" the voice over the fence asks. The person goes quiet momentarily, probably waiting for an answer. It repeats itself in a more nervous tone, "What do you see over there?"

A second voice whispers, "Where the fuck did he go?"

The voices tamper off. I shift my body around, trying to see if any angle produces results. There's really nothing in sight, and that includes Angie. I can only assume she's still on this side of the wall and is about to repeat the same bop-from-behind move.

Two men come from the left side of the house, both with pistols drawn and aimed toward the shed. Two others come from the right side. This isn't looking good for our odds. I hold four fingers through the boards so she knows she's clearly outnumbered.

As they circle in on the shed, another guy gets boosted up to stand on the wall. I wedge my thumb into the crack as well. I really hope she got out of there, or at least just stays put if she's well hidden.

"What the fuck is that?" the guy on the wall asks. I realize he's pointing at my fat fingers sticking through the cracks.

One guy from the left turns around and says, "I don't know. Mushrooms?"

The guy on the wall yells back, "Those aren't fucking mushrooms, you idiot. Go check it out!"

Well fuck. All I've got is this shitty Taser. I decide to leave my fingers unmoved in the hopes that they abort their search. This would have been a great time for Angie to be here with me. She'd probably have eight ideas already, each one successful and more creative than the last. Just my dumb ass is here now, and it's about to get a bullet put in it.

"Oh shit, man! I think they're fingers! Someone is under there! Is that you, bud?" he asks. He thinks it's their missing guard that lies possibly dead behind me. I can see the guy instructing the other guy on the left to move in on the side of the deck where I had entered.

He sticks his head in the opening and sees me. Just as he does, the sliding door of the house opens quickly, and a really loud gunshot blasts through the air. The guy inspecting my fingers collapses on the stairs. I pull my fingers away as blood slowly leaks down through the cracks.

"Get off my lawn, you fucking junkies," says a man inside the house.

The man by the deck opening leans toward the house to increase his line of sight. With his gun drawn, he quickly fires off a round. There's a loud thump that comes from inside the door. I can hear the echo underneath the deck.

BANG, BANG!

Two more shots fire off, and the men on the right both drop to the ground. I can see Angie moving around the side of the shed, still out of view of the man on the wall and the one near me.

"Someone is behind the shed! Do you have an angle?" this guy shouts to the man on the wall.

"No, I'll cover you. Move in," the man on the wall shouts back.

"Fuck that shit," this guy mutters. He keeps his focus and gun aimed at the hidden side of the shed.

I need to stop being a coward and make a move. Very quietly, I lift my body up on my toes and fingertips. My days of practicing planks were too short, but at least I had some adrenaline on my side. I'm under the belief that he thought we were both dead bodies, so perhaps I'll have the element of surprise working for me.

Slowly crawling up behind him, I pull out the taser and just stick him in his lower back. He starts to scream and shake violently. It all comes to a halt when another gunshot hits him in the head. I quickly roll back under the deck in hopes he doesn't see me.

"We need more backup!" the man on the wall yells. He jumps off the wall, and based on the sound of his scampering, he makes his way to the house.

I see Angie poke her head out to communicate with me. Scurrying back to the deck entryway, I pull the gun out from under the dead body. I navigate under the deck to the other side. There's another opening that Angie is moving toward. Moving around the perimeter of the yards, she uses the trees for temporary cover between dashes.

"You okay?" she asks me.

"Am I okay?! Are you okay?" I ask her back.

"Yeah, now we have to move fast. They may take Dakota and drive out of here."

I follow Angie's lead around a few neighbors' yards to approach their mansion from the other side.

CHAPTER 24

~ Last Stand ~

We successfully put the house on high alert. It certainly wasn't the intention, but after the nightmares they've cast on us, it seems fair. There's not a clear path inside, so we wait and study their movements a bit more.

My phone buzzes. I pull my phone out and it's a message from Cis. They took him at the same time that they got Dakota. He managed to stash his phone in his shoe and the idiots never checked there. There's a laundry room where they have him handcuffed to a pipe towel rack. He says they have a rotation of guards manning the outside of the room, but half of them drift off when they sit still for more than a minute.

He hears Dakota's and Seth's voices from time to time, but he doesn't know which floor or room they're in. There's been another bigger voice yelling at Dakota as well. Based on what he's overhearing, it's Seth's dad that runs the operation. There's a thumb drive that Dakota apparently took when she was fucked up and angry at them. It's important enough to kill people over. Dakota doesn't recall anything about it.

I told Cis to share his location, then silence his phone and put it back in his shoe. My final message to him is: 'we're coming for you, bud.' Angie and I do the same with our phones so we can find each other if we have to split up. Based on the GPS location, Cis seems to be on the same side of the house we're on. I probably should have asked if there were windows.

Angie comes up with a route around the house. Luckily for us, the mansion is the low point surrounded by a small hill. This offers a few viewpoints where we can hopefully get a decent look into a window or two.

"Wait," I whisper to her.

"What's wrong?" she anxiously asks, clearly in a hurry to make a move.

"I'm hoping I have a chance to contribute," I say. I pull out my phone and look up the mansion on the local real estate sites. It was sold two years ago, which means they probably had images up at that point. I switched over to a web archives website and am able to grab the listing from that time period.

I simply say, "Tada!" I hold up my phone to Angie and show her the floor plans of the house. It's pretty unlikely there were any huge renovations during this time. I send her a copy of the plans and we devise a plan to grab Cis first. Conveniently, he's on the first floor at a window we've basically been staring at from our current location. Somebody rolled a perfect die for us!

"Our best bet is if I can lure them away from there," Angie says, "Then you grab him from the window."

"That's fair. Going to message him to get ready. Hopefully he sees it." As I punch in a message to Cis, I try imagining what he's going through. It's all been uncharted waters and doesn't seem to be getting any better.

"Good. Have him tap the window or something when the coast is clear."

I ask, "What happens if he can't reach the window?"

"Always hope for the best. We can't afford anything short of that!"

Even with our friends on the line, not to mention our own lives, she still finds it in her to be hopeful. Honestly, the odds have been pretty much against her all day, though. And here she is.

"By the way, do you know how to shoot that thing?" Angie asks me.

"Aim and squeeze, don't pull?"

"Precisely. Aim for the biggest target. I imagine you don't have a lot of practice."

"I don't," I say, then give her a look. "How the hell do you have practice?"

"We'll talk about it later," she says.

"I honestly never thought I'd be in a shootout. I'm a fucking engineer," I say and softly snicker.

"Don't undersell yourself. You're almost an author, too!" She smiles and pokes my nose with her finger.

We hear car engines starting from the garage area on the other side.

"You've gotta be kidding me," Angie says as she migrates to the side to get a better view. She says, "Motherfuckers are leaving."

Three matching sports cars start to pull out of the garages. The windows are tinted, so we can't make out who's in what car. Two of the cars split for each of the gates, while another one sits idle. I imagine they're going to pick the cleaner route.

The main gate is much larger, so it takes its sweet time opening. The side gate opens relatively fast as the car revs its engine. Just as the gate opens enough, there's a loud squealing of the tires. I really hope Dakota's not in that car. It's as good as gone.

Half the car disappears behind the gate when there's a loud crashing sound. Then the car comes back in a rush. A big-ass Hummer with a front guard decided it wasn't go-time yet.

The third car panics and loads up behind the main gate. As the gate opens, it's a clear shot down the road. The car squeals its tires and shoots out of the gate like a bullet. As it clears the gate, a second Hummer t-bones the son of a bitch. The car gets hit so hard that the Hummer and the car both clear the gate.

The third car stays patient for clearance. It hesitates but continues to creep up the driveway to escape. Out of nowhere, a large box truck drives up and perfectly blocks the driveway. The doors of the sports car open. Seth and a bodyguard get out of the passenger side. Seth ducks behind the bodyguard as well as he can. Both are wearing Kevlar, though.

On the driver's side, Seth's dad gets out and moves low to the back door. He opens it and pulls out Dakota by her hair. He points his gun at her head as he uses her as a human shield.

They disappear back inside through the garage. I see some recognizable figures jogging away from the Hummers.

"Is that Jamal and Micah?" I mouth words to Angie.

"Sure looks like it!" she mouths back with a grin.

I text our group chat to verify and I almost immediately receive back a message from Cis reading, "Had to hedge my bets."

I gave the group text an update on what was happening. He mentions there were still several people inside as those ones tried to clear out. So we're likely looking at a dozen now.

"Tell him we're coming to get him," Angie says. As I finish typing it into my phone, she walks down the small hill and hoists herself onto the wall. She waves one arm to advise me to follow along. I run and lunge at the wall. It's not nearly as graceful as Angie's leap, but I make it, belly down on the top of the wall.

While some tall shrubs help camouflage our torsos, we are sitting ducks in this position. I think everyone is regrouping inside, so we drop down and then sprint to the window that Cis is behind. As we get close, we keep our heads as low as we can. With the stolen guns drawn, it all feels too surreal.

I text the group to let us know when the coast is clear. Jamal responds that he wrapped around the yards and is watching from behind. Micah adds that he circled the other way to watch the front and side yards that we don't have a view of. Hopefully, with all of these eyes, we don't lose track of any of these pests.

"Bad news," a text message from Jamal comes in, "Someone just went in and took Cis." My heart sinks for so many reasons. We were this fucking close to him. Angie and I share a worried look after she reads the message.

After a moment of silence, Angie looks excited and asks, "Don't you have his phone tracking?"

"Oh shit," I say as I load up the tracking app. I have Angie load the floor plans back up, and we predict his general placement based on how the dot moves around the house. If they're being used as key hostages, I imagine Seth and his dad are going to stay close to them. That's really their only ticket out of here.

The dot moves toward the stairwell.

"I think they're heading upstairs," I tell Angie as I continue to watch. The dot moves in the opposite direction. I quickly say, "No, I think they're going to the basement."

I message Jamal and Micah to look for any cellar doors around the perimeter. Looking back, I can see the very top of their heads moving around a bit.

Micah responds, "Got it. Cellar door over here. Break in shrub."

Angie's phone buzzes. It's a call coming in from Henry.

"Hey, hard to talk right now," Angie says quietly into the phone. She pauses, then turns to take a look backward. Henry and Officer White are there, each equipped with a rifle.

"It's very nice to see you," she says into the phone. I look back and see Jamal catching up with them. Officer White does a slow jog around the house. I imagine he's joining Micah to watch the cellar door.

I message the group and let them know who these men with rifles are. Then I type the most important question of all, "How are your throwing arms?"

There's radio silence as they probably don't understand the question. I follow up with, "Grab some rocks and let's break some windows!"

THUMP THUMP THUMP.

Maybe their aim isn't as accurate as I hoped. At least they're hitting the mansion across the large lawn.

SMASH!

As the first window starts to smash, I reach up with a rock and break the window to the laundry room. I toss the rock in afterward just to eliminate any suspicion. Angie looks at me in awe. She seems impressed that I'm not as useless as I thought. Now we have some level of ears inside and their general location.

"What do you think?" I whisper to Angie, then point to the window.

"Got my back?" she asks.

"Always." She nods to me. I share my location with Jamal and Micah and pass along the message: "We're headed in. You have our location. I'll message you when we switch floors."

I turn around and get a thumbs-up from Henry. Jamal gestures to Micah to make sure he sees it. After confirmation, Jamal gives us a thumbs up as well.

"Be safe, fam," Jamal messages back.

I reach into the broken window and unlock it. With the utmost care, I slide the window open. At about the at halfway mark, a gunman pops around the corner and raises his gun. As he pulls the trigger, Angie shoves me to the side.

My body halts all movements as the bullets fly out the window. Angie says something to me, but I'm unable to focus. A separate popping sound joins the ruckus then a deafening silence. There seems to be a ceasefire in his battle, but my body is no longer under my control.

Angie leans down and shakes me as I lie on the ground, facing up at her. Her mouth moves, but the words aren't audible. As quickly as it got silent, her words have sound again.

"They know our location. We have to move!" she screams at me. Our hands meet, and she yanks me off the ground. Angie reaches down and retrieves my gun and phone for me.

Henry shoots another round into the room through the window. There's a groan, and then more machine gun fire comes blasting through the half-opened window. A few bullets penetrate the wall next to us. Angie lifts her gun to one of the holes and shoots the gunman through it. The trajectory of the flow of bullets suggests he was hit and fell backward.

We turn to look at Henry, who gives us the thumbs up. Bullets come ripping out through an upstairs window as glass falls around us. Henry falls out of sight. Anger comes across Angie's face. She shoves the window open, jumps up on my bent knee, and hops into the laundry room.

Her left hand reaches out the window, and she taps the wall. She covers the door as I lift myself through the window. I can see scratch marks on the pipe that Cis was handcuffed to. Angie tucks her pistol in her belt and grabs the dead guy's machine gun. She pops the clip to verify it didn't run dry.

She points down at the phone and then taps herself on the left shoulder, right shoulder, and then at the base of her neck. I'm mostly certain she's giving me directions on how to guide her through the house. I bring up the floor plans again and tap her left shoulder. We hear footsteps upstairs above through the floor. Angie stays far left to check the opposite corner. She bounces to the right then takes a quick look down the hallway.

BANG BANG BANG.

Someone fires down the hall at her. She drops down on her knees and holds the gun sideways, firing down the hall. Another person comes in from the right and kicks the gun out of her hands. I quickly raise my gun and squeeze. POW! The man stumbles back a couple steps and hits the wall. He looks at me like I have some nerve. His eyes roll to the back of his head, and he slides down the wall, ever so limp. Angie pulls the gun back into the laundry room with us.

"Nooo!" we hear from around the corner. Bullets rip through the walls. We stay down as they hit right above us. Angie holds the gun up this time and fires back. Some moaning and coughing occur then another thumping sound follows. Her ability to locate these people through walls makes me wonder what other superpowers she has. Also, glad she's on my side.

More gunfire erupts from upstairs. This time, it's on the far side of the house where Micah and Officer White are. It's impossible to know who's winning, but it'll at least take some of the heat off of us. Angie does a quick check on either side, then moves right first. It's a dead end on that side, so it makes sense to avoid anyone else trying to sneak in behind us.

Another set of shots occurs above the laundry room. After clearing the guest area, we move back into the laundry room. We see Henry trying to pop up for a shot, but he's being held back by a couple people targeting him. I nod to Angie, telling her I've got this one. I estimate roughly where the scumbag is and unload on the floor below him. It stops the other firing long enough that Henry is able to pull himself up and take a shot. Two thumps later, we get a thumbs-up from Henry. Angie blows him a kiss.

"How fast can you run?" Angie asks me.

"I'm not a track star, but fast enough. What are you thinking?"

She pulls the few bodies into the laundry room. After closing and locking the door; I help her stack them as a barricade. I give her a puzzled look.

"Just securing our entrance back if we need it," she says. Then she gestures for me to jump out of the window again. After I essentially fall out, she hands me the weapons the guys have dropped.

"Better plan. Stay here," Angie looks out to her dad and signals she's going to run out. He lifts the rifle and gestures for her to come. She sprints across the lawn then takes cover before the shrubs. One by one, she sets the extra guns up on the wall. After the last one is placed, she runs back to me. I then watch Jamal's arm reach up there and grab each of the guns.

"Now we have four gunmen on the outside," she says and smiles at me.

"Where did you learn all of this?" I ask her. She just winks.

Angie communicates with her dad that we're going to enter the window to the right instead. It's the guest room we saw. With the laundry room barricaded now, we should have a clear path down the hall. Henry shifts down that way a bit to get a better view. Jamal reappears after delivering a gun to his brother. It just dawned on me that their friend with the box truck just disappeared after that first bit of action. I don't blame him.

I hear large vehicles approaching. Angie and I are about to jump inside the window when a call comes in from Cis. I immediately answer without considering any consequences.

"You must be Brey," says the voice from the other side.

"And you must be the maniac behind all of this madness. What's your deal?"

"I heard you have a certain jacket in your possession. We want it. We'll trade your friend for it," he says to me.

"Don't do it," Cis yells.

"It turns out my junkie of a son stashed something in that jacket and forgot."

"The tracker?" Angie says off camera.

"Tracker?" I ask, "God, that explains so much."

"You son of a bitch," I hear Dakota say. We hear a loud slap followed by her moaning.

"Get fucked!" Cis says before a thump.

"Now, now. Don't make me shoot you before we can settle a deal," Seth's dad says to Cis. He looks into the camera and asks us, "Look at this mess. Are you sure you even want him?" He turns the camera to Cis, who has a bloody nose and some gashes in his face. Seth lies on the ground, holding his own face. Then he turns to Dakota, who's now being restrained by their bodyguard. The side of her face is a deep red.

"Okay," Seth's dad says, "I'm growing impatient." He fires a round into Cis's thigh. He immediately falls to the ground, screaming in pain. Dakota starts crying loudly in the corner.

"Stop!" Angie says, "The jacket is next door. I need to go get it!"

"Okay. Call back when you have it."

Angie moves quickly to collect the jacket from the shed next door. As she gets back, I make a return call.

"We have it," I tell him, "Where's the handoff?"

"Toss it down the stairs, then we'll send him up. That is, if he can still walk."

I look behind us and see it was actually a boatload of officers that showed up. They've taken the guns from Henry, Jamal, and Micah, but at least we have some real sharpshooters now covering us.

Two officers run up to us, so I mute the phone.

"What's happening?" one asks us.

"He wants this jacket," I tell them. As they think about the next move, I ask them, "I have a plan. We're going to need some Kevlar vests."

"We can't let you go in there," the officer says with his head-to-toe armor.

"If you wanted an opinion, you should've moved faster," Angie says, "We're going with his plan." She smiles at me and nods.

I unmute the phone and say, "Hey asshole, you still there?"

"Oh yes. I'm getting impatient," he says, "Your buddy here is looking a little pale, too."

"The two of us are coming down with the jacket for the exchange," I tell him.

"One is enough," he says, "Just you."

"If you wanted that, you shouldn't have shot him."

"Fair enough. Hurry up, as I'm feeling a little trigger-happy."

Angie and I put on our Kevlar vests. The officers nervously adjust them as we just gaze into each other's eyes. There's no questioning between us on whether this is the right thing to do. We don't fear the consequences. We just wish we had more time.

I clasp Angie's hand, and we walk to the cellar doors. As we do our final march, I look up at the sky and wonder if I'll see it again. We approach the cellar doors then turn back to the wall where Henry, Jamal, and Micah look on. The looks on their faces aren't very promising for our destiny.

Angie grabs one side of the door, and I grab the other as we flip them open. I walk down the stairs first, as I'd rather take any preemptive shots from these scumbags. My eyes slowly adjust as I walk down some bright white stairs with black edging. I begin to enter a large room littered with empty casks and wine racks with not a bottle in sight. It appears no wine came with this rental.

As I turn into the room, I see the people we're here to meet. Seth's dad, I presume, holds a gun to Cis's head, who's sitting on the ground applying pressure to his wound. A larger tattooed man holds Dakota close, also with a gun against her head. Seth sits against the wall tending to what appears to be a broken nose. Dakota and Cis both look like they're in physical pain. They shake their heads at us as we meet eyes. It seems they didn't want us to join them on this little escapade.

"Ah, you brought us some Kevlar. How kind of you," Seth's dad says. He uses his gun to tell me to move to the side. As I do so, he says to Angie, "So, you must be the bitch who interrupted my men." As the words leave his mouth, he fires a round into her thigh. She grunts loudly as she falls to her hands and knees.

"Stop! We brought you the fucking jacket as you requested!" I yell at Seth's dad as I raise the jacket up for him to see.

"Cool. Take off the vests and hand it all over," he says as he points the gun at my chest.

I sigh deeply and tell him, "You don't know how much work it took to get these fucking things on."

"Take it off," he says as he raises the gun and aims it at my head.

"Okay, okay." I begin to undo a couple straps and try to slip it over my head with little success.

"Are you an infant?" Seth's dad says, "Take the fucking thing off."

"Hold this," I say as I toss the jacket up in the air to Dakota. The bodyguard loosens his grip just enough for her to reach out and grab it.

As she reaches down, I reach under my vest to try to lift it over my head. Seth's dad seems annoyed with my inability to remove the vest. I grab onto a flashbang I had wedged into my vest, pull the pin, and drop it. It rolls down my leg and I give it a kick forward. Quickly, I pull up my vest to cover my eyes. Angie drops her head the rest of the way to the ground and covers it with her arms.

POW! The flashbang pops off, blinding all five of them. Unfortunately, we had no way to warn Dakota and Cis, so they're victims of it as well.

Angie pulls out a gun from under her vest. POP POP! Clean headshots of both the dazed bodyguard and the guy formerly known as Seth's dad. The bodyguard's grip stays firm as it pulls Dakota to the ground.

"What's the fuck!" Seth screams. As his eyes stop moving and focus on Angie, he changes his tone and begs Angie not to shoot him. Dakota throws the bodyguard's arm off of her and runs over to Cis to help control the bleeding. I turn around and help Angie sit down.

While my head is turned, another gunshot goes off. I whip my head around and see Seth on the ground. His hand is inches from the bodyguard's gun. Dakota is in a state of shock as the gun she holds slowly smokes from the barrel. Blood starts covering Seth's shirt in the chest area. His eyes roll back as his head falls back on the floor.

"Move in! Move in!" I scream into the microphone attached to my vest.

Heavily armed men flood the basement and help Cis, Dakota, and Angie to get them outside. Ambulance sirens sound close outside. Based on the footsteps upstairs, another load of officers is clearing the house. There's a lot of yelling, but no more gunshots. They must be taking whoever's still alive up there without further casualties.

As I follow them up the stairs, I'm thankful to see the blue skies once again. Henry runs down to meet Angie. He dismisses the officers and carries Angie to the ambulance. Jamal and Micah watch on with dropped jaws, having no idea what they just witnessed. They give each other a hug.

Dakota stays by Cis's side. The EMTs inspect her for any serious wounds as others work on stopping the bleeding of Cis's leg. It seems both lucked out with clean wounds, so hopefully, no immediate surgery was needed for either of them. The ambulances take off in a hurry.

A few officers come up to me and ask for a quick debriefing regarding the incident. I tell them about the jacket and how they were after some thumb drive that was apparently sewn into it. One of them runs down to the basement to retrieve the jacket.

I do my best to give a rundown of the last week to the remaining officers, but I'm sure it came out like a complete ramble. They eventually just tell me to breathe and we can discuss it later at the station, after everyone has recovered a bit. The officer comes back with the jacket and feels around the patches.

"Aha," he says. He pulls out his knife to cut off a patch when he realizes it's already been cut. He reaches in with his finger and pulls out a metal device.

"That's not it," his partner tells him, "But that's definitely the tracking device."

The officer feels around with no luck.

"It's been taken already," he says.

The second officer feels around the jacket. He confirms it.

"Okay," he tells me, "stay by your phone. We'll be in touch as it's critical that we find it. Let us know if you hear anything."

Jamal and Micah run up to me as the officers move back to their huddle.

"Glad to see you up close again," I tell them.

"You all are a bunch of badasses," Jamal says, "Scary ones too!"

"It was like watching a live-action movie back there!" Micah says.

"Did y'all find what they were looking for?" Jamal asks.

"Nah. The jacket was there with the tracker, but the device was gone," I tell them.

"Who would've taken it?" Micah asks.

"Beats me. Hopefully, it didn't fall into the wrong hands," I say. Thinking about the nightmares that came with this jacket, I wonder if they're actually over now or if this is just the beginning of what our lives have become.

CHAPTER 25

~ Recovery ~

The hospitals don't seem to spend much time with gunshots. You'd think we're in the middle of a battlefield. We were told the three of them were just being treated as outpatients and we'd be on our way. Since the police were already involved in our situation, I think that helped eliminate some of the questioning.

I sit and wait with Angie as the doctor gives her sutures. She seems deep in thought and completely unfazed by the procedure. A part of me wonders if we just opened up Pandora's Box with her? The majority of me doesn't care. It all still feels a bit cinematic and I like it.

The doctor tells quick care instructions to Angie. The lack of acknowledgement reminds me of someone hearing safety instructions on a plane for the hundredth time.

"You doing alright?" I ask her. Angie looks at me with a forced grin. Her eyes look emotionally tired. I give her hand a squeeze.

"She will need plenty of rest after this," the doctor tells me.

I just nod.

*

The hospital timed all of their discharges to be together. Dakota and I push Cis and Angie down the hall in their wheelchairs. As we enter the lobby,

Dakota smiles and gives a brief wave to a woman as she's walking up to us. She seems to recognize her, which makes me assume she works at the clinic.

"Hi, I'm Hillary, I'm a therapist who has worked briefly with Dakota and Cis," she says as she smiles at all of us.

"Here to tell us we're not welcomed back?" Dakota asks her. She looks a bit hopeless and squeezes Cis's shoulder in an attempt to brace herself for the bad news.

"Quite the opposite," she says, "There's no real scientific way to know how you'll all react to the trauma you've been going through. Everyone responds differently."

"That's for sure," Dakota says.

Hillary tells us, "We not only want you, Dakota, and Cis to come back for the full duration, but we'd like to invite you, Angie, and Brey to join as well. Our therapists are equipped to handle a whole variety of issues, and PTSD is one of those. I think you'd both benefit by learning about new coping skills and seeing early signs of any psychological damage."

I look at Angie as she watches Hillary speak. Her eyes start to tear up as her lip starts to quiver a bit. She looks up at me, and I just nod to her.

"We'd love to," I tell Hillary, "I absolutely know that would be the best route for us." Angie refrains from talking but nods to Hillary while wiping some tears off her face. Henry comes up behind Angie and rubs her shoulders lightly. As she grabs his hands, he reaches down and hugs her from behind.

Jamal and Micah stand up from their seats in the corner and walk over to join us.

"We're happy to collect your things for you," Jamal offers.

"What would we do without you?" I ask.

"A lot more than we thought you could," Micah says with a chuckle.

To avoid any cold feet, we agree to immediately head to the clinic.

While we're walking toward the van that Hillary came in, I walk up next to her.

"Hi Hillary. First off, I appreciate you extending this offer to us."

She hesitantly smiles as she knows there's always more. "And?"

I laugh. "We currently have some plans we're working on for this coworking slash cafe idea..."

"We do understand it's hard to completely stop life," Hillary says. "Time can certainly be set aside on your schedule to continue your plans from inside."

"That's the thing, I was hoping to look at real estate too." My eyes grow apologetically large.

"We can work in a few outings per week. You will need to travel with one of the folks on our clinic's security team though."

"Absolutely!" I hold out my arms to give a large distant hug. She smiles at my excitement.

Henry also offers to take the trip back to Boston on his own. He has enough friends to help pack up all of our places and fill some pods. Cleaning isn't his forte, but he is in touch with the cleaning crew that works on apartments after move-outs where he lives. So we'll just pay for them to clear the place out afterward. It's remarkable how much is being achieved before even reaching the van.

As the four of us climb into the van, we say our temporary goodbyes to Henry and the twins.

"Are you sure the two of you don't want to join us?" I ask Jamal and Micah.

"Nah, we good." Jamal says as he rests his elbow on Micah's shoulder.

"Even tough guys need therapy once in a while," I tell them. They nod as though they already have a person they talk to.

I close the door and look around the van. I still find fate quite astonishing. And it all started with a "lucky" roll.

Epilogue

It's been three months since the opening of our business. I'm not back to coding yet, but I'm working on the last chapter of my novel. Hopefully, I'll make my way back after that. Things certainly didn't get busy here overnight, but I'm seeing fifty or so people now through the week.

There's a mix of small start-ups and individual remote workers. We've even had larger companies rent out the space for off-sites.

One of my customers, Alan, approaches my workspace and says, "Excuse me, Brey? Sorry to interrupt!"

"Don't need to apologize, Alan! What can I do for you?"

"There's a flickering bulb in room four."

"I'm on it!" I say as I head to the maintenance closet. There's an assortment of bulbs and I honestly have no idea which is which. I poke my head into the office and tell them, "Sorry, just got to run next door to ask Henry which bulb is correct!"

"Take your time," Alan tells me, "There's enough natural light that we just turned it off for now."

As I swing open the frosted glass door that connects our main room to the cafe, the noise permeates through our space. It's busy and booming like usual. The only time it's not full is when the front doors are locked in the early morning and late evening. I see Henry squeezed in at the counter for some lunch.

"Hey bud," I say as I lean down to Henry's ear level. "Know which bulbs I need to use for the conference rooms?"

He begins to stand up and tells me, "I can take care of it." I put some pressure on his shoulders to sit back down.

"They just turned off the lights for now, so I think it can wait if you don't mind doing it after," I tell him.

"Of course!"

"Try this new drink!" Angie says as she slides a colorful glass across the counter to me. Everything that comes out of this place is amazing, so I don't hesitate or ask any questions. It's a flavor I can't put my finger on, but it's delicious.

"Tarragon," she says.

"Aha! It's amazing!" I say as I reach across the counter and give her a high-five. As our hands connect, she clasps hands with me and gives me a squeeze.

"You should go see who's running the grill today," Angie says as she points out back.

I head to the kitchen and see Cis showing Dakota the finger check to determine how well done a steak is. They both have bandanas on their heads and smiles on their faces. It's heartwarming to see.

"Keep up the good work!" I yell back to them. As they look up, I give a distant high-five. They return the gesture.

"Excuse me," a voice says from behind me, "Could ya scoot to your left?" I turned around, and it was Faith!

"Oh my God! You made it! I thought you weren't coming out for another month or two," I say to her with excitement. Angie had run into her when she went back to finalize a couple things after checking out of the clinic.

The conversation started a whole new set of moves that included Faith coming out to work with us. And yes, she's as bouncy as ever!

"I needed the change sooner, and I'm glad I did! First day on the job!" she says. I quickly shift to the side and push open the door for her.

"Already look like you run the place!" I say as she bounces over to a far table. They're all running on expert level over here.

The door space swings open again and in walks Jamal and Micah.

"There you are!" Jamal yells at me.

"Always on one side or the other," I tell him.

"And he always guesses wrong!" Micah says with a chuckle.

"You two still up to run security tonight?" I ask them.

"You're our only client. Of course we are," Jamal says. They decided to move out and run a rentable security service.

We have a few events during the week where we keep the cafe open at night. Live music plays, and we serve finger foods. We have a BYOB license, so people can still bring wine or beer with a corking fee. This keeps crowds coming of all ages. It's working for all of us.

Our special guests tonight are none other than Steve and POP Rocks! To bring the whole crew back together, I'm surprising the others with a visit from Josiah as well. I'll be heading to the airport after lunch to pick him up.

And yes, we've all remained sober. Cis and Dakota maintain a regular schedule of meetings. All four of us attend some level of therapy. We even do a monthly group session. It helps us maintain a healthy relationship since we're both best friends and business partners.

That thumb drive was never found.

www.ingramcontent.com/pod-product-compliance
Lightning Source LLC
Chambersburg PA
CBHW050029120726
47903CB00006B/1967